1/30

D0649939

THE LION IS IN

This Large Print Book carries the
Seal of Approval of N.A.V.H.

THE LION IS IN

DELIA EPHRON

THORNDIKE PRESS

A part of Gale, Cengage Learning

GALE
CENGAGE Learning·

Detroit • New York • San Francisco • New Haven, Conn • Waterville, Maine • London

GALE
CENGAGE Learning®

LIBRARY OF CONGRESS CATALOGING-IN-PUBLICATION DATA

Ephron, Delia.
    The lion is in / by Delia Ephron.
        pages ; cm. — (Thorndike Press large print core)
    ISBN 978-1-4104-5098-2 (hardcover) — ISBN 1-4104-5098-8 (hardcover)
    1. Self-realization in women—Fiction. 2. Lions—Fiction. 3. Human-animal relationships—Fiction. 4. Large type books. I. Title.
    PS3555.P48L56 2012b
    813'.54—dc23   2012019200

Published in 2012 by arrangement with Blue Rider Press, a member of Penguin Group (USA) Inc.

Printed in the United States of America
1 2 3 4 5 6 7 16 15 14 13 12

For Jerry, heart and soul

1

Three hours south of Baltimore. Six p.m. or so. June third.

Two young women stand by the side of a rural two-lane highway. They are not sure what the road is or where it goes. In a frenzy, they left the interstate at a random exit, took one turn and then another. They are heading south, not intentionally.

They are pretty enough to stop traffic, although there isn't any to stop. Lana is wearing ripped jeans, a T-shirt, and those flat plastic shoes called jellies. Tracee is in a wedding dress and veil. She has been crying for several hours and has run out of tears. Now she is simply sniffling and her nose is red. Her dress and shoes don't match but no one can see that because her strapless gown is floor-length, a gorgeous swath of satin, beading, and lace. Even though she keeps the hem off the ground — clutching and hoisting the sides to bunch it around her hips — her copious ruffled underskirt hides black platform sandals.

Their car, an old Mustang, has a flat.

Lana slips off a jellie and smacks it against her thigh to get the gravel out. She wants to swear — she wants to let loose with a stream of expletives, this tire situation is such a calamity, potentially a nightmare, but she can't swear because she has given up swearing as a result of . . . Well, it turned out that giving up one thing led to giving up others. Giving up is becoming addictive. In addition to being five months and two days sober, she is twenty-one days without a Pepsi and six days without so much as a "damn." She feels cleaner as a result, as if fresh from a bath. But even more frustrated. And edgy. She bites hard on her pinkie nail while eyeing the flat.

"I was thinking," says Tracee, "do you think that maybe J.C. —"

"I don't want to hear about him anymore. He's a jerk. An asshole." Lana wonders if "asshole" is a swear word. Probably. Sort of. Close. "I'm swearing again."

"But you're not drinking."

"That guy is a shit." Now it's official. She is swearing again. "I mean it. My ears are falling off. Please, I am begging you. Forget him. God, the way he talks."

"Huh?"

" 'Kiss my ass' is one thing. Everyone says it, fine, it's cool, but 'How's your ass?' is not hello and 'Watch your ass' is not good-bye, but that is not the point. That is merely personally offensive to me. For your birth-day he gave you a lottery ticket that was already scratched."

Tracee remembers, how could she ever forget J.C. dancing around the room, grin-ning, teasing her to guess what was in his shirt pocket. "It's the thought."

"What thought? It was a losing ticket and it was scratched. What is the thinking here?"

The thinking? There was thinking, Tracee's sure. How had he explained it? Somehow. It's a tick away, but with Lana ranting at her, she only sighs.

"You were practically his maid," says Lana.

"I like the Laundromat. I like the smell."

"Do you like the smell of the grocery store and the vacuum cleaner?"

"Sorry," says Tracee.

"Why are you apologizing?"

"Sorry," she says, apologizing for apologiz-ing. She wiggles, trying to keep her dress from slipping. The strapless part is threaten-ing to fall, but if she lets go of the bottom to adjust the top, the bottom will brush the

9

ground and get dirty. "Would you pull up my front?" she asks Lana.

"Sure." Lana gives the fabric between Tracee's breasts a tug and then returns to the problem of the tire, taking a few steps back to see if a bit of distance might be enlightening. "I didn't realize that flats were so flat. The bottom looks melted." She walks around to the trunk and pops it.

"What are you doing?"

"Changing the tire."

"Wow. How?"

"I don't know. I've seen people change tires." Lana pulls out the jack and nearly drops it. It's steel, not that she couldn't have told you that but she wasn't prepared for the weight. She lets it rest on the ground while she tries to figure out how it works.

"Suppose someone sees us?"

"Who's going to see us?" Lana pumps the handle, trying to make the jack rise.

"Everyone. The world." Tracee is close to hysterics again. Hovering in the vicinity. She sounds like a mouse with someone's foot on its tail.

"Get in the car and scrunch. They're looking for two women, not one."

"They're looking for me."

"And me."

"Not as much as me."

10

"Tracee, scrunch."

Lana hefts the spare out of the trunk. She hops back as it thuds to the ground, barely missing her toes.

2

A woman walks by the side of the highway. She's been walking for several hours, simply putting one foot in front of the other and wondering where it will get her.

The woman, who recently turned fifty, is wearing her Sunday best: a buttoned-up polyester blouse with a bow at the neckline, a lemon-colored A-line skirt with a matching rather shapeless jacket. Her long hair, sparrow brown streaked with gray, is pinned up in a bun. The sun is low enough on the horizon that the light has dimmed. She doesn't need to squint, thank goodness, because it sometimes gives her a headache.

She expected the road to be what it is: empty. She took this route for that reason, is familiar enough with the area to know that the road leads nowhere interesting.

Way up ahead she sees a car, from this distance no more than a silver bump shimmering in the evening sun.

Tracee notices her first. She has slid down in the seat as far as she can, the voluminous folds of her skirt riding up to her chin. The car is hot. The dress — in this situation like a blanket — is suffocating. She bounces up to cool off, sees the woman, and squeaks with anxiety.

Lana looks.

"What's she doing here?" says Tracee.

Lana shrugs.

They watch her steady unhurried approach.

"Hi," says Lana.

"Are you all right? Do you need help?" The woman is friendly but not curious. She doesn't, for instance, peer in the car window or peruse Lana from head to toe. She appears merely polite.

The spare is now attached, and Lana has been trying to secure the nuts — or are they bolts? She isn't sure. She knows that if she doesn't screw them very tight, the tire will spin right off the car once they get going and then God knows what will happen.

"I'm having the worst time tightening these."

The woman considers the problem. "If I press with my foot, I think that will help."

Lana fits the long-handled wrench over whatever it is, nut or bolt. The woman places her foot on the wrench handle and then, grabbing on to the roof of the car, hoists herself up so that her entire body weighs the handle down. She's a smallish woman, about five feet, three inches, and her figure, once trim, has gone round. Lana presses with all her might. The wrench makes a satisfying half circle.

They repeat the process several times until they are confident the tire is securely attached.

"Thank you so much," says Lana.

"Thanks," Tracee calls from inside the car, keeping her face averted.

"It's nothing," says the woman. "You're welcome."

Lana tosses the wrench in the trunk and wipes an arm across her sweaty forehead. She repacks the trunk with the flat tire and the jack, refusing to let the woman help. "You'll get dirty," Lana tells her. Which is true. "Would you like a ride?"

From inside Tracee squeaks.

"Excuse me." Lana sticks her head in the window while the woman steps back to give her privacy.

"Can we trust her?" whispers Tracee.

"Of course we can't trust her. We don't need to. Tracee, they're looking for two people, not three."

She pulls her head out of the window and smiles at the woman.

3

Lana drives. She feels fantastic now. Jazzed. Better than she's felt in months. She presses on the gas, inching over the limit, and looks over at her friend, who is tracing patterns of lace on her dress.

Lana floors it.

Tracee jerks up and swivels around to see who's after them.

Lana laughs and slows the car down again. It's been such a nice day, she thinks. Their bolt out of Maryland, hammering Tracee into some semblance of sanity, the disaster of the flat, solved. The white noise of the tires rolling on asphalt is music to her ears. She turns on the radio and punches the dial, looking for something to sing along to.

The woman they picked up has to sit sideways because the Mustang, a sporty two-door, barely has a backseat. She takes off her shoes, brown pumps with stubby heels. "Excuse me?" the woman says.

Lana lowers the sound.

"Do you mind if I unfasten my bra?"

Surprised by the question, neither she nor Tracee answers, and the woman fills the gap. "I'm asking because it was kind of you to offer a ride and I don't want to do anything to upset you."

"The first thing I do when I get home . . ." Lana loses her place for a moment mentioning home. . . . "Well, not just home but wherever I'm staying. The first thing I do is unfasten my bra."

"So you don't mind?"

"No. Go ahead."

The woman untucks her blouse, reaches under, unfastens her bra, and retucks.

"I'm Lana, by the way. This is Tracee."

"Hi," says Tracee.

"Rita," says the woman. "Nice to meet you."

"Where can we drop you?"

"Where are you going?"

"We're not sure."

"That'll be fine."

Tracee shoots Lana a look. Rita settles in the backseat.

4

Two hours. Farther south.

Tracee, who is tall and skinny with an appealing gawkiness, gets sudden hunger attacks. "I need to eat," she announces, popping up straight in her seat. She doesn't threaten to faint (which she often threatens but never does); still, Lana recognizes the state, Tracee's light-headedness, a glassy-eyed stare. "I have low blood sugar," Tracee tells Rita, and then wonders why in the world she said that. She imagines Rita repeating it to a cop, "She said she had low blood sugar."

Anyway, Tracee isn't certain that she does have low blood sugar. She read about it once when she was sixteen. In the waiting room at Planned Parenthood. She and Lana had gone to the clinic to get their birth control pills refilled. As she recalls the gist of it now, eight years later, the magazine described the condition as jitters that can be cured only by eating everything in sight.

"Look." She waved the magazine at Lana. "I'm not a freak."

"You have a bona fide medical condition," Lana affirmed after reading.

Although now that Tracee is berating herself for spilling an identifying characteristic to Rita, a stranger who could turn her in, she decides that she will deny the condition. She imagines herself on the witness stand. "That wasn't me in that car. Why would I say something like that? I don't have low blood sugar. No doctor ever told me I did." This worry preoccupies her for the ten miles it takes to find a place to eat in this near wilderness . . . until Lana pulls the car into A & R, a white box by the side of the road with no indoor seating, simply a walk-up window for pickup.

"Order for me," says Tracee. "Whatever. This dress attracts too much attention." This last she adds for Rita's benefit, to account for why she hides out in the car until the only other customers leave, an older couple sharing a sundae.

"What's fast?" asks Lana, reading the menu written in plastic letters on a board behind the counter.

"Everything," says the counter girl.

"Fried chicken then. Two orders."

"That's fifteen minutes."

'Why'd you say it was fast?"

"Did I?"

"I asked what was fast and you said everything."

"Oh, right. What can I get you?" the counter girl says cheerfully.

"I don't know why you said everything was fast?"

The girl simply raises her eyebrows and waits.

"Okay," says Lana, bummed, not about the fried chicken but because she can't get a rise out of the girl. "Two patty melts, two waffle fries, and two Pepsis." Now it's official. Lana is back on Pepsi. Swearing and back on Pepsi. She takes a packet of sugar, rips it open, and shakes the contents into her mouth.

"I'll have the same, a patty melt and waffle fries," says Rita so faintly that the counter girl asks her to repeat it. "Only do you have orange juice?"

"Orange slush," says the girl.

"Oh." Rita hides a smile. "No choice then, orange slush."

When the food is ready, each identical order in a cardboard boat, Lana pulls out everything she's got, several crumpled dollars and spare change from her back pocket,

20

and lays it on the counter.

"How much again?" Rita asks the cashier. Trying and failing to divide the total by three, she has forgotten the amount she began with. "I'm terrible with numbers. Sometimes Harry says . . ." She stops, thinks about that, and doesn't finish her sentence. She unzips a small change purse, pries out four dollars folded into a wad, and adds it to Lana's contribution.

"You ladies are short a dollar forty," says the cashier.

Rita flips her change purse upside down, dumping out some change.

"Now you're short sixty-five cents."

"I can give the slush back," says Rita, but Lana runs to the car and gets Tracee to turn up the rest by scrounging around in the bottom of her purse.

They all sit in the dark at a picnic table with fireflies dancing, eating in silence for a while. Lana loses interest in her burger about halfway through. She concentrates mainly on her Pepsi, returning to the counter for more sugar, which she dumps in. "Perfectly seasoned," she says, grinning. Rita eats methodically and neatly, taking time to play with her orange slush, swirling the straw through the icy fluff while she watches Tracee drown her patty melt in mustard and catsup and then take huge bites, washing them down with noisy slurps through the straw. Tracee moans as she eats. Her fingers get sticky. She licks them. Crumpled dirty napkins pile up. Rita pushes more napkins her way.

"Maybe we can sell your wedding dress on eBay," says Lana.

"What?" says Tracee.

"No one wears a wedding dress twice."

"I haven't worn it once."

Lana waves a fry at her. "Technically, yes, you have worn it once, because you are wearing it."

"Excuse me for prying," says Rita, "but are you a runaway bride?"

Lana answers for Tracee. "Yes, no, not really." She starts laughing. Tracee bursts into tears. "Tee — come on, I'm just explaining, I didn't mean . . ." She throws up her hands as Tracee hiccups, trying to suppress her sobs. "Forget it. Who's done besides me?" Lana gets up and tosses her food in the trash.

"Would you like me to drive?" says Rita. "I've never been in an accident. I've never even had a bumper stumper."

Two hours later they pass a small sign by the side of the road: WELCOME TO NORTH CAROLINA. Lana and Tracee are sleeping,

Lana in back and Tracee in front, slumped against the window, her hand curled into a fist under her cheek. While Rita drives, she taps her cell phone.

Tracee wakes up. "Who are you texting?"

She snatches the cell and throws it out the window.

Rita reacts coolly, braking quickly and making a U-turn while Tracee goes silent, astonished at her own behavior, and Lana, sensing a reversal of direction, rouses herself to find out what happened.

Since it's black as tar out in spite of a starry moonlit sky, it's a "guesstimate," as Rita puts it, as to exactly where Tracee flung the cell. Rita pulls up on the shoulder and angles the car so that the headlights illuminate a thick tangle of lush greenery.

While she and Lana get out and stomp around, hoping to step on the phone, which seems more likely than spotting it, Tracee shouts from the car, "I get possessed, like possessed by the devil, and I do things."

"The devil?" says Rita.

"She doesn't mean the devil," says Lana, while Tracee shouts at the same time, "Not the devil devil. I mean something comes over me."

"I don't want anything to do with the devil," says Rita. "I'm living without the devil. That's what I'm trying."

Rita and Lana disappear behind some shrubbery, and Tracee can still hear their feet crushing plants.

"Did you find it?" she shouts.

"You could help," says Lana.

"I'm in my wedding dress."

"I'm really sorry Tracee did that," Lana tells Rita. "She panics."

"It's all right. I was only playing Word Shake. It's not a good thing to do while you drive."

"Suppose someone needs to reach you?"

"No one knows I have a cellular phone."

"No one knows you have a cellular phone," Lana repeats and considers this while she stomps some more, primarily for show, and strips the leaves off a fern to scratch a destructive itch. "I don't think we'll find it."

"I don't either. I don't think there's any chance at all, but thank you for trying."

Lana bends back the branches, easing their path, and then walks ahead to shield Rita from the glare of the headlights.

"Do you believe in things happening for a reason?" says Rita.

"No. Maybe. I'm not sure. I'd have to give that serious thought."

"In my opinion . . ." Rita stops and

24

proceeds deliberately, "That way of thinking is a way to accept shit."

Lana gets the impression that "shit" is a
word Rita has never used before, and using
it has given her a thrill.

5

One a.m.

Tracee drives while Lana and Rita sleep. Lulled by a repetitious clink of something in the motor, which isn't new but in the lonesome quiet becomes both noticeable and hypnotic, and bored by the straight dark road devoid of sights, Tracee dozes. Her foot slips off the gas.

The car slows as it drifts soundlessly across the empty highway and crashes into a rail.

Tracee snaps like a rubber band — thrown forward and almost as quickly pinned back, thanks to her seat belt.

Lana, jolted, bolts upright. "What the fuck?" She cranes forward to see what happened.

"Are you all right?" says Rita.

"I didn't mean to," says Tracee.

"What happened to the air bags?" says Lana. "Did that slug sell me a car with no

26

air bags?"

"Thank goodness we were all wearing seat belts," says Rita.

"What a ripoff. I could sue. Tracee, give it gas."

Tracee only sits there.

"Tracee, put the car in reverse and give it some gas."

"We'd been driving forever," says Tracee.

"I know, Tee." Lana pats her arm.

"I didn't have anyone to talk to."

"It's okay. We're all wiped. I need you to put the car into reverse and press on the gas. Can you do that? Look, I'm putting it in reverse for you. Now all you have to do is press on the gas pedal."

"I'm doing it," says Tracee.

They hear the wheels spin in the dirt.

Beyond the car, off the highway on an even smaller road that runs parallel, a large building stands alone. Not a right angle in it. A collection of panels, some of them aluminum, some a material resembling wood but possibly not wood, some vertically placed, some nailed on horizontally. If a building were a crazy quilt, thinks Rita, that's what this would be. She spots it first when they all get out of the car — from the passenger side, because the smashed driver's-side door won't open. The walls of the building rise and then tilt toward the center. The top is shaped more like a tent than a roof. There are double front doors painted a garish crimson, and a yellow neon sign over them: THE LION. The sign is more or less lit up except for a few letters. A large empty parking lot surrounds the building. It's hard to say whether this place is still happening or whether it's not.

The women look both ways. No cars in sight.

Tracee hopes her dress is undamaged. Not that it got injured in the crash but possibly after, when she had to exit. It was a trip to move herself in that huge, delicate dress over the gear and brake to the passenger side. She could easily have snagged it. She's dying to pull some fabric from the back around to the front and take a close look, but Lana might think she's off the point. Worse, or perhaps not worse but equally bad, if Tracee were to mention her dress now, Lana might think Tracee cares more about her dress than the Mustang, which Lana paid off only about a year and a half ago. Lana was a big mess then but a lot more fun. They'd hopped from bar to bar — she, Lana, and J.C. Lana showed her official owner's receipt, stamped PAID IN FULL, to everyone. She kissed it so many times it was covered with gloss, and then she lost it.

The next morning Lana said it didn't matter. She needed the receipt only if she was going to sell the car, and she would never, ever sell her Mustang, and look at her, here she is kneeling, practically caressing her car, whose fender is wrapped around the rail, tenderly touching all the dents and tangled metal the way a blind woman might feel the face of someone she loves.

"I'm sorry," says Tracee. "I'm really sorry."

"It's okay. It was used. Now it's just used-used."

"If J.C. knew."

"Shut up," screams Lana. "Sorry, I'm sorry. Just please don't."

"You do look pretty in that wedding dress," says Rita. "And with the moon shining, you're like the highwayman's lover. 'He whistled a tune to the window, and who should be waiting there / But the landlord's black-eyed daughter / Bess, the landlord's daughter, / Plaiting a dark red love-knot into her long black hair.' "

The words seem to hang in the air, a silent echo.

"What's that?" says Tracee.

"Poetry."

"Thank you. Thank you for that."

"We're nowhere," says Rita. "I can't tell you how happy that makes me."

She steps over the low rail. Lana steps over too, gives a hand to Tracee, and then strides down an embankment, leading them to The Lion.

"Do you think this is a real place?" asks Lana as they cross the parking lot.

"You mean, could we be imagining it?" says Tracee.

"No. I'm asking, could it be deserted? Abandoned?"

"I could never be imagining it, because I don't have an imagination," says Rita.

"Doesn't everyone?" says Tracee.

"Really? Do you think so?"

"I'd like to hope so," says Lana.

She checks out the front doors. They're metal, locked with a heavy chain and padlock. Close up, the crimson paint turns out to be sloppily applied — brushstrokes evident, bubbles here and there, and some missed spots where the original gunmetal gray shows through. The two windows might more likely belong on a small house. Lana tries to lift the glass on both but can't.

She heads around to the back, with Tracee and Rita trailing after.

The building is such a mishmash of materials, it's hard for her to spot the normal bits. There's a long folding door of several panels hinged together, which is also locked, and yet another window. Lana feels the dirt-encrusted glass along the bottom between the frame and the sill. She can wedge her fingers in.

Lana raises the window, groaning at the effort. "We'll put you through first," she tells Rita.

She laces her fingers together and Tracee does likewise, each making a stirrup for Rita's feet. "One, two, three," says Lana. They hoist her up. Rita pitches through and hangs there, half in and half out.

Tracee starts giggling.

"Are you all right?" Lana hopes that Rita can't hear Tracee's suppressed laughter and that she herself does not break up too.

"I'm fine. Push me."

They do and hear a thunk as she hits the floor. Then her face is in the window as she raises it higher.

"Your turn," says Lana.

"I'm scared to say it. You'll get mad."

"What?"

"I can't go through the window in this dress."

"Take it off, then."

Tracee giggles. She unzips a side zipper, and her dress collapses around her. She steps out of it, bundles it neatly, and passes it into Rita's arms.

"My goodness, it's heavy," says Rita.

"I love it." Tracee unpins her veil and hands it to Lana. She hoists herself up, relatively agile and athletic now that she is encumbered by only a bra and a ruffled organdy underskirt, and climbs through.

Lana passes her the veil and climbs in after.

Helping Tracee put the dress and veil back on proves surprisingly easy in spite of the dark room, because the satin fabric, bright white, provides a helpful glow. They take a moment to debate the pros and cons — wear versus not wear — but it seems easier for Tracee to be in the dress than to carry it in the dark.

"Where are you?" says Rita suddenly.

"Right here," says Lana.

"Here," says Tracee.

"I'm —"

"What?" says Lana.

"I'm scared of the dark." Rita is relieved that it is dark when she confesses this thing she's embarrassed about. "I got —"

"What? Spooked?"

"It's stupid."

"Why stupid?" says Lana. "We're here. Wave your arms around."

They all locate one another and, clasping hands, move through the space, banging into furniture at first, but as their eyes adjust, they begin to discern things around them — shapes — although they cannot tell exactly what they are or in what configuration.

There seem to be many small tables with chairs. Lana feels the surface of one. "Some crumbs. Eww. Sticky stuff." She runs her hand over a wood surface full of gouges. She assesses the height, slightly above her waist, and, reaching out, determines its narrow width and long length. "This must be a bar. Stay here. Sit on a stool. I'm going around to the other side."

Lana gropes her way around the bar and then gropes behind the bar, locating various things, many of which are familiar because she's worked in bars before — the spigots for beer, the faucet, the grate where the water drains. She feels around under the bar, pulls on a handle opening a small refrigerator. The women can finally see, thanks to a pie-shaped yellow light emanating up.

"What'll it be?" says Lana.

"Lana, no," says Tracee.

"I can be in a bar and not have alcohol. I'm only offering."

"Just water for me, please," says Rita.

"Tracee?"

"I'm thinking. Now, what do I want?" Tracee taps her toes.

"Tracee!"

"Fine, okay, whatever is in that spout. What does it say there on the handle? Pepsi." Tracee lifts off her veil, which has a crystal-studded crown and a long gathered net with a satin trim. She lays the veil on the bar and strokes it.

"I guess I'll have Pepsi too," says Rita.

Holding a glass under a spigot, Lana pulls the lever. It seems miraculous that the soda comes out. She sets them all up and locates napkins, chips, and pretzels as well as a jar of maraschino cherries. She drops a few cherries into her Pepsi.

"Where are you from?" Tracee asks Lana.

"What you are talking about? You've lived next door to me since we were five. Are you nuts?"

"Excuse me," Tracee says to Rita.

She leans across the bar to Lana and whispers, "I was making conversation because I thought we could find out about her, you know I'd ask you about you first and you'd tell us and then she'd be all relaxed and tell us, because I don't think she wants to tell us anything."

34

"But we don't want to tell *her* anything," says Lana.

Not wanting to intrude, leaving the young women to confer privately, Rita swivels around on her stool and stops. Far off, in the inky darkness, she sees the bright eyes of a large animal. The eyes are yellow, the pupils large circles of black. Unwavering, slightly slanted, and far enough apart that they might not even belong together, the eyes glimmer like lights in fog, diffuse and mysterious.

Rita slips off her stool and walks slowly toward the eyes.

Lana and Tracee turn. Tracee slaps a hand to her mouth to muffle a shriek. Lana goes silent, shocked as much by the realization that they are in the presence of something dangerous as by Rita's pull to it.

Rita takes slow but certain steps. Drawn inexorably. It would be easier to resist gravity.

Lana kicks the refrigerator door. It opens wider, casting enough murky glow to illuminate the shadowy figure of a lion. In an enormous cage. Thick black bars rise like spikes nearly to the ceiling.

The lion is standing in the cage regarding Rita.

Rita stares back, mesmerized.

She turns and smiles at Lana and Tracee.
The lion roars.

The women scream and run, crashing into things, heading for the window, which they all try to squeeze through at the same time.

Lana yanks Tracee. "Let her go first, it's polite."

Rita tumbles out. Tracee nearly gets stuck, but Lana shoves her through and then somersaults herself out in one leap.

For a while they simply lie on the ground and breathe.

"That was a lion," says Lana finally. "Is that legal?"

"In these country parts," says Rita, "it doesn't matter."

"Why did you walk toward him?" says Tracee.

"What?" says Rita.

"You walked right toward him."

"I don't know."

"You're scared of the dark."

"I know."

"He smelled like stale popcorn," says Lana. "The minute we saw him, I smelled him. His head is so big. That mane."

"Like a wild man's," says Rita.

"But why did you smile?" Tracee asks Rita. "That was so strange."

Rita thinks, and it comes back to her, what

she sensed when she saw him. She feels it again, something stirring inside her. Barely there, yet for most people it would be unmistakable: a sense of beginning. Rita, however, is so unfamiliar with adventure or the possibility of it that she can't tell the difference between something auspicious and a stomachache.

"I don't know," she says again. She can only articulate the obvious. "He was an astonishment."

6

"We have to go back inside," says Lana, and when Tracee protests, she points out how chilly it is outside and that the lion is, in fact, in a cage. "If an animal is in a cage, he can't hurt us, right?"

Logically yes, but at the same time, no one is sure about that. Still, within ten minutes they are back inside, flat against a wall, inching along, trying not to attract the big cat's attention. The small refrigerator is still open, providing light. They notice that the cage contains a white plaster of paris cave, extremely amateur in look. The lion is now lounging inside it.

"Does anyone know anything about lions?" Lana speaks in a hushed voice. This seems wise, although she is not sure why.

"Isn't the lion the king of the jungle?" says Tracee.

"I mean behavior. Besides eats meat?"

No one does.

"Well, I think we should move quietly and whisper," says Lana.

"He *is* in a cage," says Rita.

"But we don't want him rampaging around. Or getting aroused by our scent. What's this?" Lana feels a knob poking into her back, turns, and notes a bowler hat decal on the door. "The men's room."

"The ladies' must be nearby," says Tracee.

"I don't think we have to observe that little propriety," says Lana, walking in.

She locates a light switch where it would logically be, on the wall just inside, and a couple of lightbulbs dangling from the ceiling switch on. There are two metal lockers next to the sink, and she begins rattling their doors as Tracee and Rita use the stalls.

When they come out, they find that she has managed to open one locker and is going through the contents. She holds up a shirt and examines it — coarse cotton, red with short sleeves, a man's shirt, and on the pocket stitched in orange script, *The Lion.* She tosses it to Tracee. She then removes a small paperback and a condom, a Trojan in its plastic packet.

"Is that Sudoku?" says Rita. "I love Sudoku."

Lana hands her the book. "Do one."

"But it belongs to someone. Do you think

I should?" She thumbs through. Some of the puzzles have been completed.

"What would Harry say?" says Lana.

Rita pauses and then inquires as if she could care less one way or another, "Do you know Harry?"

"No. You mentioned him. I was making a joke."

Rita spends a moment thinking. "One little puzzle. It can't really do any harm. It's only one page out of" — she flips to the end — "ninety-eight puzzles. Who would begrudge that to someone?"

Tracee holds her purse up to her chest, opens it wide enough for a private peer inside, digs around, and comes up with a pretty pencil, silver metal with a pink eraser at the top. "Here. You can erase."

Lana pockets the condom.

7

Morning light through the small dirty window wakes Rita. Her body aches, her limbs are stiff from sleeping on the linoleum floor (on a pallet of paper towels pulled from the dispenser). She sits up, wiggling and rolling her shoulders, stretching her arms, careful not to rustle the paper towels and wake the girls. They sleep so quietly. Lana, her head cocked sideways, sits up against the wall, her long legs sticking straight out in front of her. She's wearing her sandals. Sleeping in shoes — there's something sad about that, thinks Rita. Tracee, curled up on the floor, has her legs tucked up and her head in Lana's lap. She's wearing the red shirt and her organdy slip.

Rita watches them for a minute, the slight rise and fall of their bodies as they breathe, how comfortable they obviously are together. She appreciates their innocence — Lana's face without anger, Tracee's worry-free. Especially Rita appreciates the quiet, no Harry snoring, his leg thrown over her, pinning her down.

She rubs her eyes, picks up her book, and continues with Sudoku. She had planned to stop last night after one puzzle, told herself she should, but is now in the middle of her third. As she fills in the squares, the lead in the pencil breaks.

Tracee's purse is just sitting there. Hoping for another pencil, Rita peeks inside at the mess — wadded-up tissues, a jumble of lipsticks and glosses (all sorts of fancy brands), mascara wands, quite a few. Something glitters. She looks closer and pinches out a necklace. She cradles it in her palm. It's short, more a choker, really. Rita knows instantly that it's valuable, because she has never held anything valuable before. Her own wedding ring, which she left behind, could have been mistaken for a curtain ring and cost barely more than that. It was a badge of deprivation. This fragile, pretty thing has a bit of heft; the gold is tarnished in the ways of antiques, jewelry she has admired in shop windows. The gems, tiny half-moons set in a single row, catch the light. Simply because she cannot tear her eyes away, she knows these diamonds are real.

She stands up. Looking into the cracked mirror above the sink, she fastens the choker around her neck.

It fits nicely. The small stones suit her. The chain is not tight but rests on her collarbones. The diamonds are amazing. Even in this dusty light they sparkle, brightening and animating her solemn face.

Rita arches her neck, imagining for a second she is someone elegant. Someone regal. Someone.

She lays her hand against the choker, feeling the cool links against her skin. *I don't have to be who I am.* For the first time in her life that thought wanders into her consciousness and then out again. She summons it back, what a daring thought — *Who I am is not a life sentence.* Her heart beats a tiny bit faster and that feeling is so shockingly unfamiliar, a quickening of her heart from excitement, that she unfastens the necklace and returns it to Tracee's purse.

Rummaging in the purse some more, she finds only a pen, debates whether to use it but decides no. She sits back down and waits for Lana and Tracee to wake up, which Lana does with a suddenness, announcing, "I have to go to a meeting," as though she has decided in her sleep. She shakes Tracee

awake and repeats, "I have to go to a meeting."

They all throw water on their faces and
pat themselves dry with paper towels, and,
with soap from the dispenser, rub their
teeth, which makes Tracee gag. Lana mo-
nopolizes the mirror, although no one else
wants it. She yanks her hair this way and
that, the best technique for dealing with hair
that is all different lengths and appears to
have been cut in the dark, which it was, on
a dare. She arranges her T-shirt to hide a
goldfish tattoo below her collarbone, a
reminder of the stupid things she did when
she was wasted. Her three other tattoos,
including the one she is most embarrassed
about — a guy's name, Trent (someone she
hooked up with for a week) — are visible
only when she's naked. Lana is high-waisted
with hourglass curves. After years of parad-
ing her cleavage in tight, low tops through a
slew of bars, she now keeps her endowments
hidden. Her T-shirt, a muddy green, is large
and hangs loosely. She has a coppery com-
plexion nearly the same color as her hair,
and widely set dark brown eyes, serious and
probing when they are not suspicious. Her
smiles, uncommon, are usually reserved for
moments of irony or glee. This morning, as
always, she views her reflection with dis-

satisfaction. A lifetime of compliments from men has not made up for a lack of appreciation from a mother.

While Lana scowls into the mirror, daring herself to like what she sees, Tracee clips her masses of soft black curls up and out of the way. In spite of the many glosses in her purse, she borrows Lana's, dabbing on a bit and smoothing it with her finger. She wears no other makeup, never does. Her lack of artifice, her gawkiness, and her simple beauty — porcelain skin and large gray eyes that take up a little too much space on her thin, delicate face — all tell the tale: The child she was is still very much present.

Tracee tugs her wedding dress down from over the stall where it is draped. "I'm going to carry my dress and keep on wearing this shirt and slip instead." Her voice rises as it often does, converting statements into questions, determination into doubt — a prompt for Lana.

"Good idea," says Lana. She opens the door and walks out.

They start to follow when she pivots, pushes them back inside, and pulls the door shut.

"What?" say Tracee and Rita.

Lana waves her arms. She doesn't know what to say.

"What?" says Tracee.

Still no answer.

"What?" they both repeat.

Lana opens the door a crack and they all peek out.

The lion is standing in the cage with Tracee's wedding veil on his head.

"My veil." Tracee starts crying.

"That's not the point," says Lana.

"That's not the point? The lion is wearing my veil and it's not the point?"

"The point," says Lana, "is how did it happen?"

They all consider.

"Toughie," says Rita.

"Toughie for sure."

"Could it be a miracle?" says Tracee.

"There are no miracles," says Rita. "In my opinion . . ." She stops and after a moment continues deliberately. "Miracles are simply misunderstandings. Or worse, cons."

"Whoa, dark." Lana gives Rita's pronouncement the respect it deserves, a brief silence, before continuing to analyze the mystery. "Either the lion left the cage, which means he can leave the cage at will, walked over to the bar where you left the veil, put the veil on, which means he is capable of putting a veil on his head, and returned to his cage, or —"

46

"Someone put it on him," says Rita, "and we slept through it."

"Exactly."

"Or a miracle," says Tracee. "And it means something, something wonderful that we know nothing about that has to do with me. It shall be revealed."

"So," says Lana, ignoring Tracee's comment, "someone else is either here or was here."

They put their heads out the door. They listen. They peek about.

The lion is strolling around the cage. The crystal-studded, tiara-like crown sits slightly off center, nestled in his mane, and the fluffy gathered netting poufs out. A bit of the veil appears to be in his mouth.

"We have to get it back," says Tracee.

"Do you want to be eaten by a lion?" says Lana. "Do you want to end your life being ripped to death by a lion's jaws?"

"He seems nice."

"He's a lion."

They quickly head to the exit window, checking out the place as they go.

"Say good-bye to the veil," says Lana. "Go on. Get it out of your system."

"It's sad. Don't you think it's sad?"

"Some things are sadder," says Lana.

"Bye, veil," says Tracee with a little wave.

They boost Rita up to the sill. As she is
about to climb out, she gives the lion, who
is chewing the veil, a lingering look.

It's a cool morning, overcast. Rita is the
only one with a jacket. Lana rubs her bare
arms for warmth, and Tracee jumps a bit.
In daylight the building's patchwork of
woods and metals seems even more freakish
and colorful. The parking lot, they notice, is
in terrible condition, the concrete cracked,
uneven, with weeds poking through. There
is a dumpster packed with bulging garbage
bags. Beyond the lot is a field of wild tall
grass. Directly behind The Lion, the field
lies flat, but to the left it builds to a rise.

The women walk around to the front.

On the highway where there is now light
traffic, they see the Mustang with a tow
truck and patrol car parked next to it. A
cop is talking to the tow-truck driver.

Squeaking with anxiety, Tracee spins back
behind The Lion.

"He's only there because of the car," says
Lana.

"What do I do?"

"Stay here. In back. Hang out."

"Doing what?"

"Whatever. I don't know."

" 'A, my name is Alice.' You could recite
that," says Rita. " 'A, my name is Alice, and

my husband's name is Al. We come from Alaska and we sell apples. B, my name is Betty, and my husband's name is Ben. . . .' It really makes the time pass when you're bored witless. I always do it in church. Sometimes I try to make all the words basically the same, like 'F, my name is Frances, and my husband's name is Francis. We come from France and we sell . . .' " Her voice trails off. "Well, that's three out of four. I never have done four out of four."

Lana and Tracee are silenced by that blast of helpfulness. "But I'm hungry," Tracee says finally.

"Don't be an idiot. You can't come with us. We'll bring you food."

Lana corrects herself, realizing her presumptuousness (that Rita will come along with her), realizing also that she has started to worry about Rita the way she does about Tracee. "Well, actually, you're free to go," she tells Rita. "That sounds weird, but what I mean is, don't worry about us."

"I'll stay with you," Rita tells Tracee.

"Can we hitch in another direction?" asks Tracee.

"I have to go to a meeting," says Lana. "Plus my car."

"I'm hungry."

"We can climb back inside and get more

49

chips and maraschino cherries," says Rita.

"I need protein," says Tracee in a small voice.

Lana sticks her head around the side of the building. The cop has left, her car is now hitched to the truck, and the tow-truck driver is backing up, disengaging her car from the rail.

Lana runs toward the highway, waving and shouting, "Hey, hello, that's mine. My car."

"She doesn't have any money," says Tracee.

"Does she have a credit card?" says Rita.

"Maxed. Way maxed. Me too."

"If I used a credit card, I could be found, couldn't I?"

"Don't want that," says Tracee, thinking about herself.

Rita snaps open her purse and from a side pocket extracts a MasterCard. She bends it in half, back and forth again and again until she can rip the plastic. She drops the pieces on the ground, grinds them with her heel, picks them up, and tosses them into the dumpster.

8

"You're lucky," says Bill. "You could be dead."

"I know," says Lana. She is riding into town in his tow truck, unsure of what town they are riding into and not inclined to reveal her cluelessness. She notices that the speedometer hovers around twenty-five.

"I drive slow," he says.

"That's okay with me."

"When you do what I do, you realize how it could all be over in a second. It's made me careful."

Lana guesses he's around forty. He's got a paunch, a round face, and neatly pressed clothes. His khaki pants have a crease. Probably he's been fattened up and cared for by a doting wife. A photo of a smiling little girl hangs in a straw frame from the rearview mirror.

"What's her name?" asks Lana, assuming it's his daughter. "She's so pretty."

"Anna Sue," he says.

"Are you careful about everything or just driving?"

"I see corners everywhere."

"Corners?"

"What's around them. No one knows."

"That's true. I never thought of that."

"Where are you going?"

"If you could drop me . . ." She decides to come out with it. "I'm looking for AA."

"That's me, but you're not a member."

"What? Oh, no, you're AAA, three A's, triple A. I'm looking for Alcoholics Anonymous. A meeting."

"I get you. Ask Cynthia at the café. She's one. Are you a college student?"

"Not anymore. I was. Do I look that young? I feel really old."

"How old are you, if you don't mind my asking?"

"Twenty-six."

"So you're passing through or what?"

"What," says Lana.

They both laugh.

She takes out her cell. Presses some buttons. "Dead. I need a charger. Do you by any chance have a charger for a Samsung?"

"Sam. Sung," says Bill. For some reason that amuses him and he chuckles. "Nope."

"Bill, I don't have the money right now to

pay for the repair or even the towing. Could you please hold the car and I'll let you know as soon as I can afford it?"

"Sure. If you hadn't turned up, I would have kept it until the police decided what to do. And that could take an age."

The tow truck, moving slowly, passes a big white sign with gold lettering: FAIR-VILLE.

9

Fairville is pristine, a jewel of a village, its streets lined with one- and two-story historic buildings, either white clapboard or red brick, each pretty enough to be on a postcard. A closer look reveals cracks beneath the surface, stores that have closed, their displays intact. Dishes & Stuff still has a tea set in the window. When Pete's Gardening Supplies didn't open one Monday or ever again, Pete didn't bother to remove the coils of garden hose and pyramid of bug sprays. A handful of businesses went bust in this manner — as if someone thought of a good idea for a shop, opened it one week, and walked away the next. The buildings aren't yet decaying — no peeling paint or warped timbers — simply empty. It's common to try to walk into a shop before realizing that the place isn't actually there.

Every fifty feet or so the sidewalks are dotted with wrought-iron benches, a consideration for anyone who might want to give his feet a rest. Most of the stores and conveniences are located around a main square.

Cynthia at the café directs Lana to Star Nails at the end of the block. Star Nails is another bust, and its premises have been appropriated by AA and a few other local organizations, like the American Legion. When Lana cautiously opens the front door, setting off a little bell (a remnant from the salon), the meeting has already begun.

"Welcome," says the leader, a man in a baseball cap, a starched white short-sleeved shirt, and madras pants.

"Hi," says Lana, feeling self-conscious. She must look as if she's wearing yesterday's clothes, which she is. Everyone here is neat and tidy, even the one dark soul, a young guy all in black with several piercings, nose and lip.

Her jeans are ripped too. Ripped clothes mean something, she thinks, something negative, something telling, but maybe she's wrong about that. Nevertheless it adds to her self-consciousness.

"Why don't you sit down?"

Lana hesitates. There are about twenty people scattered on miserable old couches. She decides to sit alone, on a huge beige one with dark brown stripes and what looks like coffee stains. The zipper on the bottom cushion is twisted around to the front, and as it sags under her light weight and she feels the springs, she inhales the pungent aroma of nicotine, years of it.

"Would you like some coffee?" The leader points a flyswatter in the direction of a manicure table, where there is an electric coffeepot and some styrofoam cups.

"No, thank you," says Lana, realizing that several people at the meeting have flyswatters. Pink plastic ones. "Have you already done the part where you ask if anyone's counting the days?"

"Yes, but go ahead."

"I'm Lana and I'm an alcoholic and I've been sober five months and three days."

Everyone claps.

"Oh, and also . . ." Lana raises her hand.

"Yes," says the leader.

"This is weird but I was wondering . . . I know we don't ask questions like this — I mean, I know this is not the way AA works, but I'm not that experienced as a sober person. Could I ask something?" Everyone waits for more. Lana takes this as permission and unloads. "I've been feeling strange — not high like high, maybe high. Bender high. I'm sober, but . . . how is that possible?"

"I can get that way from a treadmill," says a woman.

Lana shakes her head.

"You could be bi," says the man with the piercings.

"Bi?"

"Polar."

"Have you taken any mood-altering substances?" asks the leader.

"Not really. If you don't count sugar. We've been on the road, in a hurry. I've been taking care of my friend, barely any sleep for two days." That is the most she'll say about their bolt out of Maryland. "And it's been like . . ." She sits there struggling, trying to sort it. "Okay, it's been like if I'm happy, I'm like great happy, it's a total turn-on, but if I'm anything else . . . anything else, like the opposite, bugged, pissed, that feels fantastic too. It's all" — she slices the air — "buzzed. Could I be on a bender but sober?"

"What about medications?" asks the leader, jolting the entire membership into participation. Celebrex, Xanax, Ambien, Paxil, Ritalin. Everyone offers a trouble-maker.

"No meds," says Lana.

"If you're clean, you're not on a bender," says the leader.

Lana nods as if she accepts this, but she is not so sure.

Later a paper bag is passed for donations. Lana pretends to put money in, but instead takes out several bills, concealing them in her fist.

When she leaves, the guy with the piercings is having a smoke, hanging out on the sidewalk. "I'm loitering," he says with a smile, revealing what she did not see in the meeting, a gold tooth.

"Do you have a phone I can borrow?"

He pulls one from his back pocket and hands it over. "Addiction morphs," he says.

"Excuse me?"

"Addiction morphs."

"I'm not sure what you mean. It sounds depressing."

"It kind of is."

" 'Addiction morphs'? Does that have something to do with what I asked in the meeting?"

He tilts his head. "Could be."

"I'll have to think about that. This call I want to make isn't local. Does your plan include long distance?"

"No problem."

Lana dials. She moves away for privacy and closes her eyes as she hears the ring. Once, twice. Her stomach is churning. Is he

58

home? Yes, she hears the pickup and her father's voice. "Hello?"

"Dad? Dad, please." *Don't hang up,* she's going to beg, but before she can, she hears another click. He's gone.

Lana hands the phone back.

"Are you okay?" the guy with the piercings asks.

"I'm fine." She pretends to scan the street for where she needs to go, although she already knows, and heads to the café.

10

Clayton surprises Tracee and Rita when they are investigating the kitchen, hunting for something more substantial than a bar snack. "Hands up," he says. Tracee screams, which makes him laugh. "What are you doing here?" he asks.

"Who are you?" says Rita.

"I own the place. My name's Clayton. That's my refrigerator you're snooping in."

"Our car broke down. We needed shelter," says Rita. "I hope you don't mind."

By way of an answer Clayton blows his nose. He fights an endless battle with allergies, which are much worse in spring and the beginning of summer. His pale blue eyes water.

He's in the neighborhood of fifty, although he could be a lot older and he could be younger. Hard to tell, because he lost interest in maintenance years ago. His appearance suggests that he fell out of bed and dressed in the dark in his usual sweatpants and a sweatshirt. His gray hair, unkempt, sticks up in points. He frequently runs his hands through it backward and forward. He needs a shave.

The fact that he's a slob relaxes Tracee. She couldn't articulate that, doesn't exactly know why he doesn't seem like a threat — someone who might care about who she is and why she's here — but the reason is that he's too much of a mess.

"Your lion destroyed my veil." She leads him to the cage and shows him. Bits are now strewn from one end of the cage to the other. Scraps are caught in the lion's mane. Crystals from the crown lie scattered, looking like nothing more than drops of water.

"How did that happen?" says Clayton.

"He was wearing it."

"Wearing it? You mean on his head?"

"Like he was a bride. Wait till Lana gets here."

"What's going to happen then?"

"She'll discuss it with you."

"Discuss what?"

"Excuse me," says Rita. "I was wondering how the veil got on the lion's head in the first place. Before he mangled it."

"That I couldn't say, ma'am, because I don't believe it was on his head. How the hell could that happen? I didn't see it. Sounds wonky."

Lana turns up at that moment, having hitchhiked back in a truck full of eggs. She approaches suspiciously — noting the front doors ajar and, in the lot, a spiffy white Chevrolet Bel Air convertible with the top down (vintage, chrome polished to the max). Something Elvis might have driven.

She hovers at the door, but Clayton spies her and waves her in.

The Lion is huge — something she hadn't realized in the anxiety of the night before and early morning. It seats a ton of people, perhaps as many as two hundred, at small mismatched round tables with mismatched chairs. The lion is front and center. His cage, as large as a two-car garage, extends nearly to the back wall. The whole place is hung with old movie posters. Some films Lana knows, like *Easy Rider,* and some she doesn't, like *Blood Sisters.* Neon signs also decorate the room, mostly bar motifs — cocktail glasses or advertisements for various beer brands — although mixed in is an occasional misfit, like a palm tree.

"Finally," says Tracee.

Lana hands her a paper bag. "Grilled cheese sandwiches."

Tracee digs in the bag and hands one to

Rita. She rips off the foil and takes a big bite. "God, I'm starved. This is Clayton. He owns the place."

"How do you do? I'm Lana." She puts out a hand. They shake.

"How's the car?" says Rita.

"We're going to need at least nine hundred dollars to fix it. Maybe more."

Tracee jabs her.

"What?"

She leans in and whispers, "He owes me."

"The veil," says Clayton, in case Lana isn't following.

"It cost at least a hundred dollars," says Tracee. "Tell him."

"You should reimburse Tracee for her loss."

"Here's a little thing to remember," says Clayton. "Don't leave something you care about in the same room as a lion."

"The veil and the lion weren't in the same room," says Lana. "Technically a cage is a separate room."

"Not where I come from."

"Excuse me, but where did the lion come from?" says Rita.

"The circus was done with him. So I got him cheap. I figured it would pep things up."

Rita looks at the lion. "What's his name?"

"Marcel," says Clayton. "Not my idea. He

came that way."

"Marcel," says Rita sweetly.

"Don't go thinking he's a kitty." Clayton pushes up his sleeve and shows them his meaty arm. On the inside a gigantic scar runs from his biceps to his elbow. "I'm not giving you a penny for that wedding veil," he tells Tracee. "And you're wearing one of my employee's shirts. It's worth, if you include the special monogram, at least twenty bucks. Plus you spent the night here. So we're even."

"Do you need any help?" says Lana. "Can we waitress?"

"What?" says Tracee.

"Excuse me." Lana drags her by the arm far enough away that they can speak privately. "We've got to get the car back. If we waitress, we'll make enough. We'll be out of here in three weeks."

Tracee considers doubtfully. "Suppose someone finds me?"

"Like Rita said, it's nowhere. Course, nowhere long enough eventually becomes somewhere."

"What are you talking about?"

"Ignore that," says Lana. "Being sober makes me think more than I used to. Three weeks, Tracee, tops, I promise, and we'll be gone."

They return to the table where Clayton has been sitting, rocking backward in his chair, his arms folded across his chest, not saying a word to Rita.

"So?" says Lana.

He points at them. "I'll take one of you."

"Can't you use us both?" says Lana.

"Nope."

"How about if we split the job?" says Lana. "We'll both work but pay us one salary."

"Lana," protests Tracee.

"We'll make it up in tips. Especially if you wear the wedding dress to waitress."

"To waitress? I have to wear my wedding dress to waitress?"

"I like that," says Clayton. "It might add a little romance. I'm sorry, ma'am," he tells Rita. "The Lion needs sprucing up and you don't fit the bill. You're too old."

"That's mean," says Lana. "I don't even think it's legal. You could be discriminating."

"I'm surely discriminating. Why not file a lawsuit?"

"I might."

"She was prelaw," says Tracee.

"Then what? You flunked out?"

From the silence Clayton realizes he's nailed it.

Rita gets up and moves her chair into the table, as if to erase evidence of her presence. "He's not saying anything I don't know. I am old. I never was young, I mean in years, yes, but not really. Besides, I'm heading somewhere." She looks at the lion. "Good-bye to you, Marcel."

"We'll split the job three ways," says Lana. "One job, three ways."

"Okay," says Clayton.

"That is, if you want to," says Lana. "If you're not due wherever you're going right away."

"I could stay," says Rita.

"But you do the busing," Clayton tells Rita. "Busing only."

"Would you mind if we slept here?" says Lana. "Until we can afford a room somewhere."

"Little Tim will put you up."

"We don't know little Tim."

"He's right behind you. Tim, this is Lana and Tracee, and what'd you say your name was?"

"Rita," says Rita.

They all turn to see, standing in the doorway, a beanstalk of a young man of voting age and then some with a face fresh and wholesome enough to advertise breakfast cereal. His long neck cranes toward them,

66

because he's a bit nearsighted (undiagnosed) and more fascinated by them than they are by him. The women are struck primarily by his hair, which is that dusty pale orange known as strawberry blond. Trimmed short on the sides, it springs on top into unruly locks that flop every which way. His plaid shirt with snaps for buttons is neatly tucked into jeans that he hitches up when he wants to impress. He does that now.

"I suggested you might put these ladies up," says Clayton.

Tim smiles with such amazement and something else — possibly gratitude — that he might be a farmer who, after a drought, feels the first splash of rain.

As Lana, Tracee, and Rita gather their thoughts and their purses, Clayton hits speed dial on his phone. "Marybeth, you're fired. I've got two babes and an old lady doing your job and you can go rip off some other sucker."

11

Tim leads the way to his car, a compact two-door with a sign on the roof: WILSON'S DRIVING SCHOOL. He unlocks the trunk and spreads out a blanket for Tracee to lay her dress on, not realizing until that moment that the pile of silky white she is carrying is a wedding dress. He mistook it for a fancy curtain. Now he makes sense of her outfit. Her red shirt with *The Lion* on the pocket he recognized — he has one too. Her skirt — nearly transparent, in ruffles down to her ankles — must be underwear. A crinoline. He's heard of crinolines although not actually seen one.

He opens the passenger door, pulls a lever to flip the seat forward, allowing Rita and Lana to get into the backseat, releases the lever to flip the front seat back into place, and waits while Tracee gets in front. He makes certain that her organdy underskirt is completely inside the car before closing the door and hurrying around to the driver's side.

They drive along a country road, past verdant rolling hills dotted with clusters of very tall firs and an occasional field planted with rows of low leafy green plants. "Soybeans," Tim tells them. "You comfortable back there?" he asks Lana and Rita.

"We're fine," says Lana. "Do you teach driving?"

Tim nods. "Wilson's Driving School. Wilson's me. Tim Wilson." He steals a look at Tracee, who smiles. "I take care of Mr. M too."

"You mean the sexist pig?" says Lana.

"Excuse me, ma'am?"

"Clayton," says Lana.

"Oh, I do cleanup there and anything extra. But I mean Marcel. I call him Mr. M. Feed him. Also I work at the Pick 'n Save."

"That lion ate my veil," says Tracee.

"Your veil?"

"He owes me money."

"Who?"

"Clayton. It's his lion."

"Do you have any idea how the veil got on Marcel's head?" says Rita.

"Huh?" says Tim.

"The veil was on his head," says Tracee.

He turns into a gravel driveway at a sign, TULIP TREE MOTEL, a two-story brick building. Two white columns, whose peeling paint is visible from the car, border a yellow door shaped like a tulip. The rest of the building stretches out to the right like a long train. A white wooden staircase leads to a second-floor balcony that extends the entire length of the motel. All rooms are accessible from the outside.

"We can't pay for a motel," says Lana.

"It's not a motel," says Tim.

Tracee opens the car door to discover that Tim has sped around to her side and is offering a hand to help her out. He also helps out Lana and Rita, then takes the wedding dress out of the trunk and carries it carefully in his arms as if it's breakable.

"Are you married?" he asks Tracee.

Tracee blinks rapidly, batting back tears.

"I'm sorry," says Tim. "He died, huh? Your fiancé. He died right before the wedding. I knew you had a tragedy. I could see it in your eyes."

Tears stream down Tracee's face.

"I've got tissues," says Tim. "Fish 'em out of my pocket."

Tracee fetches a mini tissue pack from his back jeans pocket.

"Keep the whole pack. I get them for next

to nothing at the P 'n S."

"I'm not wearing my wedding dress to waitress," Tracee tells Lana.

They follow Tim up the staircase to the second floor, careful to heed his warning not to touch the railing because they might get splinters. "It used to be a motel but no one came. The owner turned it into . . . I don't know exactly what you'd call this. I guess rooms."

"How many do you have?" says Lana.

"One." He opens the door to number seventeen. "Welcome to my place. Make yourself at home."

The three women look in. A double bed with a pine bedstead takes up most of the space; the faded calico wallpaper curls at the seams. There's a wicker armchair painted red with broken bits on the arms and an old small TV. Various necessities from the Pick 'n Save are lined up on the bureau — a three-pound box of caramel creams, Ritz crackers, an extra-large jar of Excedrin, a giant jar of Peter Pan peanut butter, a four-pack of paper towels, a twelve-pack of Life Savers.

"No way," says Lana, assessing the accommodations.

"But I won't get in the way," says Tim.

"Do you get headaches?" says Tracee.

"No."

"What's all the Excedrin for?"

"Preventative."

"How could you not get in our way?" says Lana.

"May I have one?" asks Tracee.

"Help yourself. Anything here, help yourself." He slides open a closet. The door comes off its runner. He puts it back on the tracks and hangs up the wedding dress. "There's a fridge here with soda if you get thirsty." He taps it with his foot.

"It's just for one night," says Rita.

Lana and Tracee are surprised by her cheerful agreeability. "Well," Rita points out, "we're sure to make enough in one night to get a room here to ourselves. How much could it be? Tim, would you mind sleeping in the bathtub?"

"There is no bathtub," says Tim. "There's a shower. I'll sleep there."

Lana sets down her purse. "This is very kind of you."

12

Lana has showered and is relaxing in the chair, her wet hair wrapped in a very small hand towel that keeps coming untucked. Tim and Tracee hang out on the bed, sitting up against the rickety backboard. The TV is on, tuned to *Family Feud.*

Tracee daydreams about her diamond necklace. She misses it. Her fingers are itching to touch it, but there has not been a moment for secrecy.

"Look how heavy that man is," says Lana, disturbing her reverie.

Tracee focuses. He is pretty darn fat, this man who is head of the Dalton family and is trying to answer the question "What's the most common thing to lose on a vacation?" Luggage and hotel keys have already been mentioned. He's racking his brain and coming up empty.

"Your kid," says Lana, answering for him.

"That's a good one," says Tim.

"Remember that guy on our block who went on the space diet?" says Tracee.

"Jim Bonny," says Lana.

"The doctor put him on space bars," Tracee tells Tim, "these things astronauts eat. A meal would come along and he'd pick a different bar. I don't know what they were exactly. From eating these things and nothing else you drop, like, a ton of weight in a flash, but it puts your body into some sort of unnatural state. I think it's called 'tosis.' "

"It wasn't called that," says Lana.

Tim takes a pole standing upright near the bed. It's one of those things with a clamp on the end that they use in a supermarket to grab boxes off a high shelf. Tim uses this one in his job at the P 'n S and brings it home every night. He points it at the bureau, clamps a drawer pull with it, opens the drawer, and closes it. "I never need to get up," he says.

Rita comes out of the bathroom, freshened up, in time to see Tim, as a further demonstration, use the pole to grab the box of candy off the bureau. "Caramel cream?" He offers them to Tracee.

"Thank you." She hunts through for one she wants. "Look how cute they are." She holds it up for everyone to admire the chunky candy wrapped in striped waxed paper with twists at the ends.

He extends the pole with the box to Lana and Rita. Rita declines but Lana takes a handful. Then he swings the pole to the bureau, releases the box, and stands the pole back up. "If you'll excuse me, I've got some errands to run. I'll be back to take you to The Lion." He's out the door before they can say good-bye.

Tim takes the stairs two at a time and sprints out of the parking lot. He doesn't slow down until he's a quarter of a mile down the road, where he takes a turn and jogs down a narrow path through some pines to the Tar River, to a spot he knows where some people catch bass or catfish as well as run into a water moccasin or two, but that's never happened to him. Isn't it his luck that he's watching *Family Feud* with the prettiest woman he's ever met, that she's moved in, an answered prayer, and that he knows from how she says thank-you for a caramel cream that his mother would like her. Here she is, her fiancé dead and gone, probably in shock, and still she's acting positive, telling stories about space bars. Oh, man, he really screwed up. He's got to tell her. He's got to confess. He tries to reason it out. How can he explain?

He stands there throwing stones across

the river, which is nearly as narrow as a swan's neck at that particular location, while he tries to make sense of how it happened.

He stopped at The Lion the night before — well, early morning to be more accurate — before going home, because it's his job to clean up the place. Although sometimes he stops by when The Lion is closed, for no reason except to sit and watch the wild beast, who ignores him. Two lonely guys, one a senior citizen (the lion), the other a youngster (Tim), twenty-four, and two years out of Raleigh Community College, where he studied all the ins and outs of the furniture business, which turned out to be of no use whatsoever because, while he was there, the companies — and there were many — moved the manufacturing to Mexico. "Bad timing. Cutbacks. No one's looking to hire," he tells anyone who asks, but mostly they don't because everyone knows that cutbacks have pretty much squeezed the juice out of the whole county.

Tim set himself to cobbling together another living and another life.

He worked super late at the P 'n S because Ronald, who comes on after him, has a sick dog. Tim couldn't fuss about that, even though King gets sick a lot and Tami, who works the cash register, thinks Ronald is full of shit. So what if Tim clocks a few extra hours. So what that Tim is assistant manager and isn't even supposed to cover for Ronald. Tim couldn't leave Tami on her own, you never knew what could happen. While there's never been a robbery, customers can be quite pesky. The "no cash for returns" policy can get them pretty riled up. It was three a.m., a bit past actually, when he pulled into The Lion to do stuff he'd intentionally left undone the day before because he will do anything to avoid the sad, runty place he lives.

He never saw the women because he never went into the men's room. He never noticed the open window either, probably because he was preoccupied. He was homesick.

He was missing his mom's house, sixty miles away, near Wendell. Everything about it, especially the smells. His mom is always baking something, biscuits or one of her crumbles, blackberry or apple. She does his laundry, and his bed is comfortable. The sheets smell good. She dries them the old-fashioned way, outdoors on the line.

He brought his pole with him. Why had he done that? He wants to kick himself. He was unlocking the padlock, getting rust stains on his hands as usual, when he went back to his car for it. True, he needed it.

The paper towel rolls are stacked on a high shelf in the back of a packed closet. Still, it wasn't that important. He could have climbed up on a chair. Once inside The Lion, he flipped a single switch. A few sconces cast the room in a gloomy amber, which is why he was there awhile before he noticed anything. Tim conserves electricity. He uses only the lights that are absolutely necessary because it makes Clayton happy. Round-the-clock air-conditioning for Mr. M during the summer months, Clayton says, busts his balls. "I didn't think it through," Clayton told him.

The lion was asleep, lying on his side. Tim had checked — his eyes were open. Sometimes they're open, sometimes they're shut, which fascinates Tim. Why two ways of sleeping?

He'd finished sponging off the few dirty tables when way across, on the opposite side of the room, he'd noticed the mess on the bar and gone over to investigate.

Three half-drunk glasses of what looked like Pepsi, a scattering of nuts and pretzel crumbs, and a half-eaten jar of maraschino cherries. The little fridge under the bar was open. Wide open. He recalls wondering about that. He tested the door to see if it was broken. It wasn't. Someone had been careless, that was all. He dug a cherry out of the jar and popped it in his mouth. He popped in another, sat on a stool, and chewed.

They tasted delicious. He ate the rest.

Then he saw it.

He wiped his hands on his jeans before picking up the delicate thing, and turned and pulled it in several directions before he realized what it was: a wedding veil. Why didn't he put it in the lost and found, the cardboard box in the kitchen, which contained several pairs of sunglasses, a scarf, a headband, and a man's boot? It was none of his business to mess with something this precious, this obviously precious to someone, that was for sure, and now he knew who. Instead it piqued his curiosity. Who got married? Not Clayton, he'd ruled that out. You have to have some dates before you get married, and ever since his wife took off, his mother told him, Clayton's been flying solo. Solo, day in and day out.

Boy, had he been on the wrong track.

Using the pole, Tim clamped the veil by the sparkly crown. He waved it back and forth. Pretty thing, he remembers thinking as the netting fluttered, a sail in the wind. He leaned his elbow on the bar, listing sideways, looking up at the veil as, with his free hand brandishing the pole, he swooped it. God, he was tired. That memory is as clear as a bell, because it is the moment he was waiting for, the one he waits for every night — when he's so dizzy with exhaustion that returning to that empty, stale room at the Tulip Tree doesn't feel soul crushing.

I'll just try one more thing, he remembers thinking. *One more and then I'll leave.*

13

The hook is bent. The door is swollen, shrunken or mis-hung. Something. In any case she can't lock the bathroom. How did Lana and Rita do it? Maybe they didn't bother. Finally Tracee jams the hook into the metal loop, pinching her finger.

She balances her purse on the sink, opens it wide, and the necklace blinks right up at her. She rarely tries it on. Simply holding it mesmerizes her, triggering fantasies of a life she didn't have.

She lays it out on the top of the toilet tank, enjoying the sparkle while she washes her face, and lifts her shirt to splash on some cooling water straight from the tap. She's had the necklace less than a week and has found that if she doesn't see it every few hours, she worries it has vanished — fallen, or been stolen even, out of her purse.

Lana raps on the door.

Tracee scoops up the necklace.

"We've got to leave," says Lana.

Tracee tucks the necklace back in her purse at the bottom under everything.

"What?" says Lana when Tracee opens the door.

"What what?" says Tracee.

Lana whispers, "Did you just cop something?"

Tracee throws out her arms. Like what? There's nothing to take.

"You've got that look."

14

By ten that evening the women realize the situation they're in: The Lion is not popular. There are six or so tables occupied, isolated pops of activity, including a bunch of guys, workers at a local quarry, celebrating a divorce. They are on their third pitcher of beer and ordering a fourth. A couple of Clayton's friends are chewing his ear off about how NASCAR is in the toilet. A quiet couple show Tracee snapshots of their grandchildren. They have nursed the same rye and ginger for two hours, even though Tracee has politely inquired every twenty minutes whether they'd like another. She keeps refilling their bowl of peanuts.

Clayton bartends in his sweats, which the women find a depressing sight.

Rita takes her job seriously. She decides all the glasses are dirty from standing around and should be washed. "I've never had a paying job before," she confides to

Tracee and Lana. Every so often she checks on the lion, either glancing over while she buses tables or leaving the sink to stand in the doorway. From the kitchen she has a good view. *Probably he thinks I'm curious, like everyone else, like a visitor to a zoo. I'm not that,* she wants him to know. He faces away, his back to everyone. For hours he lounges on his side, his head up, still as a museum piece. His ears, round like mittens, poke through his bushy and tangled mane. Very occasionally they flick, a quick back-and-forth, the only sign of life.

"When do we get paid?" Lana asks Clayton.

"At the end of two weeks."

Lana groans.

"You can keep your tips."

She figures that will barely be anything. "You know, it flitted through my head when he fired that Marybeth, how could one waitress take care of this entire place? Now we know," she tells Tracee and Rita.

She stands at the end of the bar and broods, watching a woman play a game with her boyfriend that involves flipping pennies and chugging beer. The woman, younger than Lana, is a short blonde with way too much black eye makeup and a mouth that seems to take up most of her face, because

84

she laughs loudly every time beer dribbles down her chin. She's wearing what amounts to half a dress, her breasts are falling out of it, and the sheer fabric, wet with beer, sticks to her skin. At one point she puts a bare dirty foot on the table and anyone who wants to can see up her skirt.

When the woman bumps into a chair and then another on her way to the ladies' room, Lana follows. She stands at the sink, her back against it, facing the stall, waiting for the woman to come out. "Hi," says Lana, all friendly-like. Lana doesn't look friendly, however. She looks judgmental, like someone's mother. The woman, were she not drunk, would know instantly that she has trouble on her hands, but Lana's voice is so cheery it confuses her. She squints as if she can't quite see through the mist.

"I'm Lana."

"Candy," says the woman. She washes her hands.

"I'm telling you this for your own good, Candy, please trust me. You have a drinking problem."

Candy looks in the mirror and blinks a few times.

"You have no shutoff valve. Do you know what that means?"

Candy, her hands still dripping, unsnaps

her pink plastic clutch and takes out a cell phone. She holds up a finger, indicating that Lana should wait while she dials. "Help," she says into her phone.

"I'm helping you," says Lana. "That's why I'm here. I was you."

"Who are you now?" says Candy.

The door bangs open. They both jump even though Candy is expecting him. "What's happening?" her boyfriend shouts, as if he has arrived to put out a fire.

"Nothing, take it easy," says Lana.

"She's crazy," says Candy.

"Your girlfriend has a drinking problem."

"Fuck you."

"You can't even walk," says Lana, ignoring him and focusing on Candy.

"MYOB," screams Candy.

It takes Lana a second to differentiate between MYOB and something she is more familiar with, BYOB.

"Hey, we said fuck off, so fuck off."

Lana screams, "Your girlfriend's an alcoholic."

"Oh, shit," says Clayton, showing up at the door with some customers in his wake.

"You can't even walk," Lana screams.

"Can too," Candy shouts back.

Clayton steps between them. "Okay, that's it, we're done here." He turns his back to

Lana and smiles at Candy. "You okay? I bet you are," he adds before she can protest. "Come on, Danny, take your beautiful girlfriend back to the table." To the gathering behind him he says, "Bit of a rumpus. Over and out."

Danny puts his arm around Candy, staking his territory with a firm grip on her shoulder. She wraps her arm around his waist. "Bitch," she says as they leave.

Lana looks in the mirror and fusses with her hair. "How can you serve someone who's wasted like that?" she asks Clayton. "I hope you don't expect me to."

"If you want to quit, quit."

"I don't want to quit. I was trying to have a conversation."

"Not trying hard enough."

She follows him back to the bar.

Clayton pours himself a shot of whiskey and downs it. He holds up the bottle, offering one to Lana.

"I'm sober," says Lana, outraged.

"I can live with that."

"I don't see where it's any of your business."

"Born to spar. Fuck me. I miss Marybeth. Your girlfriend's upset." He points.

Tracee is collapsed at a table near the cage, wiping her eyes. She's wilted, her knees knock together and her arms hang limply. Lana hurries over, sits down, and leans in close. "What's wrong, Tee?"

"What were you doing?"

"What do you mean?"

Tracee jerks her head in the direction of Danny and Candy. He's at the bar now, paying the tab while Candy nibbles his shoulder.

"I was trying to help. She needs help. She went off on me, can you believe?"

"Suppose they tell someone."

"Tell someone what?"

"I don't know, that there are new waitresses and —"

"And what?"

Tracee pulls on one of her curls and twists it. "Will you —"

"What?"

"Not go off?"

"Where?"

"I mean off, like angry."

"What are you talking about? *She* went off."

"Please promise."

"I promise. I don't even know what you're talking about."

Tim hurries in the door with his grabber pole and a plastic sack from Food World. Immediately he scouts for Tracee, dying to confess — he has to get it off his chest. He's prepared an apology, a mea culpa about the veil, rehearsed it in his head many times, but decides against barging right over when he sees the women huddled together and Tracee blowing her nose. A moment of grief, he figures. Instead he waves a hello to Clayton and gets to work.

Marcel, perhaps smelling dinner, rises slowly and turns for the first time that evening as Tim sets the bag on a front table near the women. He nods, calls a "good evening" — wanting to please Tracee makes him pull manners from old movies and TV shows. Marcel moves closer as Tim takes out the five pounds of chuck (on special at $3.89 a pound), rips off the plastic and styrofoam wrapping, and clamps the steak with the pole.

"That's how your veil got on Marcel's head," says Rita.

"What?"

"I'm sorry," says Tim. "I hope you forgive me."

Tracee screws up her face, trying to understand. That Tim, not Clayton, is responsible requires a one-eighty, and she's slow on the uptake.

"Of course she forgives you," says Lana. "You're putting us up."

89

"I'll pay you back. Don't doubt it."

"It's okay," says Tracee, but her eyebrows still knot.

"You're sleeping in the shower," says Lana.

"Hell, I'd sleep in the sink."

"Marcel is hungry," says Rita.

"Right," says Tim.

"But why did you do it?" says Tracee. "I don't understand."

Tim thinks about his motives, even though he's already given them several hours of thought. "A bit of fun, I guess." He extends the pole, passing the steak through the bars. He presses a button on the pole, releasing the clamp. The meat drops. Marcel pounces.

"Is that as close to Marcel as you ever get?" says Rita.

"Pretty much."

"Is that as close as anyone gets?"

"I guess so. Unless they're crazy."

Rita watches Marcel devour his steak. The intensity, the single-minded focus reminds her of the times she secretly wolfed whole layer cakes. Sometimes she hid in the closet, vacuuming it clean afterward, poking that suction pipe into every possible nook and cranny, worried that Harry would find crumbs on his clothes.

"He must be starved for comfort."

She doesn't realize when she says this that she's alone. Tim has done his job and left. Marcel finishes, licks his paws, and rubs one over his nose. Perhaps he has an itch. He rises and, as he does, Rita moves close to the cage. The lion's big head is at the bars. She notices gray in his mane and can feel his breath on her face when she says to him softly, "Starved for comfort — I know what that's like."

"Hey, move it," yells Clayton. "Don't stand there with dirty glasses. It's not classy. And don't you have anything else to wear?"

Rita rips the bow off her blouse, startling Clayton. She picks up her tray of glasses and walks to the kitchen. At the door she looks back.

The lion is watching her. She holds his gaze.

15

Their combined tips for the night total fourteen dollars. It's a cruelty that fourteen is not equally divisible by three. Rita insists on taking four dollars and letting Lana and Tracee have five each.

Tim, driving them home, suggests they stop at the Pick 'n Save. "It's open twenty-four-seven." He assures them that since he's the assistant manager they can get whatever they need, it won't cost them. "It's the least I can do," he tells Tracee.

When they arrive he pulls Tami, the cashier, aside, and tells her to put all their stuff on his tab.

"What tab?" says Tami.

"Start a tab."

Tami ignores him and continues reading *In Touch.*

"Is Buzzard around?" Buzzard is their nickname for the owner, although the owner doesn't know it.

"In the booth," she says.

"Not happening," says Buzzard when Tim asks.

"You didn't even raise me when you promoted me. Not one dollar more. And I'm still doing all the stacking and pricing I did before, plus keeping things smooth. I'm the best at keeping things smooth, you know that. The least you can do is let me put their stuff on a tab."

Buzzard cleans his nails with a penknife.

"I'll work it off two extra hours a week."

"Fair deal," says Buzzard.

"Whatever you need, it's on me," Tim shouts to the women, who have dispersed down various aisles.

Lana calls, "One soap and one toothpaste for all three of us. And three toothbrushes. I'll get them."

Tracee tries on sunglasses. The pair she fancies has red frames and black lenses. When she puts them on she feels like a gangster's girlfriend. She slips them into her purse as Tim skids to a stop at her aisle. "Whatever you want, it's on me."

She looks at his friendly face brimming with kindness and generosity. She wants to put the glasses back. She wants them to jump out of her purse and onto the display. But it's as if they're gone, and she feels helpless to do anything about it. All she says is, "Thank you, that's really nice, but Lana will get everything I need."

Rita wanders up one aisle after another. She picks up a pack of Juicy Fruit gum, puts it back, and picks it up again. She meanders through the makeup, then gets interested in something called "butterfly washcloths," pastel-colored netting sewn together into a floppy ball. She runs one up her arm, and decides she'd like that too. At that point she gets a plastic basket to carry things. She goes to the section with stockings and tights — she's going to need more panty hose — but then on the opposite shelf notices a three-pack of women's underwear on sale for six dollars. After examining the pictures carefully on the cardboard box, she selects the relatively sedate bikini cut. Moving on, she reads all the labels on hand creams and then finds herself in the shampoos and conditioners, trying to make sense of the choices, not even sure whether her hair is dry, normal, or oily. These distinctions have always escaped her. She's never tried a conditioner and has used the same shampoo her whole life: Prell. When she spies a shampoo-and-conditioner combination with the name Fresh & Breezy, she unscrews the top and inhales deeply. A lovely aroma, not too sweet, piney. It also reminds her of dandelions.

She hopes it is just the thing for what she has in mind.

16

Rita has always been able to wake at the exact time she wants without the help of an alarm clock. At five a.m. she sits up in the chair, confused for a second to find herself in these surroundings, then relieved. It was awkward but not terrible to sleep this way, half sitting, half lying, with her legs on the double bed, which Tracee and Lana share.

She raises her legs off the spread and lowers her feet to the floor, waiting a second to see if Lana or Tracee stirs, and when they don't, she gets up and tiptoes to the closet. The rug under her bare feet feels like an old dry sponge. She nudges the closet door open, lifts Tim's pants off a hook, checks his pockets, and turns up what she wants: his keys.

She tiptoes into the bathroom, where Tim is curled up in the shower, a folded hand towel for a pillow and a skimpy bath towel for a blanket. Last night he gave them

T-shirts to sleep in, and before bed they all rinsed their clothes and hung them to dry — over the shower rod and towel racks, across the sink, and over the toilet seat (which is down).

Rita takes her blouse, skirt, bra, and panty hose, and tiptoes back out. She starts to dress but then, it's dark out, why not, she thinks, and quiet as a mouse she leaves, wearing Tim's tee and carrying her clothes, shoes, and the box of new underwear. She's hoping for a trash can on the way to Tim's car. When she doesn't find one, she sticks the panty hose in Tim's glove compartment, planning to toss them later. She dresses in the car, and soon after, enjoying the freedom of bare legs and bikini underwear, she arrives at The Lion, locates the right key on the chain, and unlocks the padlock.

Once inside, she heads straight for the ladies' room. She washes her hair with her new shampoo and conditioner. There is no hot water, but after the first shock of cold she finds the experience refreshing. Her hair reaches nearly to the middle of her back. She hasn't had it cut in years.

When she has finished, she arranges her wet hair around her shoulders as if it's a full skirt.

Rita leaves the ladies' room and walks to

Marcel's cage. Marcel is asleep, lying on his side, his front paws crossed over each other. The paws look soft, like the paws of a stuffed animal. She notices that sprays of little brown freckles form a mustache below his nose.

She sits on the floor right smack against the bars with her back to the cage. She smooths her hair.

And sits.

And sits.

She senses the lion's presence behind her. His head looms up behind hers and she hears him sniffing. The sniffs are short and then longer and more satisfied. She knows that he is sniffing her hair and that he likes it.

She stays there for a half hour at least, barely moving a muscle, simply listening to Marcel's friendly — yes, she is sure that they are friendly — sniffs.

Then she tells Marcel good-bye, locks up the place, and, under a cloudless sky showing the first light of day, drives back to the motel.

When she enters, turning the knob so there is barely a click, everyone is still asleep. She slips the keys back in Tim's pocket.

That night, when Rita buses tables, the

lion follows her, moving from one side of the cage to the other.

17

The next day Rita asks Tim if he'll drop her at the library. He's giving a driving lesson to a sixteen-year-old named Debi, and the ride over is a herky-jerky experience. Every time Debi makes a turn, she accelerates, changes her mind, and hits the brakes. When they get to the library, in spite of Tim's careful guidance, Debi drives right up on the curb.

The librarian is helpful, setting Rita up at a computer where she can use the Internet. *Who is this woman plain enough to be a maiden aunt in a period novel?* the librarian wonders. *What is she doing at the Fairville Public Library?*

She sneaks a look over Rita's shoulder to see what Rita is Googling. On the screen is a picture of a lion jumping back and forth through a hoop. Below which it says, "Never try anything when the lion is hungry."

As the librarian goes to answer the phone, Rita scrolls down and reads more.

THE LION

Clayton built The Lion twenty years ago, when the North Carolina furniture business was booming and tobacco farming was profitable. The design was his wife's idea. "A hodgepodge," Helen called it. "Keep it cheap — buy whatever they've got at the scrap yard, mix it all together. The crazy construction will get attention," she said. She was right.

He remembers the night they came up with the idea. All their friends had children, and Helen didn't see herself as the mothering type, but they wanted something together, a project. They went out for steaks — it was their second-year anniversary. They sat in the corner booth at the Outback Steakhouse. Everyone they knew drank beer, but Helen always ordered, "White wine, whatever you've got." She smoked through the meal, letting the cigarette burn in the ashtray, taking a satisfying drag now and then. "We're night people," she said, and that's what led to the whole notion of opening a bar, a big one with a jukebox and dancing.

Afterward, even though it was a cold night in December, they'd taken a ride in the Chevy with the top down. Helen took off her scarf and let the wind rip through her carefully curled bouffant. She always set her hair in hot rollers the size of frozen orange juice cans. They tooled up and down back roads hunting for For Sale signs, and were exhilarated when they saw a couple of flat acres available on Winstead Road. The property was convenient, right off the highway.

Helen was angular. Her hip bones poked out. She had thin arms with sharp elbows, narrow hard shoulders, and pointy breasts. You could get stabbed hugging that woman, which should have been a tip-off. She wore flowered dresses in slinky nylon that weren't exactly sexy but clung. Her skirts flared and stopped above the knee. She had good legs. And she was sociable. She kept the customers happy, moving from table to table. "Clayton's Place" — that's what The Lion was called then — was popular. One night an old beau of Helen's roared up on a motorcycle. He'd stopped in Fairville and had asked if anyone knew where she was. Everyone knew exactly where she was every single night. A couple of days later she told Clayton she realized it had been him all along.

"She's gone," was all he'd say when people asked. Folks were forced to speculate. They figured it out because a few had seen her eyes light up when that man walked in, and had noticed that she didn't table-hop that night.

Clayton never let on, even to himself, that he was bothered. So what if Helen took off and told him it was someone else all along. So what if that made all their years together something of a delusion.

Then Rocky died.

Rocky was a black mutt, mostly Lab, sleek-furred and graceful. Rocky went everywhere with Clayton. He loved the Chevy Bel Air. He sat up proudly in the front seat after Helen left (before that, in the back), and was handsome enough to do the car justice. He died of cancer — a quick death — and while Clayton couldn't allow himself to grieve for a wife who took off with another man, he went to pieces over the death of his dog. Of course, it wasn't only Rocky he was mourning. It was the double whammy, all that loss. He tanked.

He stopped taking care of his house, lived basically in the living room, sleeping on the couch. Sweats were the easiest thing to put on. He got sarcastic too. Couldn't help it.

Clayton's falling off a cliff emotionally co-incided with tobacco farming and furniture manufacturing hitting hard times. Some farmers switched to soybeans but didn't make as much. Everyone had less to spend, and going to Clayton's was depressing because Clayton was depressed. Many of the customers were depressed already. Only a few regulars came by out of loyalty, to cheer him up or because they couldn't give up the habit.

And that's the way it was until two years ago, when his aunt died. His mother's sister. She was his last living relative and she named him in her will as beneficiary. Clayton had to go to Florida to sell her small condo.

He drove down. It felt good driving around Miami. His 1957 Chevy blended in with the surroundings, all those spruced-up fifties buildings, many of them in orange or trimmed in orange, like his car's leather seats and dashboard. The ocean breezes pepped him up too. He spent a week getting his aunt's stuff sorted and found a Realtor to handle the condo sale. In the evenings he sat outdoors under a beach umbrella at a local bar eating fish tacos and drinking mojitos. No question he was buzzed when he picked up a newspaper that someone had left behind on the next table, read the classifieds, and, under "Animals for Sale," saw an ad for "big cat." He somehow knew what was going down. Someone was unloading a lion.

He called the number. The woman who answered had an accent he couldn't place. That she sounded foreign made him more circumspect. Instead of saying, "What's the deal? Are you selling a lion?" he said, "I'm interested in what you're selling."

She was polite. "We'll be happy to meet you, sir, at nine this evening in Jefferson Park."

He walked through a fancy wrought-iron gate into a tropical garden, an oasis of large, leafy plants and palm trees, their giant fronds in silhouette against the night sky. The couple was waiting.

He could barely see them. The garden was all darkness and shadows, and they were shadowy figures — olive skinned, dressed in black, with black eyes and shiny ebony hair, hers long and straight, his long too, wavy and tucked behind his ears. Clayton assumed they were Gypsies, a conclusion based on his fantasy of a Gypsy rather than any direct knowledge, and the fact that she wore large gold hoop earrings and a bracelet that jangled. She had a low, sultry voice, which made the experience even more novel and enticing, and Clayton more inclined to go with the flow.

No names were exchanged.

They led him to the street, where a horse trailer was parked.

"The circus is done with him," the woman said as Clayton looked into the trailer through a small square wire grate.

The lion was facing him. The remarkable yellow eyes, rimmed in a brushstroke of black, were flat. They gave nothing away. His head hung low. *He'll die if I don't take him,* Clayton thought. Maybe he was thinking of himself. This was *his* last chance too. At the same time, it didn't seem that the animal wanted to be rescued. It turned its head away, uninterested.

Clayton believed the story — that the lion was from the circus. It made sense. He knew the circus summered or wintered in Florida, whichever season it wasn't touring.

"Why aren't you giving him to a zoo or one of those safari places?"

"No one wants him." The woman knew how to close a deal. She was certain this explanation would hit home, that Clayton would identify.

"You'd think someone would."

"He's old. Believe me, sir, it's not easy to find a home for a wild animal."

The man said nothing, only kept his hands in his pockets and nodded whenever the woman spoke.

"We tried to give a parrot to a zoo once, a beautiful bird, and it was not possible. She took up much less space than Marcel."

"Marcel? That's his name?"

She wiggled her fingers, showing off silver nails. "Marcel, yes."

They followed Clayton to an ATM. He withdrew six hundred dollars to add to the four hundred he already had. Was he saving himself or the lion? Was it folly? A balmy night, two Gypsies, a garden as lush as a jungle, the intoxicating scent of gardenia and jasmine. A man could do something crazy, like fall in love or buy a lion.

They helped him attach the trailer to his Chevy, and as they drove off, the woman called out the window, "When one door closes, another opens."

"A goddamn cliché," Clayton said to himself. Yet it resonated.

He renamed his bar The Lion. He used the money from the condo sale to make it lionproof. He built the cage, added drainage and several accordion doors along the back to open the place wide. The cat needed fresh air. But after an initial flurry of interest, business lapsed to what it had been before, only now instead of one depressed soul in the bar (Clayton), there were two (Clayton and Marcel).

When Clayton discovered Tracee, as pretty as a spring day, snooping in his refrigerator, and then Lana, tough and sexy, strolled in, he remembered the door-closes-opens thing. He'd never been able to shake a belief in it, still harbored a tiny hope. The lion, now these women. Gypsies were fortune-tellers, weren't they? Then the very first night, Lana tried to stage an intervention in the ladies' room, browbeating poor Candy. When he was home later microwaving some mac and cheese, he laughed about it — how loony tunes was it of him to imagine they were some sort of salvation? Still, they weren't dull. He sat on the couch in his ratty blue terry-cloth bathrobe listening to a Braves away game on the radio. His TV was shot. A few weeks before, when the sound was static, he'd taken it apart. The wires were still strewn about.

The game was in extra innings, tied 6–6, when it occurred to him: *Lana is like Rocky.*

Rocky could get obsessed. He would scratch the same spot, trying to dig a hole in the wood floor, which was impossible. But if Clayton threw a ball, Rocky forgot all about the floor and chased the ball. Perhaps like Rocky, Lana needed redirecting.

The next night he pointed to the back of the bar — all the bottles and glasses — and said, "Do something with this. Make it nice."

She started organizing and reorganizing the liquor bottles by height and color. Sure enough, it turned into an obsession. Lana returned to the task whenever she wasn't waitressing. Clayton, pleased with himself, foolishly thought it was that easy to keep her out of trouble.

18

Tracee flutters around Lana and Rita as they approach the motel office. "Cash," she says. "Just pay cash."

"Of course cash," says Lana. "We don't have anything else."

"And don't sign."

"What?"

"Anything."

"I'll handle it, Tee. Don't I always handle it?"

They have been paid for their first two weeks' work.

"A grand total of two hundred thirty." Clayton pulled it from the register with a flourish and counted it out. Enough to get a room of their own, and worth it, they decided. They all feel guilty about Tim's sleeping in the shower, especially because he is cheerful and obliging and acts as if they are doing him a favor, allowing him to curl up every night on the damp, cramped concrete floor. He shares his clothes with Tracee too. She wears his shirts as mini-dresses. And he drives them everywhere.

Rita, who has been making daily secret early-morning visits to Marcel, knows that Tim doesn't lock his door and she can continue to sneak his keys and borrow his car.

"Maybe I don't want to go in. I don't want to be noticed," says Tracee.

"Fine," says Lana. She does not point out that Tracee works in a bar every night. Rita has gotten used to Tracee's intermittent paranoia. One morning when Marcel was sniffing her hair and Rita was sitting cross-legged with her back to him as usual, she said, "We're all hiding from something." She just put it out there.

"I'm staying out here for sure, but don't do a lease or whatever," says Tracee. "No matter how much that lady insists."

That lady, whose name is Marlene, is talking on the phone. "For Pete's sake, it's on the second shelf," she says, and then to Lana and Rita says, "Two hundred a month, cash. Where it always is," she says into the phone.

She's a large woman in small clothes — a tank and shorts she's bursting out of. She wears a black knit hat pulled down low on her round face. It hides her hair. A black knit stocking cap in summer. This curious fashion choice, a mite threatening, makes Rita wary and Lana more inclined to provoke. Marlene counts their money while she keeps the receiver clamped between her ear and shoulder, picks a key off a hook, number nineteen, and slides it across the counter. Rita notices that the shades are drawn and they are blackout shades. Behind the counter, taking up all available space, is a maroon Barcalounger with the back down and the footrest up. It faces a TV on a wooden box. The TV is on, tuned to *Iron Chef.*

"How come there is cable in the office and we don't have it in the room?" says Lana to Rita in a loud voice.

"Hold on." Marlene puts the phone down.

"That's an awfully big chair," says Rita. "How many positions does it have?"

"Four." Marlene keeps her beady eyes on Lana, who looks everywhere but at her, pointedly uninterested.

"You got complaints?" says Marlene.

"Oh, no, we're fine," says Rita.

"Get cable, who's stopping you? This isn't a motel."

"It is to me," says Lana.

"It's not."

113

"Just because you rent rooms by the month doesn't make it not a motel. It looks like a motel. It's called a motel."

"Don't forget your telephone call," Rita tells Marlene. "Would you happen to have an empty cardboard box or two we can use?"

"Outside, around the back."

"Thank you. We appreciate it." Rita holds the door for Lana.

"It's a motel," says Lana, when Rita has almost but not quite pulled the door shut behind them.

"What did she do? Did you have to sign?" says Tracee.

"She has cable." Lana gives the finger to the closed office door.

"I don't get it."

"She was watching *Iron Chef.*"

"So?"

"She has cable and we don't."

"We've never had cable." Tracee looks to Rita for clarification.

"She has a box or two we can use," says Rita. "Isn't that good news? She says they're around the back."

Tim follows them as they pack their few things, even though there is no space in the room to follow them. Stepping this way and that, he pleads his case from one to the other. "It's not necessary to move," he repeats again and again.

"We can't impose on you anymore," says Lana firmly.

He insists on carrying the two boxes to number nineteen, two doors down.

"Just leave them at the door," says Lana. "You're going to be late for work."

"Thank you, Tim," says Rita.

"I'll carry the wedding dress too," he says.

"That's not necessary," says Tracee.

The nine of number nineteen is missing. There are two nail holes and, in the old paint, a shadow of a nine. The doorknob rattles a bit — it seems to be loose — as Lana unlocks and kicks open the door. Their new room, a twin of Tim's, has a slightly moldy smell. Rita pulls up the blinds, some of which are bent, and opens the window. Lana tosses what remains of her pay on the bureau. "All I've got left is twelve dollars."

Seeing that crumpled ten and two singles really drives it home. "We're never going to make enough to have the car fixed. We're going to be stuck in this shithole for fucking ever."

"Don't say that," says Tracee, her bottom lip trembling.

"It's true."

Lana goes into the bathroom and slams the door.

Rita takes Tracee's dress and hangs it up for her. She slides the closet open and shut several times as if testing it. She doesn't want Tracee to see how happy she is and that she is smiling.

Lana empties her toiletries out of a paper bag into the sink and then arranges them in a row on top of the toilet tank. She pats her back pocket, remembering it's still there, and slips it out. That's the last thing she sets down, at the end of the row: the condom. She stands the packet on edge, resting against the Noxzema.

19

Rita has insisted from the beginning that Lana and Tracee sleep in the double bed while she bunks in the chair with her legs resting on the mattress. She pointed out the logic — she's smaller, it's an easier fit. Usually Tracee crashes first, falling asleep before the TV is off and the lights are out, and Rita conks out shortly thereafter. Lana, plagued by insomnia ever since childhood, secretly takes a Tylenol PM, something AA would disapprove of.

Tonight, with the unsettledness of a new room and the prospect of spending a lifetime in it, everyone is wired. The television has a loud hum, making it impossible to watch. They lie there wide-awake with the lights out.

"Who wants a cherry Life Saver?" Tracee passes around a roll that Tim has given her. "Have you gone to another AA meeting?"

"Why are you asking a question you know

the answer to?"

"Sorry." Tracee moves closer to the edge of the bed. She allows herself only a sliver of space. She worries about getting in Lana's way even while they sleep. Lana kicks. Even sedated with a Tylenol PM she's restless.

"Do you want company? I could go with you," says Rita.

"It's not that kind of thing. Besides . . ." Lana thinks about the guy, the one with the piercings. He knows her dad hung up on her. She tries to wipe out the memory. It's harder to wipe out memory when you don't drink, harder to make embarrassment and humiliation and guilt go away. He knows her dad won't have anything to do with her. He's guessed the truth, she's sure, that it's all her fault, that she deserves it. "I don't need to go to AA, I'm fine."

"It must be hard to work in a bar," says Rita.

"No it's not. Lots of AA people work in bars."

"I didn't realize that. Still —"

"Does anyone care if I eat the whole roll?" Without waiting for an answer, Lana stuffs all the Life Savers in her mouth at once.

She crushes them with her teeth. They lie there quietly while she chews and then sucks the last of them into extinction.

"Have you noticed how little that lion moves?" says Lana.

Tracee giggles. "He's like furniture. It's so weird. I'm getting someone a beer and walking past a lion. Yet I don't even think about it. Because he's not there."

"He gives us his backside. It's so 'fuck you.' Way to go, Marcel. Why doesn't he hide in the cave?"

"Because his home is sad," says Tracee. "That white hut. It looks like an igloo."

"It's elegant," says Rita.

"What?" says Lana.

"The hut?" says Tracee.

Rita hesitates. Harry always told her to keep her thoughts to herself. "No one wants to know about *you*. No one cares what *you* think." He drilled it into her, but Lana is persistent. "What do you mean, elegant?"

Rita tries to say this clearly in order to be worthy of their interest. "Facing away is elegant because it's simple. What are his choices? He's in a cage. How does he maintain his dignity? Every single day living in a cage he's less of who he was." Her voice trembles here, and she talks faster to compensate. "How does he hold on to something that perhaps he never had?" She has said more than she intended and fully

119

expects them to burst out laughing. She always amused Harry when she didn't mean to.

But Lana and Tracee seem to consider her words in a friendly silence. "Cool," says Tracee eventually.

"He follows you," says Lana.

"Oh?"

"That's the only time he moves at all. When you're around. I've noticed that."

Lana turns on her side and tucks the pillow closer to her shoulder. Tracee knows that means that Lana will be asleep shortly. She listens for Rita's soft and regular breathing. Rita sleeps so quietly. One night Tracee worried that she was in a coma. After a few minutes, certain that her roommates are deep in slumber, she draws the diamond necklace from under her pillow. She wraps the choker twice around her narrow wrist. The stones are so pretty, she thinks, like tiny stars.

TRACEE

The first thing Tracee stole was a scrunchie. It was the Christmas season and she was in Squires, a small variety store in Fosberg, Maryland, where she and Lana grew up. She was nine years old and had wandered the six blocks to Broad Street by herself. Broad Street, festooned for the holidays with silver-and-green garlands spiraling up lampposts, had all of Fosberg's fancy shops and, at the ends, a few low-rent stores like Squires. Broad divided the town, stately houses on double lots with grand trees on the north side, and, on the south side, where Tracee and Lana lived, small identical one-story houses with aluminum siding originally built for veterans after World War II.

Tracee wasn't tall — that came later, when she had a growth spurt at thirteen — and as she stopped here and there in various aisles, she had to stand on her toes to see the merchandise laid out in compartments on the counter. She played with the scrunchies, rolling them on and off her wrist, pulling at the elastic. The assortment was enormous, at least it seemed so to her. They came in every color and fun fabrics like shiny plaids, polka dots, denims, and velvets. Mr. Squires was behind the counter, smack-dab in front of her, when she found herself slipping a red velvet one into her pocket. It was sparkly, sewn all over with sequins.

"What'd you take, missy?"

It was strange to be called that.

"Nothing."

Quick as a flash he was around the counter and pulled the scrunchie out of her pocket. "Where's your parents?"

Tracee shook her head.

"Who you with?"

Tracee shook her head.

He grabbed her arm and yanked her past staring customers into his little dark office in back. "You're bad news." He stared down at her, his face flushed and puffed with anger. To Tracee he looked like a red balloon. She thought he might explode. "I'm calling your parents, what's the number?" He had to ask her three times before she could tell him, because she was shaking all over.

While he dialed he glared at her. Tracee blinked, trying not to cry. "Sit down," he said, but she didn't move as he waited for her mom or dad to answer. No one did. They weren't home.

"Sit," he said again, and this time she obeyed.

"Keep your butt in that chair." He went out and slammed the door. She thought he was getting the police and didn't move a muscle while she waited to be arrested. But he turned up a while later and phoned her parents again. Still no answer.

"I'm sorry," said Tracee.

"You're not getting out of it that easy."

He didn't realize that she was apologizing for her parents, for their not being there.

"Where are your parents?"

Tracee shook her head. She had no idea. She never did. Her dad did short-distance trucking, day trips or hauls lasting two or three days. Often her mom jumped in the cab at the last minute and took off with him. They'd be laughing, nuzzling — her mom basically climbing all over her dad. Occasionally they waved good-bye. Usually not. Tracee had to fend for herself.

Mr. Squires left again.

The next time he came back to call, he sat down at his wooden desk and tapped it impatiently as the phone rang. Giving up, he banged open and shut a few drawers, finally locating a transistor radio. He set it on the blotter next to the scrunchie and turned it on. "Fiddle with the dial. Find something you like. Don't steal it." He laughed at that and left again. Tracee didn't touch the dial and for two hours listened to Christmas music. She hummed a little to the songs she knew.

When it was six o'clock, time to close, and there was still no answer at Tracee's house, Mr. Squires said, "Christ, you're a stray cat. What am I supposed to do with you?"

"I could go to Lana's."

"Who's that?"

"Next door."

"I'll drop you."

Tracee got up, and at that moment he noticed she was wearing her parka. She'd been sitting there for hours in a heavy coat.

"Weren't you hot? It's pretty hot in here."

She shook her head.

"Let me try one more time." By this time he knew the number by heart and put the speaker on. The scrunchie was still on the desk blotter, and he spun it while they listened to the phone ring. Finally he gave up.

He offered the scrunchie. "Why don't you

keep this, an early Christmas present."

Tracee started to shake her head no but stuck her hand out instead.

He drove her home in his large car, and when he pulled up at Tracee's, she was certain he noticed that her house was the only one on the block without a wreath or fancy red bow or lights strung through a scraggly bush or neatly rimming a porch. Lana's house had all those things, and a big plastic reindeer too.

"I'm sorry," she said to Mr. Squires, again not for stealing, this time for her house.

"Don't do it again."

He didn't drive off until she rang the doorbell at Lana's and Lana's dad let her in.

Tracee took the scrunchie home and stuck it in her dresser drawer as if, when she was considering what to wear, it was simply one of the possibilities, albeit one she never picked. "What should I wear today?" she would ask herself every morning, although the choices were meager.

Lana knew that Tracee stole, but she learned about it so gradually, she didn't think much about it. Lots of kids stole things. A group of girls in sixth grade used to laugh about their raids on Costco, bragging about what they took and who was the decoy and who was the thief. Tracee simply never outgrew it. She went through a Hello Kitty phase (key chains, pencils, pins, plastic wallets decorated with that pink-and-white cartoon kitty), all of which ended up in a heap on her closet floor. For a while she favored stealing from Rite Aid, where it was understaffed and easy to scarf a Maybelline eyebrow pencil or a pretty tin of mints. But mostly her plunder was random, born of a sudden urge wherever she happened to be and for whatever caught her eye.

Folks in Fosberg knew that Tracee's parents were often away and left the young girl roaming around a fairly empty house. They also knew that Bob Byrne, Lana's father, looked after her and that she and Lana were inseparable. Tracee had a wide-eyed innocence, and she was such a skinny girl — no matter how much she ate it never stuck to her. She was not only a waif, she looked like one. She got used to the sad smiles people bestowed when they said hello. She didn't mind the pats on the head, although she didn't understand why she was getting them.

Boys quickly learned that compliments went farther with Tracee. Needy for affection and approval, she liked to please. With a little flattery they could have their way with her. Thanks to the routine and help at Lana's, she got through high school, but she had to be cajoled to study. She preferred to watch *The Cosby Show* in reruns every afternoon and evening. She loved that TV family: Cliff and Clair Huxtable and their four kids, especially Denise, the sassy teenage daughter. She loved the Huxtable house, cozy and crowded. Theo's bedroom was such a mess. She loved how Cliff and Clair were always figuring out what trouble their kids were up to and paying a visit at bedtime to have a heart-to-heart about it. And they were all so funny. It seemed like everyone in that family was having fun.

After high school, when Lana moved to Baltimore, Tracee moved with her. They shared a room at the top of a three-story brick row house. Four hundred dollars a month. Lana went to the university until she flunked out, while Tracee worked a succession of jobs — Ace Same-Day Photo, Betsy's Hair (she gave shampoos, swept the floor, and cleaned the bathroom), and then the Sun Spot, a tanning salon where she met J.C., who liked a fake bake every now and again. Tracee answered the phone, greeted customers, and took the money.

J.C. thought she was hot, and knew she was gullible because he underpaid her for his tanning session and convinced her she hadn't counted properly before relenting and admitting the truth. He took her for buffalo wings and slept with her that first night, and when he woke up the next morning he found she'd cleaned up his room, put everything away, and he appreciated that. She got to be a habit.

Tracee thought J.C. was gorgeous. He had a wicked sexy grin, wore sunglasses with reflector lenses, and his brown hair was streaked the color of Velveeta. She soon took over the job of keeping his hair looking exactly the way he liked it. She was a pro with Clairol, had a real knack for highlighting. She'd learned from observing at Betsy's Hair.

J.C. was a weight lifter, and, because he liked an audience, Tracee often accompanied him to the gym. She sat on the stationary bike, not pedaling, and watched him bend over, grunt, and raise one hundred fifty pounds over his head. He could lift her too like a barbell, and often asked to do it, and then dropped her on the bed. She hated it, it frightened her, but she didn't want to tell him. If she ever complained, like about the time he slept with Joanne, a trainer at the gym, he said, "You want to break up?" He jumped right to it. Tracee backed off.

She put up with being lifted like a barbell and J.C.'s barely concealed transgressions, and never told Lana about it. Lana and J.C. were oil and water.

After three years with Tracee, J.C., who worked at the bar in a Hampton Inn, enrolled in audio school part-time to become a professional in the music business. Even though he had no real gift at the computer engineering part, barely passing those courses, he thought he'd be good at spotting talent. He was going to graduate, finally, on June fifteenth — twelve days after Lana and Tracee left Maryland in haste. All through spring, Tracee and J.C. talked about how they would move to Nashville. "And get married, right?" Tracee would add. J.C. didn't disagree. They'd get a U-Haul, pile everything in, and take off. Tracee was excited, figuring that J.C. was about to pop the question. Wondering each day if today was the day.

On May thirty-first, a date she does not forget, she was driving J.C.'s car along Route 9 on the way to pick him up from audio school. They were going to an Orioles game. She stopped at an antique mall to use the restroom, and afterward took a few minutes to browse. At a stall that sold vintage clothing she tried on a crocheted hat that hugged her head and flared around her ears. The saleslady called it a cloche, a word Tracee had never heard before. Then she spied a jewelry booth, and, with rare confidence and entitlement — after all, she was about to get engaged — she strode over to peruse the rings. She was surprised to discover that Karen Hofstadder's mother was there. It was her booth. It had a sign on it, HOFSTADDER'S, so she knew that Mrs. Hofstadder didn't only work there, she owned it. Tracee had gone to high school with Karen.

The booth was fancy, perhaps the fanciest at the mall. Glass vases inlaid with swirls of gold were locked in glass cabinets. There were several cases of jewelry — the rings, necklaces, pins, and earrings displayed on sheets of black velvet.

"Hi, Mrs. Hofstadder," said Tracee.

"Hi, Tracee," said Mrs. Hofstadder, friendly but not paying attention. She was busy helping a mother and her teenage daughter. The mother favored pendants on long chains. "I like things that land on my cleavage," she said, which made her daughter squeal, "Mom!" Tracee loved that. "Mom!" she said to herself, as if her own mother were there embarrassing her. Tracee leaned over to check out the rings. *What will*

J.C. give me? she wondered. She admired a thin gold band with a bow of tiny diamonds and another narrow band studded all around, diamonds alternating with red stones that she assumed were rubies. *Probably J.C. can only afford semiprecious,* she thought. *As long as it's from you,* she imagined herself saying, *that's all that matters.*

"Ooh, don't you love this?" Tracee thought they were talking to her, but the mother and daughter were exclaiming to each other about a necklace that the daughter was wearing. "Diamonds and gold, eighteen-carat," said Mrs. Hofstadder.

The daughter posed this way and that in front of an oval mirror set on the counter. Each time she adjusted even slightly, the diamonds seemed to shoot off sparks.

"What kind of cut is this?" said the mother.

"It's called a half-moon," said Mrs. Hofstadder. "The necklace is from the 1920s."

Tracee had a way of fading into the landscape. She was so unimpressive, people often forgot she was there. No one noticed her staring, coveting that necklace.

"How much is it?" said the mother.

"Three thousand dollars, although I could do a little better," said Mrs. Hofstadder.

"Good grief, take it off, sweetie." The

131

mother laughed, and, at that moment, two other women pressed in to see the rings. Tracee got bumped sideways, closer to Mrs. Hofstadder, who undid the diamond necklace, set it down, and selected something that was cheaper from the same tray.

"How's Karen?" asked Tracee.

"She married Greg, didn't you hear? Hold your hair up, that's good." She fastened silver and turquoise around the young girl's neck.

It was a perfect storm — a bit of a crowd, the saleswoman preoccupied, the object within reach. Tracee's hand, like a magician's, skimmed the velvet, and the diamond necklace was in her pocket.

"Bye, Mrs. Hofstadder," said Tracee.

Mrs. Hofstadder didn't bother to answer.

Unlike other things she'd stolen, which went directly from her pocket into the bowels of her bag, Tracee fussed over the necklace at the first rest stop she came to. She held it up to the light, touched every single stone, examined the tiny claw settings. Something old, something new, something borrowed, something blue. This necklace solved two problems in one. Old and borrowed. *Tracee, we want you to have this.* Tracee saw it so clearly: her mom and dad hovering, and she the center of their attention. All snug on a couch that looked remarkably like the one in the Huxtables' living room — big and comfy, pale gray. Her dad beams while her mom weeps with happiness. *Tracee, we want you to have this. Your mother wore it at our wedding. You'll wear it at yours.*

Then a car pulled in and parked next to her, stopping Tracee from what she was about to do: try the necklace on. She tucked it away in her purse. *I will wear it at my wedding,* she thought. *Borrowed, I'll tell everyone. It will go perfectly with my dress.*

She had her eye on one already. Satin and lace shimmering with beads as tiny as dewdrops. She hadn't tried it on but had fallen head over heels. It cost a fortune. Tracee was sure the store would let her buy it on time.

She started up the car and pulled back onto Route 9. She didn't want to be late. J.C., an Orioles fanatic, hated to miss even "The Star-Spangled Banner." He never left a game before the final out.

20

One night at The Lion when it's the usual slow, Lana flops into a chair at the kitchen table, where Rita is cutting limes. The paring knife is dull; she has to saw them.

"It looks pretty out there, how you arranged the bottles and glasses," says Rita.

"I should do the wall stuff next. All the neon. Maybe groupings." Lana jumps up, turns on the faucet, sticks a hand under it, shakes off the wet, and bounces down again. She sits there, her leg jiggling.

"Are you all right?"

"Some beer splashed on my hand. I thought I might lick it by accident and start down a slippery slope." She laughs.

"Were you tempted?"

"I don't know. Not really." She takes a piece of lime and sucks it. "I used to drink things with limes. Screwdrivers, cosmos, lemon drops — well, that's with lemons, but same difference. I only drank fancy

134

drinks when someone else was buying. It was never hard to get someone else to buy." She grins. "Beer with lime. That's delicious. Sometimes I drank boilermakers. When I was showing off." Lana enjoys the word, "boi-ler-maker." For a second, looking back, it all seems romantic. A happier time. "I drank tequila too. I love tequila." She sucks the lime ferociously until there is no pulp or pith. The activity is intense. Rita stares, she can't help it. Lana starts gnawing the skin.

"I wish I could be addicted. I'm too scared of life to be addicted. I suppose that's why Harry . . ."

Lana stops gnawing and hangs on for more.

"What's it got to do with God?" says Rita.

"What?"

"It's Harry's favorite saying. If you said something, that's what he'd say back."

"Buzz kill."

"Huh?"

"That means, like, it's a joy buster."

"Yes. I would say so." Rita piles the slices in a tumbler. "We don't have bowls. I've looked in all the cabinets."

"AA's all about God. Giving it up to a higher power."

"Giving what up?"

"Who knows. I'm not giving anything up

to God, even though they say it's not God, not necessarily, but if it's not God, what is it? I don't get it. These are sour. My tongue's shredding." Lana drops the rind on the table and starts on another. "I screwed up college. My dad doesn't speak to me."

"Because of college?"

"No. Something else. Worse." Lana slaps her own cheek. Hard.

Rita grabs her hand and holds it. "Why did you do that?"

"I don't know."

"Please don't do that again. Please." Rita lets go, but her hand hovers in case she needs to stop Lana again.

But Lana only takes another slice of lime. "You don't want to be an addict."

"I know. I only meant, I wish I were reckless." Rita pushes her chair back and walks to the door. From here she can see Marcel, and as soon as she appears, he rises off his haunches and moves slowly to the corner of his cage closest to her. His long tail drags along the ground. It always drags. That bothers her. It doesn't seem right.

Clayton shouts, "Hey, Lana, get out here."

"Creep," says Lana.

She dumps her lime bits in the trash and heads to the bar. "Tracee's got it covered. What do you need me for?"

"Eye candy."

Lana, irritated, leans back, resting her elbows on the bar, and plays a game she invented where she assesses the customers: *How many bars have you been to?* When six young guys knock the door back and stroll in, she guesses: This is their second. They're cocky. There's a jacked-up confidence in how they walk, and they keep talking, not too loudly (which would signal their third), but they don't stop joking around as they pass from outside to in. A lack of curiosity, that's a tip-off. Definitely The Lion is their second bar.

Lana's always been a sucker for stocky men. One of them is built solid and muscled. His hair is the same coppery color as hers — more reddish in some light, more brownish in other. They have similar coloring, tan without being tan. Lana calls it a twinny thing, likes it when she and the man look like they go together before they get together. He's not taller than her, five-foot-six to her five-foot-seven, but that's okay, because he's hot and she's bored.

"Hey, Clayton," he says.

"Hey there, Tucker, how's it going?"

Clayton sets Tucker and his friends up with Coors, and Tucker notices Lana. Lana pretends not to notice him. He lifts his bottle in a greeting, and Tracee pokes Lana with her elbow to say, *Check him out,* but of course Lana already has.

Rita comes out of the kitchen and puts some quarters in the jukebox. She's never used a jukebox before but has decided that Marcel might like some music.

The jukebox, a big shiny old thing, is a mass of dazzling colors — turquoise, pink, lemon, and lime. To make a selection Rita pushes a button and the choices spin on a silver roller — Dolly Parton, Patsy Cline, Tammy Wynette, George Jones. All traditional country. Then she finds someone she loves, Julio Iglesias. She has listened to him on the radio. She presses another button to stop the roller and a third to start the song "Bamboleo," one she's never heard before.

Julio on the jukebox stops everyone cold. At the few occupied tables glasses are set down, looks exchanged as if everyone has suddenly found themselves in a foreign country without intending to go there. "Bamboleo" is a salsa, a bouncy, happy beat, and Julio's voice is smooth and seductive, as if he himself is swiveling his hips around a dance floor. No one understands a word of it.

Rita, oblivious to the effect of her musical taste, looks over to see if Marcel appreciates it. His tail slightly elevates. It swings once back and forth. What a charming, even comical tail it is, with that burst of fur at the end like a feather duster.

She hopes the music will help make the time pass for him as well as for her, and she returns to the kitchen to dry some glasses.

Clayton storms in. "What the hell noise is that? Are you trying to clear the joint?"

"What do you mean?"

"I wouldn't gargle to this shit."

Rita doesn't say anything.

"You're only here as a favor. Out of the kindness of my heart."

He leaves.

"But it was on your jukebox," she says softly.

He storms back. "I didn't pick the songs personally. That jukebox came secondhand. He's not singing English."

"It's Julio."

"Julio?"

"The singer. Julio Iglesias. He's from Madrid." Rita says the word "Madrid" as if it's "wonderland."

"Have you ever been to Madrid?"

She shakes her head no. She hasn't really been anywhere.

"Madrid is a dot on a map. That's all we are. A bunch of dots." He takes out a handkerchief and blows his nose, which really does put a period on the conversation. He goes back to the bar.

Rita picks up a tray to bus some tables and goes out of her way to pass Marcel. She leans in very close to the bars and softly sings along with Julio. "Bamboleo, Bamboleo." She wiggles her shoulders in the tiniest suggestion of a salsa move. Marcel's tail bounces up and flicks.

At the end of the evening, Tucker, the one remaining patron, ropes Lana into sitting with him. She tangles her leg in his, flirting shamelessly. Lana, who has a smoky voice, works it when she flirts. She sounds as if she is simmering on a low flame. They discuss scary movies. Her favorite is *Scream;* his is *Saw.* She deflects all personal questions with teasers like, "Wouldn't you like to know?" Intrigued by her evasiveness, he doesn't notice that she asks him nothing personal either. Lana feels powerful, a puppeteer pulling strings.

Tim is doing a serious cleanup of Marcel's cage. First he uses the pole from the P 'n S, clamping it to a dustpan. He skillfully manipulates it through the bars to scoop up the poop. Then he folds open all the back doors, exposing a huge span of outdoor space, and hoses down the cage (as well as replenishing the water trough). A moonless night glittering with stars provides a storybook backdrop for Marcel, who now appears to be in a cage in the middle of the wilderness. Rita finds the sight simultaneously depressing and enchanting.

Tim's final task is to mop up around the bar. He can barely concentrate because he is too busy admiring Tracee. He's been obsessed with her all night. How gracious she is to customers. She thanks them for coming and waves good-bye. He loves her long curly hair, which bounces, and thinks he could drown in her eyes, which look to him gray sometimes and at other times green. Her pale skin is inclined to freckle. A few new ones have turned up on her nose, and he wants to tell her, "Hey, cute freckles," but he doesn't have the nerve. Her spontaneity is amazing. Once she got out of his car during a sun shower and stood in the road getting soaked and grinning. His favorite thing ever — he keeps a mental record — was when she spied a hummingbird zinging this way and that, and made Lana, Rita, and him come out to the field.

"How crazy is that bird?" she said.

Watching her tonight, he marvels at how quick she is to smile. She's generous with her smiles. They're like gifts she's handing out.

Tim's not without experience. There was his community college girlfriend, a short affair with one of his teachers, as well as some quickies in the storeroom with a Pick 'n Save cashier (no longer employed), but Tracee's something else. She casts a spell. When she's around he simply can't stop staring.

Lana untangles from Tucker. "Tracee, come on. Come with us. We'll drop you."

"We'll drop her?" says Tucker.

"Yes, we'll drop her. You too, Rita. And then we'll go to your place. Do you have a place?"

He drapes an arm around her and they leave.

"Thank you for lending me your clothes," says Tracee to Tim. "I got beer on this shirt."

"I'll wash it. Don't worry."

"Thanks." She runs out to join Lana and Tucker.

Seeing Tim yearn for Tracee is giving Rita pangs of sadness. She comes up to him and offers this: " 'Then look for me by moonlight, / Watch for me by moonlight, / I'll come to thee by moonlight, though hell should bar the way.' "

She leaves, and after a second Tim rushes after, catching up in the parking lot. "What's

142

that you said?"

"A poem."

"Did you write it?"

"No. I just memorized it." She quotes again. " 'I'll come to thee by moonlight.' "

" 'Though hell should bar the way,' " says Tim. "It's my feelings."

"Then you're the highwayman."

"I'm the highwayman."

A honk. Rita hurries to Tucker's pickup and crams herself into the cab, sitting on Tracee's lap.

The truck rumbles out of the lot.

Tim, alone with the mop, watches it go.

21

Lana wakes up. She turns her head left. There's a clock, a cheap black digital on a wooden box, Tucker's bed table. It's 5:02 a.m. She sits up and looks at Tucker. He's naked (as is she), sleeping on his stomach, his face smashed into the pillow. He smells awful. Beer awful. There are several empty cans on the floor as well as Lana's Pepsi, and Lana is careful not to step on them as she pads into the kitchen and opens the refrigerator. Nothing but six-packs. Budweiser is the beer of choice, although there are also a few Pabsts and a Coors. She drinks some water straight from the tap, and then uses the bathroom, which doesn't appear to have been cleaned lately.

She goes back to the bedroom and tugs on Tucker's feet. No response. He's passed out cold.

Their clothes are strewn about where they dropped them after ripping them off in a heat. Lana picks up stuff, sorting his from hers, getting dressed as she does, and when she lifts up his pants, his wallet falls out. She picks it up and sees, pinned inside, his badge. Tucker is a cop.

A cop.

She had no idea.

Lana tears into the living room to find the phone. Where might it be? She has to call Tim to pick her up, even though it's the crack of dawn. She has to get out of here fast. What will she tell Tracee? Well, she won't. Maybe it will never come up. She's flipping up Tucker's couch cushions, imagining a handset might be buried between them, when she spots car keys on the TV. A round metal tag hanging off the chain identifies them as Fairville PD.

Out the front window she sees the car, one house down.

Lana forgets her mission — the phone hunt, the need for rescue. It flies right out of her head. She forgets even her panic in the face of an opportunity, enticing and naughty.

She takes the keys, leaves the house, crosses the street to Tucker's patrol car, and drives off in it.

When Lana takes off in Tucker's car, Rita is

pulling into the parking lot at The Lion for her morning visit with Marcel.

Once inside, she goes straight to the jukebox, drops in some coins, and punches "Bamboleo."

The song wakes Marcel in his cave. He pokes his head out and, seeing Rita, rises to his feet, stretching his legs and yawning. His back legs are stiff, Rita has observed, he doesn't move quickly. Not that he has anyplace to go, so why would he? Still, he's agile. She didn't realize that lions had such thin, sinewy legs. He ambles to the side of the cage nearest Rita.

"Isn't this music simply . . ." Rita pauses and then uses a word she's never used in this way before: "hot." Swaying and snapping her fingers, she improvises what she imagines is a salsa step.

The lion roars.

Rita laughs. "Take it easy, Marcel."

She picks up a thick rope, loops it loosely around her neck like a long strand of pearls, then takes two packages of beef patties out of her purse.

She rips off the wrappers and slips the patties between the bars. Marcel eats eight practically in one gulp.

She tries several keys on Tim's chain before finding the right one. When Marcel has finished eating and is licking his chops, he turns his head to observe Rita turning a key, lifting off the padlock, and tentatively pushing back the cage door.

She takes a deep breath, exhales loudly, and pats her chest — preparing heart and mind to enter the lion's den. She steps inside.

The door clangs shut behind her. She flinches, but the lion stays unperturbed and quiet.

She unwinds the rope from around her neck and moves closer. When she is near enough to reach out her hand and touch him, she lowers her head and lets him sniff her hair. She resists the desire to thrust her hands into his mane and tousle it. "Marcel," she says, "you've got to see the sunshine."

She loops the rope around his neck. Marcel allows it, remaining still while she knots it.

She pulls the rope. Marcel sits. It's not clear he wants to leave.

She tugs. And tugs again.

Marcel rises, and Rita leads him out of the cage. They walk toward the front door, knocking into chairs now and then. Every so often Marcel's tail swishes, dusting the tops of tables.

Rita peeks outside. No one is about.

"I've thought a lot about this, Marcel. If something happens to you, like if you go berserk in the outdoors and fresh air, it's still better than spending your life in a cage."

She tugs Marcel out.

She walks him around the parking lot. She walks him as if he were a dog, only he's a lion. Occasionally he stops to sniff some stray grass, but mainly he keeps moving, staying right by her side. Around and around they go, and then Rita thinks, *Why not? We've come this far.* They cross the road into the field.

At the top of the rise Rita sits. The damp, sharp grass prickles her legs. Marcel settles beside her. He lies flat on his stomach, his long legs stretching out front and back.

There they rest and enjoy the dawn. The dark sky has faded to a translucent gray. Soon it pales and brightens. Rolling hills, waves of grass, and in the far distance, a border of tall firs gradually come alive with color.

Rita and the lion stay until the sun rises high enough to spill a golden glow over the trees and light up the fields dotted with lavender and yellow wildflowers.

22

Lana cruises along the highway in the patrol car. Her head nearly swivels off when she catches sight of Rita sitting on the rise with the lion. She pulls over onto the shoulder, gets out of the car, and looks back.

They are tiny figures on the horizon but they are unmistakable.

It is extraordinary to be struck by lightning twice in a minute. As soon as Lana sees Rita and Marcel, she understands that she may not have to spend her life in Fairville. She gets a plan. Perhaps it is that "eureka" — the notion that she may have a way out — that startles her into a serious look at Tucker's car. The gold stripe across the white door with POLICE in bold black letters brings it home to her that she has committed a serious crime. She has stolen a police car.

The squawking on the walkie-talkie, a turn-on up to now, suddenly agitates her.

Although there is no attempt from "head-quarters" to communicate with Tucker, she is eavesdropping on a summons for another deputy to report to the elementary school because a window is broken. The situation needs investigating. This is all real, she realizes, not that she thought it wasn't before, but in some way it actually wasn't. It was a lark.

She has to return Tucker's car. Before anyone notices she's in it. She's worried that she might not find her way back to Tucker's house, but she does, and he is exactly where she left him, naked, dead to the world (although not dead) on his bed.

Leaving the car where she found it and the keys where she found them, she hurries to Fairville's main street, but heads the wrong way, has to flag down a jogger to figure out where she's going, and, breathless, finally arrives at Star Nails, whose door is locked. Is there a meeting this morning? She paces up and down, relieved when a car, and then several more, pull into the angled slots. A small crowd of AA members gathers, waiting for the one with the keys. For reasons she doesn't understand, she resents how cheerily people at AA greet one another. Lana keeps to herself, arms crossed, head down, and aims straight for the same hideous couch she sat on before. The guy with the piercings smiles and nods. Lana returns the greeting with a cool half wave. She keeps an eye on the coffeemaker, edging around the perimeter to pour herself a styrofoam cupful, and douses it with a stream of sugar from the dispenser. There are glazed doughnuts too, and she takes one, rips it in two, and devours it in a few bites, a ravenous display worthy of Marcel. The caffeine and sugar hit is instantaneous. To add to her confusion and guilt, she is now wired.

The member who speaks today is a stooped man with a Southern accent so thick she can't understand him. Perhaps she's too rattled. Every so often he raises his hand, points a bony finger, and mimes a jagged line. She notices a white plastic band on his wrist, probably a hospital patient ID. Is he miming the needle on a heart monitor? Was he released to attend the meeting? It's all confusing. On the next couch over, a heavy woman who is fanning herself taps her flip-flops while he speaks and says, "Yes," every now and again, as if she's at a revival meeting. It bugs Lana. In Fosberg and Baltimore, where she has attended AA meetings, no one ever provided a hallelujah chorus. This isn't church.

Still, when the speaker is finished and the leader asks if anyone wants to share, Lana's hand shoots up.

"I stole a cop car," she tells them. "This guy Tucker. I don't even know his last name. Tucker. I picked him up, had sex with him, and this morning while he was still asleep — well, more like passed out — I took his keys and took a ride. Why did I do that?" Her hands whirl around, illustrating her frazzled state, her utter confusion about her own behavior. "Why?"

To her horror and embarrassment, she has to suppress a smile. Where did that come from? Even now, even as she realizes how destructively she acted, something about the episode amuses, a fact that further distresses her and produces an additional onslaught of self-disgust. "I brought the car back, he never knew, so no harm, no foul. Still . . ." She considers how she could be in jail right now instead of plotting her exit from Fairville. "I guess that's all I want to say."

The room seems unnaturally quiet. *That must be one of the worst things they've ever heard,* she assumes.

"Is there anyone else who wants to share?" says the leader. He acknowledges someone sitting behind Lana.

"Last time you came you stole money out of the donation hat."

Lana, preoccupied with herself, registers this a few seconds after it's said. "What?" She turns around. The woman is knitting and doesn't miss a stitch.

"I was planning to pay it back. It wasn't for me. It was for Tracee. She was starving."

"You owe us six dollars."

Lana digs her wallet out of her purse. All she's got left in life is a ten. "Does anyone have change?"

Someone does.

Lana is cringing, her T-shirt sopping with sweat. She wants to walk out. The distance to the door seems huge, not that she could travel it. Mortification has paralyzed her. She is trapped here with her torturers. Is someone even allowed to do that in AA, level a charge at another member? There's a tiny hole in her jeans above her right knee, and, for the rest of the meeting, she digs her thumb into it, working it wider, pinching her skin. Finally the end, the worst, the Serenity Prayer. She has to stand up and hold hands in a circle, and that woman, her accuser, scoots in next to her. Lana is cursing Tracee for being hungry, for always acting like she'll die if she doesn't eat, for sucking Lana right in and playing on the

153

goodness in Lana's heart. *It's not my fault, fuck you all,* she is thinking while everyone chants, "God, grant me the serenity to accept the things I cannot change; courage to change the things I can; and wisdom to know the difference."

Lana leaves quickly, unaware that the guy with the piercings is chasing after her. He taps her shoulder. "Hey?"

She stops. Waits for more.

He offers a Nicorette. She shakes her head. He pops two and chews. "Do you know how to tell the difference between an addict and someone who isn't?"

"No."

"An addict will touch a hot stove, burn himself, and touch it again."

She thinks about that. "You mean why I took the car?"

"Beware of your need for trouble."

"Fuck you." Lana speeds off down the street and doubles back. "I don't know why I said that. I shouldn't have said that. I'm trying to stop swearing. I truly am. I shouldn't have — Is 'fuck' a swear word? Maybe it's just ugly. Maybe I'm trying to give up ugly. Good luck to me." She's tired, it's only nine in the morning and already it's sticky out. "I don't even recognize the air."

"Strange place, I get that."

"At least someone gets something." Lana moves a little farther down the block to avoid any other stray AA members. "What's it got to do with God?"

"What's that?"

"That stupid prayer. That prayer," she amends, taking the "stupid" out, feeling guilty even for that.

"It's not God. It's whatever."

"The prayer says God."

"It could be anything. Buddha?"

"Buddha's god. Are you into Buddha?"

"I light candles. That's kind of an India, Asia thing." He tugs his earring. "I like those monks. The Tibet ones."

"What's it got to do with God?" I'm echoing Harry? Why in the world? From the few tidbits Rita has offered, he's awful, got to be. In any event, surely Harry meant, If it doesn't have to do with God, shut up about it, whereas Lana means something different. "There is no God," she says flatly.

"Heavy."

"Could I ask you a favor?"

Anticipating her request, he hands over his cell.

"Thank you. Thanks very much. I need privacy. If you'll wait one minute." She points down an alley. "I'll just be . . . I won't

155

run off with it." She hurries down the narrow alley between buildings to the rear of Star Nails. There is a lot of debris — several broken manicure tables and a few chairs. Lana sits at a lopsided one and dials, knowing her father isn't home. It's a weekday, he's an electrician. He's off installing someone's kitchen fan, rewiring, flipping switches on a fuse box. She rehearses her message while she dials, deciding it will be grown-up, not begging, simple. *Dad, I'm sorry for what I did. I just want you to know that I'm sober now, sober six months.* Then she hears his voice. He has a wonderful voice, deep and warm. Inviting, friendly. She loves her dad's voice. But on the machine it's strangely blunt and cold: "I'm out, leave a message." She hangs up. He's erased her. She was the one on the machine. "If you want to reach me or my dad, start talking." She'd recorded it when she was thirteen. Even when she went to college, he didn't erase it. He didn't erase it when she flunked out. He didn't erase it when she spent the years since floating from one job to another. Now he has.

She returns the phone.

"Bad news?" he says.

"No, it's fine. I was calling my father. He's

not home. He's going to be very upset to miss my call, but, you know, *c'est la vie.*"

23

To put her plan into action, Lana insists that Rita needs better hair. They all crowd into the bathroom, and, with Lana supervising, Tracee trims it to shoulder length.

Now it looks like hair and not a long drape.

Rita, viewing herself in the mirror, is struck with the thought that she looks younger. She's never even considered younger as a possibility, but she likes it. She asks for bangs. Tracee obliges.

She also needs an outfit. "Something dramatic," says Lana, who has noticed a rack of one-dollar clothes at Goodwill.

Tim drives the women over, and on the way he tells them about loggerhead turtles. He's been searching for something to charm Tracee and hopes this might be it.

"The babies hatch at night on the beach in sand pits. Like two hundred eggs cracking at once, round eggs shiny like pearls, and the turtle babies walk toward the moonlight to find the ocean. They're sea turtles," he adds, realizing that information might be helpful. "One summer I volunteered at a beach, Sunset Beach, going from place to place — stores, bars, houses — asking folks to shut off their porch lights or draw the shades to make sure the baby turtles walked in the right direction."

"Why are they called loggerheads?" says Lana.

"Because they have big heads," says Tim.

Tracee says nothing. All those tiny turtles needing guidance make her want to cry. Tiny turtles scurrying to the ocean and a bright white moon lighting the way. She sits quietly thinking about that. Tim doesn't know if he's charmed or bored her.

While they shop, he goes for a soda.

"Do you think Tim is hot?" asks Tracee as they hunt through the mash of clothes.

"I think it's possible to have too much imagination," says Lana, laughing. "That's what I think."

"But he's so" — Tracee fishes around for the right word and comes up with it — "sensitive."

"I agree," says Rita.

"Last night he hung an air freshener on the ceiling. He's a genius with that pole."

"Island syndrome," says Lana.

"What's that?" says Tracee.

"Isolation creates whatever — an attraction that, if you weren't stuck on an island, you wouldn't have."

"I think," Rita says, and then proceeds deliberately, "that having too much imagination must be like having too much happiness. Impossible." She pulls out a dress — a mint green wash-and-wear with billowy sleeves and a minimal shape, barely a nod to the female form. On Rita it will look like a potato sack. "I love this. Especially the color."

"Rita, we're counting on you to save our lives and get us out of here," says Lana.

"But I don't want to leave here."

"We're still counting on you." Lana pulls out something short in leather. "What about this?"

"I prefer this."

That night The Lion is filled with the usual sparse crowd, about fifteen people. While Clayton is wiping off the bar where he has knocked over a bag of peanuts, he hears Julio on the jukebox. That dammed "Bamboleo." He swings around and sees Rita in the mint green dress walking toward the lion's cage. Her hair is down. She's wearing lipstick and a bit of makeup, which he doesn't quite realize, only that she looks different. Her face is set with a purposefulness he hasn't seen before.

Rita stops at the cage, face-to-face with Marcel.

An uneasy quiet settles as customers notice. The few who don't, Lana and Tracee nudge.

Rita and the lion are communicating. No one doubts it. The communication is silent but the bond is unmistakable.

Rita slips her hand through the bars, reaches in, and places her index finger on Marcel's nose.

Lana and Tracee forget to breathe.

Rita pulls her hand back through the bars and returns to the kitchen.

She is up to her elbows in soap suds when Clayton storms in with Lana and Tracee in his wake.

"Are you crazy?" he screams. "Is your brain sawdust? One chomp and you'd have four fingers, no, one chomp and you're missing a hand — are you right-handed? — yeah, one chomp and you're missing your good hand, maybe an arm, and there'd be blood spurting all over the place. And I'm out of business and that big kitty has a bullet between his eyes."

Rita rinses a glass and places it on the dish rack.

"I should fire you for that stunt."

Rita turns to meet his eye. She rubs her hand against her cheek and gets some suds on it. She looks like a little kid.

"Would you do it again?" says Clayton.

"Do what?"

Clayton places a finger on his nose the way Rita touched the lion.

"Right now?"

"No. Tomorrow. Give the folks some time to phone their friends."

Behind him Lana and Tracee silently leap and pump their fists in a cheer.

The next night The Lion is half full. "More customers at one time than I've seen in years," says Clayton. And Rita's finger is once again on the lion's nose. She pulls her hand back through the bars, turns to the audience, and nods shyly.

Everyone applauds.

24

Lana, Tracee, and Rita fly out of The Lion, high on happiness. Lana waves the sheaf of bills they got in tips. Tracee jumps and twirls. "We made a fortune. You did it." She throws her arms around Rita.

"How amazing. You are amazing," says Lana.

Rita smiles. "It was really Marcel. I owe it to him."

Tim opens the car door and bows like a footman with a coach and four as Tucker's pickup roars into the lot. Tucker, carrying a Coors, nearly falls out of the cab, and hurls the can at Lana, barely missing her. "You stole my patrol car."

"So what?" says Lana, while Tracee, startled, realizes that Tucker is a cop.

"I'm suspended. The chief says they don't know anymore if I'm law enforcement material. They're reviewing me."

"Don't blame me. You were drunk. You

163

were passed out cold. The car was sitting there. You left your keys."

Tracee moves slowly and quietly backward, away from the fight.

"I left my keys in the house," says Tucker.

"Same thing."

"Not hardly."

Tracee gets into Tim's car, closes the door, and slowly sinks from sight.

"Who told you?" says Lana.

"The chief is AA."

"That rat. What a person says in AA is supposed to stay in AA. He violated the code."

Tucker tries to assemble himself into a sober state, tries to keep his words from tripping over one another. "This job I have, as an officer . . . being on the force . . . it has a pension."

"You're worried about a pension? How old are you?"

"I'm twenty-five, and I can retire at forty-two with a full pension and health insurance until I die. That's security. That's job security. I can have a family and know I can take care of them. That's big."

He climbs into his truck. "I'll get you back. I don't know how but I will."

He floors it. The truck throws up stones as it screeches out of the lot.

"Jerk," screams Lana as loud as she can.

On the way to the Tulip Tree, Tracee starts squeaking with anxiety. At first Tim thinks the noise is coming from the motor. He pulls over. Then he realizes it's Tracee next to him, in the front passenger seat.

"Put your head down," he says.

Tracee drops forward, her head between her legs.

"Breathe." He rubs circles on her back. "Breathe, breathe, breathe. That's good. That's real good."

The squeaks come less frequently, then faintly. Finally they stop.

Tracee sits up. "Thank you. I feel much better."

"I took CPR."

Tracee leans close and brushes a piece of lint off his shirt. "Fluff," she says. How good he smells. Is it aftershave or is he simply one of those people with a wonderful natural scent? For Tim the light brush of Tracee's hand across his chest is the most exciting moment of his adult life.

"Would you mind if Tracee and I talked privately?" says Lana.

Tim gets out, hurries around, and helps Rita out of the back.

As soon as the door is closed, Lana starts in. "How would I know he's a cop? Think

about it. How would I know?" She is reasonable, calm, soothing. She leans forward
between the seats, speaking softly. "Tracee,
I am a victim here. I go to AA to feel safe,
it's my salvation. What would I do without
it? And look what happens. Somebody rats
me out. I took a hit for you."

"Huh?"

"I forgive you. It's okay."

"What?" Tracee is getting all twisted up.
Lana forgives her? Isn't she mad at Lana?

"Remember when you were starved and
we had no money? I borrowed some from
AA to get you and Rita grilled cheese
sandwiches, and the other day a woman at
the meeting accused me of stealing. Like I
wasn't going to pay it back. It was awful. It
was a gigantic public humiliation."

"Sorry."

"It's okay."

"It's my blood sugar."

"I know. You should always carry around
M&M's. We should get a big box of them at
the P 'n S."

Tracee wants to mention the car. How
could Lana kidnap a police car? But she
doesn't want to point it out, she hates to
confront. Besides, she gets so lost when
Lana explains.

Lana flops against the backseat. She flicks

the ashtray open and shut. "That whole thing with the cop car has to do with hot stoves."

"You were cooking?"

"Not exactly."

"He was cooking?"

"No one was cooking."

Tracee sits and blinks. Blinking is something she did when she was little. It was an activity.

"It's a very complicated, sophisticated thing to understand about sobriety.

"Tracee?" Lana says when she doesn't get a response. "Tee?"

"I'm going to end up in jail." Her voice wobbles.

"He's suspended. He's not even on the force. You're completely safe. Besides, it's just a dress."

Tracee pulls in: knees against her chest, arms wrapping her legs, head tucked down.

"Where's Tracee?" says Lana, as if Tracee is a baby.

She hears a muffled sniffle.

"Why are you so worried anyway?" says Lana. "Is there something you're not telling me? Something I don't know about?"

This all feels familiar, even though Tracee can't identify what feels familiar — some way the conversation goes, the way she gets trapped.

"Not the handkerchief you copped at Goodwill," says Lana. "I saw that. I mean something else. Something bigger, besides the wedding dress?"

"Bigger?" Tracee feigns innocence. She hates Lana's intuition. Or is it telepathy? — they have known each other so long. "No." She denies it with insult and outrage, the way people do when the opposite is true.

Outside Tim is pacing back and forth, glancing in the car window, trying not to snoop but worried about Tracee.

"I have to apologize, Tim," says Rita. "I've been borrowing your car."

"That's okay, anytime. What for?" He slaps a mosquito on his neck.

"In the morning I walk Marcel."

"You walk Marcel?"

"Yes."

"Where?"

"Outside. Just around."

Tim thinks about that, imagining the lion on a leash leading the way, which isn't how it works at all. Rita is the leader. "I bet Mr. M likes that."

"I think he does."

"How'd you get my keys?"

"I go into your room when you're asleep and take them out of your pants pocket.

You never lock your door."

Lana sticks her hand out the window and waves them in.

25

The next night at The Lion, Rita sits in front of the cage, facing the customers. She sits there for a half hour while Marcel sniffs her hair. The customers gasp when his big head looms up behind hers. The sniffing is fascinating, the sound, the variety, sniffs so dainty you could believe it of a kitty, and snorts so loud you might think Marcel was planning to eat her head. Both she and the lion have rusty-brown hair flecked with gray, and, for customers, there is something vaguely erotic about the fact that Rita and the lion share the same color palette.

Rita loves sensing Marcel's presence behind her and feeling his breath, which is hot.

Clayton is riveted. The Lion is packed, not an empty table, but as hard as Clayton works, he still finds that he can't take his eyes off Rita.

Later, when everyone has left, they all

celebrate.

"I've been thinking about this," says Clayton. "From now on, no busing tables. You can waitress."

"Thank you," says Rita.

"We want three jobs, three salaries," says Lana.

"You got it." He uncorks some wine. "Bordeaux?"

He pours them cheap wine, making a point to serve Rita first. Lana takes a Pepsi from the fridge and they all toast. "To us," says Clayton, "and a damn big future."

"To Marcel," says Rita.

26

The AA meeting has already begun when Lana slams in, rattling the door so fiercely that the bell over it falls off. "Who is the police chief?"

No one answers — identities at AA are private — but a few heads inadvertently swivel toward a bald man in his fifties sitting on a couch in the corner. His eyes widen slightly behind thick black-framed glasses, the only indication that it might be him.

"You used my private confession, things I said in here in total secrecy, to wreck someone's life. Because of you an innocent man may lose his job and his entire future. You —" She is about to say "suck" but thinks better of it. "If there is such a thing as expelling a person from AA, you should be, and I sincerely urge everyone here to do that."

She whirls around and leaves.

27

Rita never thinks about the past. It's as if she were born the moment Lana and Tracee picked her up on that highway. She is so grateful. Now that they have their own room, she leaves little presents on their pillows, like mints in a fancy hotel.

"What's this?" says Lana, spying a mini-corsage of pretzel sticks tied with a bit of ribbon.

"Nothing, really," says Rita. "Just something."

"This is so cute," says Tracee, nibbling it.

Another night Rita cuts quarter-moons out of the *Fairville Times* (a free four-page weekly devoted to classifieds and local happenings) and leaves them as pillow presents, each moon placed carefully, tilted as if it hangs low and lazy in the sky. Another night she gives them each a mini-galaxy — stars cut from newsprint. Sometimes Lana and Tracee find simply a wildflower or a stick of gum. They love the presents and begin to look forward to them.

Unlike Rita, Lana can't stop thinking about the past. Being stuck here in limbo until she can pay for the damn car has trapped her between the past and the future, creating a void that shame and guilt have rushed to fill.

After a night of drinking last January, Lana awoke in her apartment flat on the floor, fully dressed — boots, miniskirt, sweater, down vest. Everything except her underpants. She stood up and, in spite of a splitting headache, had a dawning suspicion. She placed a hand on her thigh and slowly slid it up for certain confirmation. She had no idea, not a clue, how her underpants had left her body.

When Tracee came home from J.C.'s later that morning, she found Lana in the kitchen drinking coffee and eating Frosted Flakes from the box, shoveling handfuls in her mouth. "I have to stop drinking. I have to go to AA. Will you come with me? Because I'm worried I won't go. I'm worried I'll drive right past it and buy a six-pack instead."

On the way over, Tracee asked, "What happened to your nose?"

Lana twisted the rearview mirror to look.

Her nose, swollen at the bridge, was red heading toward purple.

When she had managed to stay sober for seven days and still recalled nothing, she thought, *Give it a month. Maybe a bit more.* Recovered memory, something she'd either read about or seen on some TV show or other — the trauma would reveal itself later. But that night remained a blank. She speculated: sex with someone she either knew or picked up — a quickie in a car? outside behind the bar? in a narrow hallway near the restrooms? — all things she'd done before. Or things she hadn't done, like sex with several men? A gang fest. And what about her nose? Had someone punched her? Had she been raped? She examined herself for other bruises, didn't find any. She took a pregnancy test, an AIDS test. She got tested for every possible venereal disease, waiting, hysterical with worry about the outcomes, which were negative, and believing that she deserved every ounce of suffering. She didn't want to go to the many bars she frequented to ask what had happened. Even contemplating such a thing was degrading. She wondered if she'd danced on a bar. Had she stripped? Had she tossed some stranger her panties like a bouquet at a wedding? What vulgar acts might she have performed in public?

What had happened was this. She'd been with a guy named Duke. He'd picked her up at Dario's, a dive bar on the seedier side of Baltimore. He was a biker and showed her his shark-nose Harley. She tried on his helmet. It was huge, and when he took off down the road speeding, weaving, with her sitting behind him, the helmet fell forward, smacking her nose. She was riding blind, laughing hysterically. By the time he finally wailed to a stop back at the bar, she was weak from laughing. That was the crazy thing about drinking. Emotions came out backward. She'd been frightened to death, and instead of screaming in terror, she'd laughed deliriously. She was a confusion, especially to herself.

Afterward they sat at Dario's bar, matching each other shot for shot, seeing who would fall off his stool first. "Whoever does has to tip the bartender their skivvies," said Duke. He wasn't wearing any, although she didn't know that. In any event, she lost. She peeled them off right then and there (on the floor where she landed) without giving a damn who saw, actually hoping that people would appreciate her brazenness. She left her thong on the bar with Duke's thirty-six dollars for the tab. She gave Duke a blow job to get rid of him and drove herself home, weaving all over the roads but arriving safely.

Now, at The Lion, whenever she sees someone toasted, or hears a woman in a stall throwing up, or even merely steps outside for fresh air (something she did the other night) and hears a couple laughing a little too loudly, she remembers that she doesn't remember. It hits her like a ton of bricks.

The truth is trashy, nothing worse, but she has no idea. She spends her nights guessing at her humiliation, which is worse than knowing. Guessing about what happened, who it happened with, and how many people know it.

She hates herself. How could she not?

LANA

When Lana became a serious and committed drinker she understood how alcoholics provoke and manipulate, by turns begging, angry, hostile, seductive. Feelings dulled by booze left one free to feign anything. But when she was a child, she understood only that her mother was volatile and unpredictable. Lana, Tracee's protector, who had scared off many a bullying boy, was scared of her own mother.

One freezing winter night when Lana was nine years old, her mother slammed her fist against Lana's bedroom door, which flew open and hit the wall. Lana awoke as if shot with a bolt of electricity.

"Leave her out of it," said her dad.

"I hate you," her mom screamed.

He pulled the door closed as her mother kicked him in the shins.

A few minutes later Lana heard her outside. She scrambled over to the window. Her mother was in a fight with her roller bag, cursing as it twisted on the icy walk. Her mom kicked it and went down on her rump, swearing and falling again when she tried to get up, finally grasping handfuls of the hedge to stand. She rerouted, dragging the bag to the curb over patches of slush and stubby grass. "Fuck." She couldn't get the key to work in the trunk. Finally it did. She tossed the bag in and slammed the trunk with both hands, then slammed the car door loudly after she got in. The car skidded on ice as she sped away but then righted itself. The taillights didn't go on until she was at the end of the block. The car spun again on the turn and disappeared from sight.

Lana yanked off her pajama bottoms and struggled into her jeans in the dark and then waited under the covers, pretending to be asleep when her dad came in to check on her, which she knew he would. "Lana," he said softly, and when she didn't answer he kissed her forehead and left. She waited longer, she didn't know how long. She heard the TV in his bedroom as she tiptoed down the hall, pulled on her snow boots, and slipped out the back door. The small yards in their neighborhood were separated by chain-link fences, and she ducked under, dragged a garbage can to Tracee's bedroom window, stood on the can, and climbed in.

Tracee was asleep. Lana tugged her hair.

"What?" said Tracee.

"My mom's gone."

"Where?"

Lana shrugged and Tracee moved over so Lana could squeeze in bed too.

The next day she and her dad played hooky. It was his idea. "How about you skip school and I cancel my jobs?" They dressed warmly — they "layered up," as her dad called it — and drove two hours to Chesapeake Bay. They didn't talk much in the car or on their long walk along the pebbled beach. It was a blustery gray day, which suited them, the water choppy and forbidding. They brought bag lunches and ate them at a picnic table, the paper, plastic, and napkins all secured with rocks. They ate so quietly that a tern landed on the table, scavenging crumbs.

"I don't think she's coming back," said her dad. "She's got problems. We can't fix them."

"I don't want her," said Lana. "If she showed up right now, I'd throw a rock in her face."

That seemed to make her dad even sadder. He put his hand against his head, holding it as if *he'd* been hit by a rock, helpless about how to make amends for a cruel mother and longing for that crazy, angry woman in spite of himself.

Lana's father was popular in Fosberg. "You have such a nice dad." Lana grew up hearing those words over and over again. Lester, who owned Baskin-Robbins, told her that every time they went for ice cream — peanut butter fudge for her, chocolate for her dad. She heard it from strangers for whom her dad had done electrical work, from her teachers after open-school night. Bob Byrne was polite, he was curious, asking people about themselves and remembering what they told him, but in spite of his manners, he was essentially shy, never boisterous, and revealed little about himself. He was self-employed, honest, charged reasonable prices — some might say too reasonable, he was a soft touch — and was skilled in the work he did. He wasn't handsome but he was good-looking — of medium build, about five feet, ten inches tall, with a broad, open face and warm dark eyes. His hair, like Lana's, was a thick, straight reddish brown. "Your dad is not only a gent but he has the best hair in Fosberg," the barber told Lana. He was steady too. Before her mother left, they always went to the movies on Saturday afternoons and duckpin bowling on Friday nights. Her mother, who never bowled, drank one scotch after another and chatted up anyone she could. Sometimes she disappeared and, when the evening was over, returned, vague about where she'd been.

After his wife left, Bob Byrne's life was his daughter and his work. Sunday afternoons he and Lana took a walk. She would race ahead, double back, circle around, waving her arms, raging about one thing, raving about another, confiding while he listened and advised. Every school night he made dinner. Usually Tracee was there. The girls helped with the dishes. Afterward they all hung out at the kitchen table, she and Tracee doing their homework, her dad engrossed in his hobby, building miniature trains.

Outwardly Lana was fine. A fierce, bright girl who got good grades and always got her way by arguing people into capitulation. But she stopped sleeping. She could be dead tired, out before her head hit the pillow, but inevitably around two in the morning, she woke up. For hours she would wander the house. Her dad had no idea. One night, when she was eleven, she wandered into the kitchen, where her dad had left a bottle of Pabst with some dregs, about two inches or so. She drank it, more from curiosity than anything. And slept like a baby.

Her dad wasn't much of a drinker. She understood that later. Nobody who loves liquor leaves anything in the bottle. From then on she finished his beer and soon began sneaking and drinking whole bottles herself.

Alcohol, the perfect cure for insomnia. She was medicating her pain — the emptiness of abandonment, the guilt that it was somehow her fault, the sadness that she was too proud and angry to acknowledge.

In high school she drank more. Party drinking, mostly. She had more fun buzzed. She was a champion at snapping bottle caps. She could snap a beer bottle cap clear across the street and into a garbage can, and often challenged guys, getting her beer paid for by winning. She branched out, trying sweet drinks with cool names like Singapore Sling. She was careful, limiting herself, because her father waited up. He never went to sleep until she was home. Anyway, it was easy to fool him, because he trusted her.

When she got to college on a scholarship, the University of Maryland at College Park, and away from the watchful eye of her dad, she started getting drunk every night.

Which is how Lana became the last person she wanted to be: her mother.

28

Rita and Marcel take daily walks to see the sunrise. One morning Rita braids wildflowers into a chain, something she learned to do when she was a child. That night, when she performs, both she and Marcel wear a crown of wildflowers.

Clayton sheds his sweats and begins to dress up. He bundles all his collared shirts that he hasn't worn in years and drops them at the laundry for a wash and iron. Light starch, he tells them. He digs out his old jeans, discovers that they still fit and that, if he wears them with his leather embossed belt with a large square silver buckle, he doesn't look half-bad. He notices a purple rayon shirt in the window of the local men's store and buys it. He makes them take it right off the mannequin. He doesn't even try it on before buying because he's embarrassed about his sudden interest in self-improvement. Late at night he pays a visit to the Pick 'n Save, where he locates a jar of hair gel for men. At checkout he feels the need to explain himself. "We're getting popular," he tells Tami. "I've got to look the part."

But he knows the real reason he's dressing up is for Rita.

He's fascinated with her. When she crowned the lion with that wreath of flowers he couldn't get over it. She's graceful. So solemn. Purity itself, he concludes. He offered her a ride to the motel after closing but she refused. He offers it every night, and every night she refuses.

"No, thank you," she says. "I appreciate the offer but Tim will take me."

He thinks her manners are impeccable.

The audience is growing. One night Clayton arrives to find a line at the door. It is standing room only, and all because of Rita. She enters the cage now as part of the show, and when she does, you can hear a pin drop. She lets Marcel sniff her with no bars between them.

Rita observes that often when she approaches Marcel, he bats a paw at her. It makes her nervous. He does have powerful paws and sharp claws. But then she thinks maybe he's telling her something, something he would like to do.

The next afternoon before The Lion opens for business, she enters the cage with a box of paper towel rolls. She tears off a longish strip and holds it out, stretched tight between her hands. After several attempts Marcel karate-chops it with a bat of his paw. They rehearse this for days. The night she unveils the new trick, the audience goes wild. She gets a standing ovation.

Rita raises her arms, acknowledging the appreciation. And then bows.

29

One afternoon the women borrow Tim's car and drive to a nearby freshwater pond. "A prettier spot you won't find," Tim assures them.

Rita drives while Tracee reads Tim's directions aloud, appreciating his pointer about changing lanes early to prepare for left turns. And his thoroughness. It is impossible to get lost when a person tells you how many stoplights to count. They buy a picnic lunch from a diner they pass on the way, including a sweet tea (jumbo size) for Lana. She has become obsessed with this local drink that Clayton calls "liquid diabetes."

As they thread through the trees along a narrow path, Rita marvels at the strange North Carolina pines that have foliage top and bottom but are bare in their middles, providing a clear view to the parklike clearing and a smooth, glassy pond gleaming in the sun.

"Isn't this beautiful?"

"Tim's idea," Tracee reminds her. "He's so reliable. Have you noticed?"

"He's a sweetheart," says Rita.

"Yes, a sweetheart," says Tracee. "That's what he is." She kicks off her shoes and walks barefoot on the dense, mossy grass, enjoying the soft sponginess. She picks flowers for each of them, exotic spiky blossoms in purple and magenta, tucking one behind her ear, while Lana and Rita spread a ratty motel blanket under an enormous shade tree.

Lana and Tracee can barely recall how drab Rita once was, because now she laughs easily and her intelligence, long suppressed — a quiet ability to assess a situation — is so apparent. The caution that informed her every move has given way to curiosity and spiritedness. She is still modest but not shy, small but no longer invisible. They admire and trust her. Because trusting someone besides each other is not familiar, they don't know that they trust Rita, only that they like being around her. They feel safe. While they lounge on the blanket, eating tuna fish sandwiches, Lana and Tracee find themselves talking about the past, regaling Rita with stories.

"My favorite sandwich when I was little was —"

"Butter and sugar on white bread." Lana finishes Tracee's sentence. They high-five and burst out laughing. "High-fiving is so dumb. We high-fived our way through high school."

"Have you been best friends forever?"

"Forever," says Tracee.

"She was always at my house. Her parents were useless," says Lana.

"They were never home."

"She'd come over in the morning for scrapple."

"Is that a game?" says Rita.

"No, it's food. It's a loaf made of pig parts. You don't want to know what parts."

"The head," says Tracee.

"Remember the couch," Lana asks.

Tracee groans.

"What?" says Rita.

"When Tracee's dad wasn't trucking and her mom riding with him, they were at the racetrack in Bowie losing their money. One day she answered the door —"

"I was all alone."

"She opened the door and there were two guys —"

"As big as barns, I swear."

"They walked right in and carried out the couch."

"It had splashy red flowers."

"How old were you?" says Rita.

They ponder that, what they were wearing at the time, and that Lana's dad felt so bad for Tracee he took them for ice cream — so it was most likely summer.

"Probably twelve," says Lana.

"Oh, my," says Rita.

"They never replaced it," says Tracee. "I had almost no place in the whole house to sit but my bed."

"At night we'd do homework. Well, I did. You weren't too big on school." Lana falls silent, thinking about how much she loved school and drank her college opportunities away. "My dad built miniature trains. It was his hobby after my mom split. We had little cabooses and engines everywhere. Locomotives galore. The Silver Streak, the Prairie Princess, the Sunset Limited. He took me to all the conventions where these train-obsessed guys get together."

Lana shoves her straw into her tea, bobbing what remains of the ice, remembering her dad, Tracee, and her all together at the kitchen table — her dad wearing his big magnifying lenses over his glasses, concentrating hard to screw tiny wheels on tiny

191

axles, gluing in itty-bitty windows, fitting parts together with ant-size pincers. He would flip his lenses up every now and again to give Lana a smile or a wink. "How's it going, baby?" If she or Tracee needed help, he slid his chair around. "What's the problem?" Sometimes he was as clueless as they were, but usually they figured it out together.

Tracee has the diamond necklace in her pants pocket. She stretches out and turns away from them, hoping they will nap so she can play with it a bit. Instead she finds herself thinking about the other day, when she was in the kitchen picking up a tray of clean glasses and caught sight of Tim out the window. It was nearing sunset on a hot night and he was washing his car. He was shirtless and as slick as a wet seal, tossing on pails of soapy water. Tracee had seen Tim shirtless before, when they'd shared a room, but never shirtless and slippery. She'd never seen him stretch and scrub half naked under a violet sky.

Lana moves to the water's edge, reading a book Rita has brought her from the library, *Lit* by Mary Karr, all about being an addict. Rita, who could not astonish Lana any more than she already has, given her relationship with Marcel, goes skinny-dipping. Lana looks up to see her pass by, her naked ample bottom white and dimpled. She walks into the water without even dipping a toe first, swims out a fair distance, and rolls over. She floats on her back, the sun on her face. Blissful.

A splash. Rita splashes upright, rubbing her eyes to see.

"Mary Karr gets religion," Lana calls from the shore.

"What?" says Rita.

Tracee struggles to focus, having lost herself entirely in Tim perched on his car roof soaping the sign, WILSON'S DRIVING SCHOOL. She sees Lana raging back and forth. "Catholicism, how sick is that? The Bible, church, the works."

Rita, treading water, squints, locates the book bobbing not too far off, swims over, and pushes it to land.

"That's what saved her," says Lana. "That is so fucked."

"Could you get me that blanket?" Rita wades ashore with the now useless stack of soggy pages. "Would you mind, Tracee?" she adds, because Tracee is lying on it.

"Religion!" Lana is scathing.

"I had no idea." Rita takes the blanket from Tracee and wraps herself up like a squaw. "The librarian recommended it."

"She should be shot. I'm not giving it up to God."

"Giving what up?"

"Who the fuck knows." Lana drops back down on the ground and sits there glowering at the beautiful day. Rita notices how tired she looks. Beat up. She wears herself out.

"Marcel could help," says Rita.

Lana erupts. "Marcel?"

Rita decides maybe now is not the time.

Lana smacks the water with her feet. "I'll pay for it. Tell the library. Do you think my head is too big?"

"Is this about the book? I'm getting confused. I don't mean to." Rita sits down next to her.

"No. I've just always wondered about my head in relation to my body." This is something Lana would have asked her mother, but her mother wasn't there to ask.

"Your head is a perfect size. You are perfectly proportioned." Rita slips an arm out of the blanket and around Lana, pulling her close. Lana sighs. Her head conks onto Rita's shoulder as if she has been waiting her whole life for the opportunity.

30

One night at closing time Clayton approaches Rita and hands her a book. "I heard you like this," he says.

"Sudoku? Oh, thank you, I do."

"I don't know what level you are at, so it's got all three levels."

The next night when Rita comes out of the ladies' room, Clayton is there, stopping her in her tracks. He's wearing cologne, a scent so sweet she nearly sneezes.

She moves sideways. So does he.

He backs her against the wall. "I want you," he says.

"Excuse me?" says Rita.

She ducks under his arm and slips away. He follows.

"I can't stop thinking about you."

"Please try."

"I can't. You're" — he almost loses his nerve but decides to tell the truth — "erotic."

Rita is surprised. No one has ever said that to her before. But still . . . "No, thank you." She hurries away.

At the library Rita continues to educate herself on lion behavior. She reads that lions like to hang over the branches of a tree. At first she imagines Marcel standing on his hind legs with his front paws drooping over a low branch, as if he's a person chatting over a backyard fence. But then she sees pictures of lions in Africa, stretched out on the thick limbs of thorn trees, lounging like the cats they are.

She wants Marcel to have a tree.

There are none around The Lion. The closest, a cluster of scraggly firs a mile away, have twiggy branches that would break under Marcel's weight. Besides, she would never risk walking Marcel any farther than she does.

One morning when she and Tim are making a grocery run, they pass a lot where two men with a buzz saw are about to demolish an oak tree. "Pull over," she says to Tim. "Stop here, please."

Rita knows that the tree has been struck by lightning. She has seen its effects before. The tree is a skeleton, all foliage gone. The bark is sheared off one side of the trunk, although the hardwood beneath is still

196

intact. The men have already cut off the burned upper branches, which lie scattered where they fell, but what remains is substantial: a strong trunk and several low, mighty limbs. "More a sculpture than a tree," she says as she and Tim look it over. A sculpture — the men are impressed by the idea, but they are already impressed with Rita, because they have seen her show.

She offers to buy it. "It's for Marcel," she tells them.

"No charge," says one.

"Where do you want it?" says the other.

They dig it up, load it onto their pickup, cart it to The Lion, and replant it next to the parking lot.

Clayton, arriving that night, isn't thrilled to find a fairly petrified oak tree on the property, but he keeps quiet about it because he wants Rita.

The next morning, when Rita and Marcel leave The Lion for their dawn walk, they turn right instead of left. Rita leads him to the oak tree, hoping he will climb it. The low limbs aren't that high and she can still keep Marcel leashed. How nice it would be for him to loll on a branch.

Marcel doesn't react at all to the tree. She might as well be introducing him to a mailbox.

They stand there awhile. Eventually he moves close and rubs his side against it. Back and forth. Rita hears a low hum like an air conditioner on the fritz. It seems to her that Marcel is purring.

From then on, every so often, for a change of pace, they visit the tree in the morning for a rub before heading to the rise.

31

One afternoon at the café in Fairville, when Rita, Lana, and Tracee are sharing a slice of buttermilk pie, Rita tells them about a crime that happened right in the next state. In Selmer, Tennessee.

"One night when the minister was lying in bed asleep, his wife took a rifle and shot him in the back. Bang." She pops a bit of crust in her mouth.

"He must have been a meanie," says Tracee.

By way of an answer Rita recites, " 'Law, says the priest with a priestly look, / Expounding to an unpriestly people, / Law is the words in my priestly book, / Law is my pulpit and my steeple.' "

"Hey, lion lady," a dad with a brood of six yells from the back. "Come say hello." He lifts a toddler for a better view.

"I'll be right back," says Rita.

They watch her shyly greet people on her

way to the man's table, autographing a few napkins simply "Rita," shaking hands with all the children. They can't hear her because she always speaks quietly, but they know she is giving all the credit to Marcel.

"That poetry," Tracee whispers to Lana, "what's it mean?"

"What you said. The priest is a meanie. Well, more a tyrant." Lana pours a pile of salt onto her plate, presses her finger in, licks it, and considers the implications.

Rita slides back into the booth. "It could have been the potato salad."

"What?" says Tracee.

"What set her off. Making it for the umpteenth time."

"Who?"

"The wife. Potato salad after church every Sunday. Let's see, fifty-two weeks a year. Let's say she was married thirty years —"

"How old was she?"

"I don't know. Let's say twenty years, then. Fifty-two times twenty . . . What's that? I can't do math. Harry would know," she says grimly.

"Couldn't she make coleslaw instead?" says Tracee.

"Is Harry a minister?" asks Lana at the same time.

"Yes," says Rita.

"And he's your husband?"

Rita fidgets, folding down the corners of the napkin.

"Did he beat you? Is that why you left?"

Rita still makes no reply.

"Did you shoot him?" says Tracee.

"My goodness, no. I would never shoot anyone. Too messy." Rita picks up the bill and studies it. Lana continues to eat salt. It's making her tongue raw but she can't stop herself. Rita slaps the bill down. "I'll tell you what I think. Why she snapped. Suppose you're the wife of a minister and you're unhappy? Who can you tell? 'Don't you dare tell anyone your problems because it will reflect on *me*.' I bet you anything he said that. I bet the town was so small that if she turned around she bumped into herself. It's surprising she even knew what she felt if she could never say it. Everything bottled up. All the pretending. That her husband was loving, that he was kind. Everyone projecting goodness onto you, but it isn't you at all, it's some idea of you. The minister's wife. The expectations. The isolation. The loneliness. Feeling invisible. I don't think about her at all."

"Who?" says Lana.

"Me. Then."

Sensing that Rita needs to leave the café

right now, Lana checks the bill and lays the money on the table. Because she is worrying about Rita, it's a moment before she notices Tracee's terrified eyes and her fixation out the window.

On the sidewalk opposite, Tucker slouches along, head bowed. To Lana it seems that he's ashamed for people to see him, although it could be some new cool way of walking. Yes, that's it, she decides. Sometimes people decide to walk differently.

Tracee twists in her seat. She wants to escape but it's a booth, Lana's in the way, and Lana only stares as Tucker crosses right in the middle of the block, heading toward them.

"What wrong?" says Rita.

"Tucker," says Lana.

"That police officer?"

"He's not one anymore," Lana reminds Tracee.

Tucker, reaching the sidewalk and sensing he's a person of interest, looks up. The women could almost touch him were it not for a pane of glass between them.

Lana's hand closes around Tracee's.

Tucker summons a swagger, takes a step closer, and points his finger at them.

No one moves.

He walks in.

They suspect correctly that once inside he pauses to intimidate them again, although they don't turn around for the faceoff. They are also certain that he takes a seat right nearby, at the counter, because his voice seems quite close when he greets Cindy. "Hey, there."

"How are you doing, sugar?"

Cindy calls everyone "sugar." In fact, Lana, Tracee, and Rita have noticed that everyone calls everyone "sugar," but in this case Cindy sounds genuinely concerned for his well-being. Lana assumes she knows his circumstances, the suspension. Does she know Lana's role in it?

"I got screwed," says Tucker. "But hey. It's an opportunity." Which makes him and Cindy laugh, like that's true. "I'd like a coffee. Black."

Lana detects a slur in his voice. Well, not precisely. What she detects is something she used to do herself — she enunciated especially clearly because she didn't want anyone to think she'd been drinking, but the slur usually sneaked in anyway.

"Large glass of OJ too," he says.

Lana speaks quietly in Tracee's ear. "Stand up, take your purse, walk out, don't squeak."

They are in Tim's car, on loan, driving to The Lion when Tracee finds her voice. "Did he point a gun at us?"

"It was a finger," says Lana. "He pointed a finger."

"It was a finger pretending to be a gun," says Rita.

"Rita!" says Lana.

"Just saying. I'm sorry. I guess I've got Harry on the brain."

32

After several days of hundred-degree-plus heat and humidity, a storm blows through, cooling the air, chasing the clouds away. Clayton opens up all the back doors. The sky is a clear, crisp cornflower blue. There's a refreshing breeze that Rita knows Marcel is enjoying. He stands at the far end of his cage, looking out into the field, while Rita sits at a table doing Sudoku. It's about five in the afternoon, an hour before they open.

Clayton, busying himself behind the bar, glances Rita's way now and then. Finally he moseys over. When she looks up, he sits down. "I have to know why you don't want me."

The question throws her. She doesn't want to explain, but he is looking at her intently and she can see he means to have an answer. "I'm not attracted to you," she says.

"You're not attracted to me? How is that

possible?"

"I'm sorry, Clayton."

He gets up and walks away.

"Clayton," says Rita.

In a snap he's back and in the chair, jamming it against hers. "You changed your mind?"

Before Rita can answer, Marcel roars, and the force of it blows the Sudoku book right off the table. "My goodness," says Rita.

Clayton retrieves it. "Wasn't that critter at the other end of the cage a second ago?"

"He can be quick," says Rita. "And quiet. You know a lion's paws have very soft padding."

"I didn't know."

She laughs. "They don't like competition."

"Who?"

"Lions."

"Oh."

"In the pride the male lion provides protection."

"Is that what he's doing?"

"I couldn't say." She blows Marcel a kiss.

"Are you goofing on me?"

"Why would I do that?"

"Did you change your mind?"

Rita hesitates.

"What?" says Clayton.

"Remember that thing you said about how

we were all dots? Just dots?"

"No."

"That was a terrible thing to say."

"Is that why you're not attracted to me? Because if so, I take it back."

"That's not why."

"Is there hope?"

"No."

That night Clayton gets all his orders mixed up. He has to recruit Tim to help behind the bar, and Tim, sensing his distress, works like a demon. When Rita enters Marcel's cage and touches his nose, an act of bravery and gentleness all mixed up together, Clayton knows his heart is broken.

RITA

Rita and Harry got engaged when she was a sophomore and he was a senior at Henderson, a small college in Virginia. They married that summer. Rita was twenty. Painfully shy, she was relieved to marry a man who seemed to have all the answers, and when he didn't, he simply opened a Bible to find one. And there was a role waiting to be filled: the minister's wife.

"And the Lord shall make thee the head, and not the tail; and thou shalt be above only, and thou shalt not be beneath." Deuteronomy 28:13.

Harry quoted this when he proposed while they were walking home from the library one night. First he bent over — Rita thought he was picking up litter, because he often did, but instead of a candy wrapper, he plucked a daisy and presented it to her.

"And the Lord shall make thee the head, and not the tail."

In the years after, when Rita considered everything, including that moment, she realized the meaning of that Bible quotation. "Thee" meant people as opposed to animals. People, mankind, human beings, Christians were the head and not the tail. But in Harry's interpretation he was the head and she the tail, and therefore she should leave school and be his wife. Which to her was a relief. What would she do with a college degree? If she were a teacher, as she planned, would the students run wild? Could she even speak loud enough to be heard?

She was flattered and surprised that he wanted her.

Her mother, who had never expected her shrinking-violet only child to marry, cried when Rita phoned to say that Harry had proposed. "I hope you said yes," said her father.

They first met when she was a freshman sitting alone at a table in the cafeteria eating some chicken and rice. She had noticed him because his voice had a penetrating quality. Not that it boomed, but it had a high timbre that pierced the din. He always sat with the same group of guys. From the Bibles next to their trays and the fact that they said grace before eating (uncommon but not rare at Henderson), she figured they were all studying for the ministry. Her table was on the route to the tray return and he stopped as he passed. He'd eaten everything except an apple. He asked if she was all right.

"Fine," she said.

"You're sitting alone."

She wanted to say, "I like to," but was too bashful.

When he left, having found out which dorm was hers and that she was an English major, he gave her his apple.

Harry wasn't handsome, but Rita was too much of a mouse to expect or attract a good-looking man. His face was square, his chin broad as a shelf, his nose wide and a bit flat. His narrow eyes set in deep crevices had shadows around them. His smile, which did not light his face and in fact seemed to exist separate from the rest of his features (always causing some confusion about whether he was smiling or not), revealed a set of small, identically sized teeth. One in the front was discolored gray. Harry wasn't friendly-looking but he had presence. He walked erect, with a purposeful stride. Rita liked walking alongside him. It was as if she had a steel support pole to grab on to if necessary, although Harry disapproved of public demonstrations of affection. The support was therefore theoretical rather than real. He approved of her modesty, which was born of self-consciousness, Rita's desire not to be noticed. "Vanity is a sin," he told her by way of a compliment. Rita wore only a touch of pink lipstick and kept her long hair off her face with a white plastic headband.

The most romantic thing Harry did in their years together was, the first time he kissed her, he took her headband off.

They began meeting for coffee. He showed her his writings, his preliminary attempts at sermons. He expressed himself in the passive voice, and she changed his sentences to the active, teaching him how to write and speak more forcibly. (Later she kept all his sermons filed by subject and cross-filed, often misfiled by accident, by date.) They went to prayer breakfasts, which Harry sometimes led, and on Saturday nights to sing-alongs. He filled up her life. For her birthday, he gave her a record: Sister Mead singing "The Lord's Prayer." It had been a top-ten hit on the pop charts, and serious Christians like Harry saw the hand of God in that freak happening.

What Harry did have was dreams. He was going to be a missionary and save souls in

Ghana. When he told her, his eyes were shining. Fantasies of the church he would build, the poverty he would cure, the souls he would save with the words of Lord Jesus Christ Our Savior poured out of him. Rita was captivated. She envisioned herself at his side, holding babies with their stomachs distended from malnutrition, comforting sick mothers, hiking through the jungle with monkeys hanging from branches above her. While he carried on, she listened, enraptured. She was his first worshiper. His first taste of what it would be like when he stood in the pulpit, where he would eventually confuse God's words with his own and God with himself.

A month before they were supposed to leave, in the midst of getting shots to prevent at least seven horrible diseases, Harry was offered a position: pastor of a church in Ambrose, Virginia, population three thousand. It was permanent. Harry didn't want to pass it up. "Closer to home but the challenges will be as great," he told her.

Thus began a life in which wanting was a sin.

They settled in a modest house, a gift of the parish. The furniture, donated, was all secondhand: a wooden rocking chair, a denim-covered couch with buttons and plaid patches, a small round ottoman covered in brown velvet, a knotty pine table in the kitchen with six chairs. Upstairs consisted of two bedrooms, one for them and one for children, and a bathroom. A carpeted basement had shelves where Harry put his Bibles, books about Bibles and saints, and the complete works of C. S. Lewis. Rita's poetry books and novels remained packed in a cardboard box and stored in the small coat closet.

"Three children," Harry said. "No point in waiting."

Dutifully she had them — three boys in three years. Three boys under the age of four and no help. It wasn't right for the minister's wife to hire help, he told her. No babysitters even. She nearly went mad.

Did he beat her?

No, but Rita could never confide the casual cruelties to someone as young and innocent as Tracee. She doesn't want her to know. She's ashamed that they hurt, and it hurts her to remember.

"Why'd you marry Rita?" a member of the congregation asked Harry, and the reason Rita knows this is that Harry told the story, holding forth to a group of parishioners at Sunday lunch several years after they were wed. " 'Why'd you marry Rita?' the man troubled in his own marriage asked me," said Harry. " 'It was an act of charity,' I told him."

Everyone laughed. It was the closest Harry came to telling a joke, and it wasn't funny. Rita knew instantly that it was true. She finally understood. He'd married her because it made him a better Christian to marry a woman no other man wanted.

Of course, Harry wasn't owning up to his own insecurities.

She longed for a friend, but Harry disapproved. Probably he worried that she might tell his secrets: that he sweated through two shirts when he addressed the congregation and got terrible stomachaches in anticipation the night before, that he bit his nails, although that was out there for anyone to see. Harry was human. It was a hard thing to conceal, but he tried.

Rita learned very early that he was a creature of habit. Instant oatmeal with sliced banana and brown sugar every morning for breakfast. Dinner at six. Sunday lunch after church — presliced Virginia ham, Parker House rolls, homemade potato salad, and a green salad with Wish-Bone dressing. Harry loved Wish-Bone dressing. Like a dog, nothing made him happier than the same thing at the same time. When life was good, tomorrow was never another day; it was the same day. He ate each meal with a large mug of milk. Every night he rolled over on her in bed, grunted while they made love, rolled off, and then got up and went into the bathroom to wipe himself off.

Evenings, after she put the boys to bed, he liked her to sit with him and rub his feet. "Come sit with me, I'm all alone," he'd call. If she dawdled, she could hear panic in his voice. "Rita!"

She knew that the head was lost without the tail, even if the head didn't know it.

She was expected to account for the money she spent. He gave her an allowance and kept a record in a small black notebook. On Sunday nights they would sit up in bed while she read off the receipts and he jotted them down. He enjoyed these moments, opportunities to lecture about saving money. "Don't simply compare prices, compare per ounce." "Is hand cream necessary?" "Painting your nails is self-worship" — not that Rita ever would. Lunches out were frowned on. He was a waste hunter. Inevitably she would lose receipts or forget to ask the cashier for one. The account rarely balanced, and Harry often suggested, patting her hand, that she pray for guidance in this area of her life.

Rita loved Sudoku. Discovered it in the weekly paper, where they ran a puzzle. Doing the puzzle was the high point of her week. "Strange," said Harry, "you can fill in those boxes but you can't keep track of your pennies." Until Lana handed her that paperback unearthed in the men's room locker, Rita had never held a book of Sudoku. A whole book. It would never pass the usefulness test. Or the more acid and higher bar of acceptability: "What's it got to do with God?"

Harry didn't like her to say anything negative, even things that were obvious to all, like "This food tastes terrible" or "That woman is mean." They were uncharitable thoughts, she had no business even having them. In the beginning he tried to redirect her with the admonishment "Smile, be a princess." As he grew more arrogant, a consequence of being leader of a flock, the arbiter of all things to do with his parish, consulted on crises of every kind, he began to shut her down bluntly. "No one wants to know what you think."

She learned to keep her opinions to herself.

Rita's secret shame was not that she did not love Harry. Once there were children and an entire parish that depended on him, love seemed beside the point. Her shame was that she didn't enjoy being a mother. She wanted to. She had expected to, and did on occasion, reading to the boys in bed, cuddling them after a bath. But she was overwhelmed and exhausted almost all the time, trying to please Harry, worrying that the children would displease him, guilty that she didn't know how to stop Peter from wetting his bed, certain that if she weren't so hapless Luke would be better behaved, sure that Andrew's being picked on was her fault because she was a wimp. She felt inadequate so much of the time. As far as Harry was concerned, it *was* her failure — it couldn't possibly be his — and above all no one should know. "Our family is a building with no cracks," he often said. The demand to appear in public as if nothing rattled her also took its toll.

Housework, cooking, washing dishes, and laundry were her responsibility. If the good Lord wanted her to have help in the kitchen, Harry told her, he would have given her girls.

She wasn't surprised to hear that. It was something her father would have said.

The boys loved their mother, but as they got older, they began to treat her as their father did, with condescension. They couldn't help it, he was the role model.

One day, five years or so before Lana and Tracee picked her up on the highway, Rita read an article in the dentist's waiting room. She told Harry about it (knowing she was talking about herself without speaking personally, which afforded some self-protection). The article had troubled her. She needed to discuss it. She waited until after she'd rubbed his feet.

"I read an article today."

"Where?" said Harry.

Rita hesitated. "The *Smithsonian*." She wasn't sure that periodical was on his acceptable list, but apparently it was, because he only waited.

"Did you know that some immigrants forget their first language but never get fluent in their new language? No one can ever really be fluent in a second language the way they are in their first. They're stuck with feelings and ideas they can't express. So I was wondering, Do they eventually stop having feelings or thoughts, or simply the language to express them? Or both?"

"What's it got to do with God?" said Harry.

There was that brick wall. She felt foolish for bringing it up. Even berated herself for

her own stupidity. But her anxieties per-
sisted. By never saying what she thought, by
being prevented from speaking, silenced,
was she losing the ability to observe, to
articulate? Was she losing the very emotions
and thoughts themselves? Could she lose
herself? Would Rita be gone? Would there
be a shell of a woman in her place? Had it
already happened?

The fears grew worse.

She began to think about leaving. About
escape. To save what was left of her.

She tried to quash the desire, forcing
herself to consider people worse off — child
brides in Afghanistan, people starving in
Darfur. Besides, she had no options. Harry
doled out the money. Her MasterCard had
a two-hundred-dollar credit limit. How far
would that take her?

She dug the box out of the closet and
began reading poetry again, romantic poets
like Keats, Shelley, Alfred Noyes because he
wrote "The Highwayman," a fairy tale of
passion and longing like nothing she would
ever experience. There were others she
loved: Tennyson, Yeats for his chaos and
density, but especially Auden for his wisdom
and pain. She loved one poem in particular
that began, " 'O where are you going,' said
reader to rider, / 'That valley is fatal where

furnaces burn.' " It was about fear, which she was trying to confront, or, put another way, about being brave, which seemed so out of reach.

She read the poetry secretly when Harry was out.

She started bolting. The urge would come upon her — almost trancelike, a subconscious command over which she had no control. She'd take off her ring, place it on the mantel, leave the house, and start walking. Wishing that the world were flat and she might reach an edge to drop off.

Eventually Harry would find her. She'd hear a car rolling slowly by her side. A tap of the horn. "Get in," he'd say. And she would.

33

The next Sunday, when Tim is all alone at The Lion, after he's cleaned and hosed the cage, Tracee strolls in. She's pretty much figured out where Tim is and when, and she arrived during his final mop-up.

"Hi," says Tim.

"Do you want to do it?"

Tim drops the mop. He grabs Tracee and starts kissing her while at the same time trying to take off his shirt and hers.

"Tim, wait." Tracee pushes him away, stunned by his ardor and amazed at their chemistry. She feels like mush.

"What?" says Tim.

"I like a bed."

Tim grabs her hand and pulls Tracee through the parking lot to his car. He opens the door, she gets in, he slams it closed, tears around to the driver's side, jumps in, and guns it, lickety-split, out of the parking lot.

Tim drives like a maniac. He runs a red light, passes on the left, passes on the right, takes a shortcut through a gas station, blows through a stop sign. He is kissing Tracee while he drives and tries to keep an eye on the road. This involves attempting to see sideways and taking quick breaks from the kiss every few seconds or so.

When they hear a siren, at first they think their passion has set off alarms.

Then Tim realizes something is up and checks the rearview mirror. Behind them a patrol car flashes its lights.

He pulls over.

Tracee doesn't quite realize what's happening until the cop is at the window, peering in at them.

"Hi, Tim," says the cop, an older man with a tired voice.

"Hi, Rudy."

Rudy leans down and takes in the view, front seat and back. "Who's this?" he says of Tracee.

"Sheila," says Tracee.

Tim is surprised by that but says nothing.

"What's going on?" says Rudy, although he's got an idea, because they are both rumpled and flushed. Tracee's cheeks are as pink as poppies. Tim's face is practically on fire. "You ran a red light, you did not come to a full stop at a stop sign, you were going fifteen miles over the speed limit, you passed on the right. Plus I'd say you were driving recklessly. That's five violations."

Tim can't think of anything to say. Truth is, he can barely focus.

"That's your license," says Rudy. "And your job. You teach driving. What kind of an example are you setting for young folks? How about your students? They look up to you."

Tim thinks about Debi, how she's going for her driving test next week. Suppose she hears about this? Maybe she won't pass. He feels like shit.

"Get out of the car," says Rudy. He leans down and says to Tracee, "Excuse us, Sheila."

Tim follows Rudy back to the patrol car. Rudy takes out a book and starts writing. "I don't want to wreck your life, Tim. Or upset your mom. I'm just giving you one. For running a stop sign."

"Thanks, Rudy. Thanks."

Tim gets back in the car, sticks the ticket in the drink holder, and drives responsibly to the motel. The mood has changed. They ride in silence.

"Do you still want to?" says Tim as he pulls into a space.

"Do you?" says Tracee.

"I've still got a hard-on. I had a hard-on the whole time I was talking to Rudy. Who has a hard-on when they're about to get five moving violations?"

Tracee starts giggling.

They bolt from the car, race up the stairs, and tear off their shirts as they kiss their way into Tim's room and fall on the bed.

"Wait." Tracee pushes him away.

She jumps up and unzips her jeans. She pulls them off and stands there as cute as can be in her bra and thong.

"Wow," says Tim. He's dizzy from the heat and the excitement and the sight of Tracee nearly naked. "Why'd you say your name was Sheila?"

Tracee bursts into tears.

"Oh, man, darn, shucks. I blew it. Why'd I say that? Why?" He slams his fist into the mattress. Slams it again and again and again while Tracee sinks down in a heap.

"Is your name Sheila?" he asks.

"No," says Tracee, crying. "It's Tracee."

He puts his arm around her and she weeps into his shoulder. He gazes with wonder at the little freckles on her pale and trembling shoulders. Her breasts press against him as her chest heaves. He wants to be comforting, that's his noble intention, he takes his role seriously, but his penis, hard as a rock, is getting harder.

Not wanting to let go, even a little, he reaches out with his unoccupied hand, grabs his pole, and uses it to clamp a ten-pack of tissues off the bureau and flip it his way. "Whatever it is, you'd better get it off your chest," he says, and ends up opening one pack after another. Recounting her unhappiness unleashes nonstop tears, sniffling, and blowing.

"The Orioles were ahead," she says. "Which seemed like a sign. It was the seventh-inning stretch and we had really good seats in the all-you-can-eat picnic perch. J.C. could really pack it away."

"J.C.?" says Tim.

"J.C. is this guy — he was my boyfriend, steady, nobody else for ages, like, five years. Sometimes he kind of strayed, not his fault because women were so hot for him, but anyway, we were at the game and I was keeping my eyes glued to Diamond Vision, thinking that any minute it was going to light up for the whole world to see, 'Tracee, will you marry me? J.C.' when J.C. went to get a hot dog. He sent a text: 'It's over.' There I was, looking for my future on Diamond Vision, and instead it came as a puny text message. He never came back."

She hiccups a few times and Tim thinks he has never seen anyone look so cute hiccuping. He opens another mini tissue pack for her.

"I had my wedding dress all picked out, because I was sure J.C. was going to propose. I said to Lana that I had to try on that dress anyway. It was like it had my name on it, you know? So a few days later we went to the store and I tried it on. And I don't know what came over me, I just ran out of the store and jumped in the car. Lana tore out after me and said, 'What in the world are you doing, Tracee?' and I said, 'Hand me the car keys, Lana,' and she did. She handed over the keys and I drove. We took off the hell out of Fosberg and ended up here."

"Fosberg?" says Tim.

"Maryland. It's near Baltimore. I kind of have kleptomaniac tendencies. There's probably an all-points bulletin out for me."

"For stealing a wedding dress?"

Tracee picks at some crumpled cellophane ripped off the tissue packs while she thinks about the stolen diamond necklace now stashed under stuff in the bureau drawer.

"A wedding dress?" Tim continues to mull it over. "I don't know. I don't think so. Although it sure is beautiful."

"It was a designer dress. The most expensive in the store. By far."

"Like how much?"

"One thousand and ninety-five dollars."

Tim makes a sound like he's choking.

"A lot, huh?" She leans over and her mostly bare butt pops up, nearly in Tim's face. His breath shortens. She yanks her purse up and onto the bed, reaches in, and pulls out sunglasses with the sales tag still dangling. "I scarfed these at the P 'n S. I never wore them. I felt too guilty."

"Don't worry. I'll take care of it."

"See how bad I am." She opens her purse wide and shows him all her lipsticks, glosses, and mascara wands, enough to open a drugstore. "These aren't from here."

"You're not bad," says Tim. "No way." He speaks so emphatically that she believes him. He stops her tears.

Of course, believing that won't last long. How can it? She's been ignored and neglected since forever, and what is she good at? Shoplifting. Still, it's the loveliest, lightest feeling while it's there. *I'm not bad. No way.*

"How'd they know your name? I mean, at the store. You walked in, tried on a wedding dress, escaped with it."

"Everyone knows everyone in Fosberg."

227

Tim thinks about it all. "So that's the whole story, why you're here, as far as you and Lana are concerned?"

Tracee tells the truth, simply not the whole truth. "As far as me *and* Lana." She's careful to emphasize the "and" to ease her conscience. "Do you still want to go to bed with me?"

He jumps her, and in a second they are rolling around skin-to-skin.

Their lovemaking is great. Tim adores every inch of her and spends time exploring — stroking her breasts, sucking her nipples, kissing the curve of her hip, her belly, as well as a sweet spot at the nape of her neck before moving on to more exciting territory. He is considerate, insatiable, and kind of crazy. They invent a few positions, and he refuses to shut his eyes because he can't believe his good fortune. Whenever Tracee opens hers, there is Tim gazing at her with the most obvious appreciation. It's a turn-on.

She is happily snuggled in postcoital bliss when Tim disentangles. "I got Debi at four." He mimics steering a car. "Stay here as long as you want. Hell, stay here forever."

He pulls on his jeans and shirt and goes into the bathroom, where he throws some water on his face, towels off, and returns to

228

the room.

Tracee is dozing, hugging her pillow. She opens her eyes, lazily stretches, and wiggles her fingers at him.

"I just want to say," says Tim, "that I love you and I'll marry you right now if you want." He walks out, leaving Tracee startled and deeply moved.

34

A couple of weeks later Tucker gets his badge back.

"I hope I'm not making a mistake," says the chief. He hands him his badge, his gun, and his car keys. They stand there squinting into the sun as if they're outside a saloon in Dodge City. "I don't need to remind you of your responsibilities."

"No, sir," says Tucker. "Thank you for giving me another chance. I'll make you happy you did."

First thing Tucker does is drive to the gas station to get his patrol car filled up. There he sees Lana's car. No coincidence, he knows it's there and that it's her car — everyone in town knows that the car at Bill's station belongs to the waitress at The Lion. That's why Tucker drove to this station instead of the Texaco, which is closer. He strikes up a conversation with Bill, who tells him he's replaced the door on Lana's

Mustang and is waiting for parts to replace the fender.

"Very nice lady," says Bill. "Got a drinking problem — well, had one — but she showed up a couple of weeks ago and put down three hundred of what she owes so I could start the repair, and she picked up the check when my wife and me went to see the circus act."

Tucker scopes out the license plate. Maryland. He jots the number down. "Do you know her last name?"

"Don't you?" says Bill. "She ran off with your patrol car, so I figured . . ."

"I was toasted."

"She goes to AA. Maybe you ought to think about joining up."

"Just give me her last name, okay?"

"Just a suggestion. I'll get the receipt."

As they walk to the office, Tucker changes the subject, asking about the difference between real oil and synthetic oil. He doesn't want any more personal advice from Bill.

"Here's her name. Lana Byrne." Bill shows Tucker the receipt. "Don't know why you're investigating her. What about the other?"

"Tracee?" says Tucker.

"No. The lady with the lion. That's a wonder."

35

The next morning, on their daily walk, Rita and Marcel leave The Lion, turn right instead of left, and visit the tree. Marcel sprints up the trunk. Rita, shocked, nearly drops the rope. He settles with his haunches anchored against a large knot in the limb, his paws drop to the branch below and rest there for balance. When they planted the tree Rita forgot to consider the view. Marcel's "savanna" is the parking lot and the two-lane highway beyond. She didn't consider how to get him down from the tree either. She hasn't read a thing about how lions leave trees. Will he leap? And what might that mean? Will he refuse to leave? She worries that she has gotten him into a pickle of some sort, or gotten herself into one.

After sitting for a while, Marcel stretches out along the long limb and hangs his head over, looking down at her. It seems to Rita that he is smiling.

She waits until, in her judgment, he is extremely mellow, and gives the rope a tug. Marcel jumps down, landing surprisingly lightly.

"You are remarkable," she tells him.

36

"I want to hold you close under the rain. I wanna kiss your smile and feel your pain."

Clayton has had the jukebox rigged and the place wired. Julio's voice can now be heard in the parking lot. He is relieved that Julio turns out to sing in English, and on the jukebox Clayton discovers a song he likes, "When You Tell Me That You Love Me," Dolly Parton and Julio in a duet. Julio must be okay if he's singing with Dolly.

Tim has taken photos of Rita and Marcel. He hangs a bulletin board outside the entrance with the photos blown up and tacked on. For a festive feel he sets out pots of red and pink geraniums.

Marcel is happy. Anyone can tell. He's often close to the bars, watching, his ears flicking, his tail scooped up, following the daily activities — setup, cleanup, deliveries, chatter, and especially Rita. She sweeps in front of the cage, not because the floor is dirty but because she got it into her head that a broom whisking back and forth would amuse Marcel, and it seems to. He follows it up and down, keeping his nose to the ground as if the broom is an animal he's tracking. She slides the broom, which has stiff bristles, through the bars. Marcel twists and turns as she gives his coat a brush and scratch. He's noisier too — Rita loves listening to his intermittent, unprovoked, and undoubtedly friendly gargle-y grunts.

"Marcel, your voice is beautiful," she tells him, and thinks that his chest puffs up. "Although," she says to Lana and Tracee, "that's not supposed to be a good sign, puffing up — that might happen just before a lion charges, but not with Marcel."

On their morning walk he often gives her a playful bump or rub, and while they lounge in the tall grass he lies very near so their bodies graze.

Most afternoons Rita simply keeps him company, pulling a chair close to the cage, sipping Lipton tea while Marcel rests, his eyes shuttered in lazy contentment.

Tracee and Tim. Tim and Tracee. They have quickly become inseparable, wrapping themselves around each other every chance they get, giggling at private jokes. Tracee is delighted to discover that Tim can do accents. His imitation of a French veterinarian examining a duck puts her in stitches.

Every day Tracee wakes up happy in Tim's arms.

She avoids stores, worrying that the urge to steal will come over her, and mostly, between living at the Tulip Tree and working at The Lion, this is not difficult. She pushes the diamond necklace out of her head. It's as if someone else stole it and she is as innocent as a downy newborn chick.

She trumpets Tim's accomplishments to Lana and Rita — how industrious he is, how every single one of his students passed the driving test with a grade of ninety or over, how he gives some of his earnings to his mom.

"He's a rube," says Lana, unimpressed.

"So am I," says Tracee. She invites Lana to come to Clarkson's Furniture Land with them. "Tim says North Carolina is the furniture capital of America."

It seems to Lana that Tracee quotes him nonstop.

"He says, 'No way can you be in North Carolina and not visit a furniture store, because they are awesomely large.' This one, Clarkson's, takes up more than a mile and has to be seen to be believed."

"Steal me a couch," says Lana.

Tracee shuts up like someone slapped her.

"Does he know?" says Lana.

"I don't do it anymore."

"It's that easy?"

Tracee puts her hands over her ears. She doesn't want to hear. She wants to believe what she wants to believe, but when Tim bounds up the stairs after buying a six-pack of assorted throat lozenges because she coughed once or twice the night before, she tells him she doesn't want to go. "Suppose I misbehave?"

"There's not one thing in Clarkson's small enough to fit in your purse," Tim assures her. "These lemon ones are best. They're magic on your throat. My mom swears by them."

He unwraps one. Tracee opens her mouth. He pops it in and watches while she sucks. "See what I mean?"

She kisses him, transferring the lozenge from her mouth to his. "I'll have another," she says.

Tim offers to take Lana into town and pick her up on their return. She declines. She doesn't want to risk bumping into Tucker. Clayton has told her he's back on the force. She hasn't told Tracee.

She doesn't want to cross paths with any AA members either. She hasn't been back and has no intention of ever returning. Sometimes when she lies in bed at night, she blasts the police chief all over again and berates each AA member for collaborating.

"Spend the day with me," says Rita as Lana stubbornly stares out the window.

"It's too hot," says Lana.

"I know. I'm going to sprinkle some water on Marcel. See if he likes it. I know I would. We're practicing a dance."

Lana shakes her head. She's sick of the bar. Detests the smell of the liquor. Has run out of improvement projects. Sees visions of her former self nightly. That hideous Candy, whom Lana waylaid and tried to save her first night on the job, following her into the ladies' room, drinks herself into a stupor twice a week. Lana takes it personally. Tracee got her into this mess and now Tracee's gone wiggy over a guy who thinks visiting furniture stores is a fun way to spend a Sunday. She could ask Clayton for a ride to the pond, but she knows if she relaxes next to the water in that calm, beautiful wood, her mind will veer right to her dad and how he doesn't want anything to do with her.

After Tim and Tracee drive off, taking Rita with them to drop her at The Lion, Lana finds herself walking into the motel office.

Marlene is reclining on the Barcalounger,

looking like an inflatable raft on which one could set out to sea. Dressed in her usual outfit, shorts and a shrunken tank, with the black knit cap pulled down to her brows, she's watching the Food Network, Paula Dean. The room, lit by a dim ceiling fixture, smells of sardines, which Marlene is eating from the can, swiping her mouth with a paper napkin after every swallow. All the yellowing blackout shades are lowered over the windows. The air conditioner, which whirs and rattles loudly, keeping the place icy, works a million times better than the contraption in Lana's room.

Lana hoists herself onto the counter, swings her legs over to Marlene's side, and stares at the TV.

"Who said you could watch?" says Marlene.

"You've got cable. Our TV sucks. There's zero reception, in case you forgot."

Marlene raises a tubby arm, points the remote at the TV, and hits mute. She seems to consider saying something but doesn't. She hits mute again and Paula's voice, laced with "y'all," "hon," and "shug," resumes mid-sentence.

"Paula Dean's a fake," says Lana. "A big fat phony."

"Mind your business."

"She's on television. She's everyone's business."

"Paula is a hero," says Marlene.

"Excuse me?"

On the TV Paula unwraps a hunk of cream cheese, drops it in a bowl, dumps in a scoop of sugar, and talks over the hum of the mixer about cheesecake.

"How is she a hero?"

"Take a hike," says Marlene.

"Come on, I want to know."

"She used to be like me. Now she's a conglomerate."

Lana laughs. "How is she like you?"

"Agoraphobic, smarty-pants. That's someone who never wants to go out."

Agoraphobic. It doesn't register for a moment; then Lana takes in the cavelike atmosphere, a room that hasn't seen sun since God knows when. She jumps down from the counter, tugs on the shade, and it retracts with a snap.

"Hey," says Marlene.

The drive to Clarkson's Furniture Land, normally an hour and a half, takes two because of some county fair traffic. Tracee and Tim take the scenic route, all back roads, past neatly planted fields of soybeans and tobacco, sunflower farms, split-rail fences, and mini-forests of firs. They stop for tangy barbecue, pulled-pork sandwiches, and get sidetracked having sex in a not entirely hidden duck blind that Tim knows about. As they come around a curve, the gigantic three-story building surprises them. Tim laughs out loud at Tracee's shock, because built right into the facade, spanning from the second story to the third, is a fancy wood-and-glass cabinet tall enough for a giant's house.

Tracee poses in front of the building. Tim crouches down and snaps a photo, aiming the lens up to get the freakily large armoire in the background. "Smile," he says, which is unnecessary, because Tracee is always smiling at Tim.

Lana yanks a second shade. It spins up. Sunlight pours in. Marlene flails, trying to bounce to a sitting position. She is helplessly horizontal unless she pushes the correct buttons, one to lower the footrest and the other to raise the back, but in her panic has forgotten to do it. Lana snatches her knit hat, pulls it right off her head, grabs Marlene's purse, a large bubblegum-pink plastic number. She smacks the door and, leaving it ajar, strolls into the empty parking lot, a flat, open space perfectly designed to send an agoraphobe into the stratosphere of anxiety.

Lana waves the purse. "Come and get it."

Marlene peeks out. Usually when she leaves the motel, her son pulls up right to the door, thereby allowing her to scoot into his car. She hasn't actually walked into the parking lot in years. She hasn't walked anywhere.

Lana twirls Marlene's hat on her finger, holding it high, teasing her. "Come on, take a few baby steps." Marlene lowers her head and charges.

Lana turns tail and runs. She's faster than Marlene, who suddenly swerves away and up the motel steps, grunting and swearing. She gets to Lana's room, barges in, and reappears carrying the TV. It's heavy, but hefty Marlene is strong as an ox. "You hate it," she screams. "Eat it." She heaves the television over the railing. There's a stunning split second of silence while the set is in flight. It crashes on the concrete, fantastically loudly, cracking open. Metal and glass fly in every direction.

At that moment, having forgotten some scribbled notes for her dance with Marcel as well as some paper towel rolls for his karate trick, Rita pulls into the parking lot driving Clayton's Chevy Bel Air with the top down. She's small for the car; it almost seems as if a child is driving it. She doesn't notice the wreckage because she's concentrating on making the turn — even though there's power steering, it's vintage power steering, and that takes a lot more muscle than modern power steering. Besides, driving Clayton's pride and joy is a responsibility. Since Rita has rejected him, she'd feel especially awful if she wrecked his car too.

She gets out and within a few steps feels the crunch of glass under her shoes. Looking more widely around, she realizes the lot is strewn with large and small hunks of debris. What she initially takes for a large laundry bag on the balcony is actually Marlene on the floor in a crumple. Lana stands at the far end of the motel holding a purse and hat that Rita recognizes as Marlene's. It doesn't take a genius to conclude that Lana is not an innocent bystander.

Marlene scoots along the balcony on her rump and descends the stairs scooching from step to step.

Stepping carefully through the rubble, Rita meets her at the bottom, helps her up, and escorts her back to the motel office as Lana shouts at Marlene, "You owe me. Because of me you left the room." Rita then goes upstairs, collects the stuff she needs, closes the door, which is now askew, and comes back down. "Meet me at the car," she says to Lana, taking the purse and hat from her. She delivers them to the office, opening the door only enough to slip them inside.

"It turns out she has red hair," says Lana as Rita stashes the paper towels in the back-seat and slides behind the wheel. "Dyed magenta hair. Didn't you always wonder what was under that hat?"

Rita reaches over and squeezes Lana's shoulder, and Lana realizes that Rita has tears in her eyes.

They drive the familiar route back to the bar without speaking. When they can see the skeleton tree in the distance, Rita pulls over and stops the car. "It's not working."

"What?" says Lana.

"You."

Rita sits there tapping her fingers together, thinking about it, and then rubs her eyes. "You have to let go of the pain you're carrying around."

"It's just the bar. I'm stuck here."

"You need a better personality, that's the truth. All this raging and yelling. The mean stuff. It has to stop. You have to give up your anger and your guilt and all your sadness. You have to give it up to Marcel."

Lana is struck dumb.

"I spent years of Sundays in church listening to Harry —"

"Marcel? Hello? Earth to Rita."

Rita continues blithely. "Harry would stand up there in that pulpit waving his arms, ranting and raving about sin and redemption, and I would be the proper minister's wife, watching raptly, wondering why anyone would think there was a God if he had Harry representing him." She presses her hand against Lana's cheek. "When I got in the cage with Marcel . . ." Rita thinks about the first time, the door clanging shut behind her, gazing into the soulful depths of Marcel's eyes. "When I did that, I discovered what it meant to be at peace. Marcel is a force."

"I'm not getting in the cage with Marcel."

"Of course. It's not necessary."

"Marcel is going to be my higher power?"

"Yes."

The sheer size and volume at Clarkson's are astounding. Furniture of every fashion in stylish groupings as far as the eye can see. Living rooms, dining rooms, breakfast nooks, cozy dens. Fancy beds layered with shiny duvets, coverlets, and quilts. Sexy beds with black silk sheets. More throw pillows than Tracee has seen in her life. Tailored, modern, and masculine spaces, others as frilly and feminine as a petticoat. Bunk beds and cribs ready and waiting.

Clarkson's aims to satisfy every fantasy and create some Tracee didn't know she had. One step inside and she balks.

"What's wrong?"

She looks like a terrified calf.

Tim whispers, "You're safe with me."

She shakes her head.

"Do you want to leave?"

"I wish I could live here," she tells him.

Tim takes her by the hand and leads her to a glossy mahogany table and matching buffet that Tracee thinks are fancy enough for the White House. He pulls out a chair in matching wood, with curved legs, an arched back, and a needlepoint seat cushion. She sits and he pushes her chair in. No one has ever pulled out a chair for Tracee before. "How many children do you want?" she asks.

He takes the chair at the other end as if they are mother and father with a brood in between. "I guess, I don't know, maybe three."

"Me too," says Tracee.

They move from one arrangement to another. Tracee rests her feet on an ottoman with carved frog feet; she opens every single compartment of an Oriental desk. They play a game: "What if . . ." "If, say, we were furnishing a house." Tracee vetoes anything molded in plastic — too outer space. Tim agrees. He likes wicker. Of all the things in Clarkson's, what Tracee loves the most is a glamorous white leather couch that has a corner in it — on one side it's longer and on the other shorter. "It's called a sectional," the salesman informs them.

"A woman who owned this," says Tracee, "would wear a diamond necklace."

"You're way prettier than diamonds," says Tim.

He's not looking at her when he says this. He's checking to see how the sectional is put together, if the parts are attached. *You're way prettier than diamonds.* If Lana were here she would point out that the response doesn't even track. Tracee's saying that a woman who owned this white leather sectional would wear diamonds has absolutely nothing to do with Tim's saying that Tracee is way prettier than diamonds. Thank God Lana isn't here, because muddleheaded Tracee, not burdened with logic, has a moment of clarity. She must give the diamond necklace back. *Is it too late? It can't be too late.* In a life that has been generally devoid

248

of impulse control, she finally understands
that she went too far. She really will end up
in jail, and now she has something to lose.
Something wonderful. Tim.

"Sit right here," Rita tells Lana, indicating a
chair at the table closest to Marcel's cage.

"He's asleep," says Lana.

"Oh, that doesn't matter. He'll wake up
eventually. Anyway, he doesn't need to wake
up for you to get what you need."

"But what am I supposed to do?"

"I couldn't say. I'm sure you'll figure it
out. I'll be back in an hour." She blows
Lana a kiss and leaves.

Lana feels ridiculous. Solo, ringside, like
she's waiting for a cocktail, only instead
she's at a zoo. "Hey, Marcel," she calls. He
doesn't react. He's lying on his side, eyes
open, unblinking. He could be dead. Does
he even know his name? Can he hear? He's
pretty old for sure, probably he's deaf. She
plops her feet up on another chair. She
chews on her thumb. A few minutes pass.
She squeezes her biceps, puts her feet back
on the floor, and jiggles her legs. Thoughts
are bouncing. *Marlene's crazy. Stupid hat.
My throat's dry. Rita's nuts.* She stands up,
paces, sits, gets up, walks over behind the
bar and stares at Marcel from a distance.

She opens the small refrigerator — a solid wall of Budweiser. "Fuck it." She takes a bottle and looks up. Marcel is awake. Yawning. His yawn is enormous. Between the frightening spikes of his incisors, she can see down his throat. She can see practically to China. He turns his head and looks at her.

Lana sticks the Bud back in the fridge. She takes a glass, scoops ice into it, shakes some into her mouth, and crunches as she carries the glass back to the table. She sits down.

Marcel rises and pads closer to Lana. His walk is slow and deliberate. His stomach sways with every step. He settles, lounging on his side, his big bushy head held high. Lana shifts in her chair, crunching more ice, thinking, *Fuck you, Marlene,* wishing she'd smashed *her* television. It was all Marlene's fault. Lana was utterly provoked by that major chubette psycho lady's refusal to provide decent accommodations. Lana drifts right to default mode, rage, but Marcel keeps interfering. For one thing, today he smells like damp, dirty socks. For another, he breathes loudly, the way people do when their noses are clogged. She keeps being drawn his way.

She begins to study him. No question, the

cat understands that gestures have more power when made rarely. He remains absolutely still, except on occasion his tail swings up or his head turns, and the move seems elegant, understated, majestic. He doesn't seem as if he wants to eat her. He doesn't seem remarkably interested in her at all, simply accepting.

"Ha, ha, I'm inside, you're out," says Lana. Then, realizing she got it wrong, "I mean, I'm outside, you're in."

It's quiet. Lana is now as still as the lion.

A fat fly that somehow got into the bar is buzzing around Marcel. He seems not to care or notice.

"I flunked out of school," says Lana.

Marcel only coughs. He sounds like a cat attempting to regurgitate a very large hairball. Lana takes it as a sign that more is expected.

"I get angry too much. I think I like it. I like the feeling.

"I had a scholarship and I drank all night and slept through all my classes. I lied to my dad about it. Also I did something degrading. I don't know what it is. I'll never know. I'll never, ever know, and every day I imagine something new, something else awful that it might have been. I need to stop. Help me let it go. Help me let it be something that's over and done.

"I stole from my dad."

She says it louder. "I stole from my dad."

Marcel stretches out on his stomach, facing her, and rests his head on his paws. His eyes are kind, she thinks, and understanding.

37

It's a courtesy to loan out officers to other towns in need. On Tucker's first afternoon back on the force, he was sent to Johnston for several days, then Rutherford to direct traffic at their county fair. At Rutherford, near the western border, he bunks with a local cop. The work is boring but he clocks a lot of overtime. A good week and a half goes by until he can get back to his desk at the Fairville station and do a search on Lana Byrne. One night, when he's the only one holding the fort in Fairville, he puts her name into the computer with the directive: "Outstanding warrants, Maryland."

Nothing turns up.

Assuming the folks who do the entries are prone to typing errors, he runs her name through every which way he can. After spelling it properly he misspells it — Lynn Burn, Lana Burn, and so forth. There are two Linda Burnses, one wanted for bank robbery, but he can tell from the descriptions and photos that neither is her.

He runs her license plate. Nothing there either.

His brain is getting tired, muddy. What could wake it up? A beer, he thinks. There should be one hidden in his bottom desk drawer, unless someone cleaned (or searched) the desk while he was on suspension. Yes, stashed behind a used book of parking tickets is a bottle of Bud. Warm as hell but who's complaining? He bangs the top down against the edge of the desk — an art form he's perfected. It pops right off. He chugs the beer, downing half, and a familiar feeling of calm and confidence washes over him. He begins Googling.

An hour later the chief walks in. He left his glasses in his office, the ones with the progressive lenses. He's lost without them. He finds Tucker, his grin as wide as a Halloween pumpkin's, lit by the computer screen, an empty bottle of Bud on the desk.

"I've found something," says Tucker.

The chief considers which to discuss first: drinking on the job or police business. "Found what?" he asks.

38

The next Saturday Rita unveils her dance with Marcel. She salsas circles around him. The lion wears a wreath of flowers and Rita has flowers in her hair.

The dance is Marcel and Rita's best collaboration yet. Rita takes several bows in the cage, several outside, and then she turns and bows to Marcel. He lowers his head, paying homage in return.

Lana now goes to the bar in the early morning with Rita, waits in the kitchen with the door closed where it's safe, while Rita takes Marcel out for his daily constitutional. Afterward, when he's back in the cage, Lana takes a seat at the table closest and they spend an hour alone together. Sometimes she talks, sometimes she doesn't, but when she leaves, the edge is off. Her face is noticeably softer. The crease between her eyebrows is gone. So is the permanent scowl. She sleeps better. She doesn't always need a pill.

255

Some of the kicking and tossing stops. Her tips improve. Not that she's all smiles and chat like Tracee, who knows what everyone does for a living or how many kids they have or whether their girlfriends cheated, but at least Lana no longer bangs the pitcher down on the table hoping to splash customers with beer.

Such is the power of Marcel.

She tells him random bits, that she and her dad played chess, that her dad taught her a train song, "When the Choo Choo Chugs to Cheshire." She sings a line to Marcel, " 'Chugging off to Cheshire, glad that I'm aboard.' " She tells him Cheshire is in England, that her dad built miniature trains. "His were the most beautiful. Everyone at the conventions said so."

One day she lists every lie she told her dad. They're endless and mundane, like, "I'm having pizza." "I was in the library." "I sound groggy because I was up all night studying." "I need money for books." Another day she rages, "If there is a God, why did he give Tracee deadbeat parents? Where was he when my mom split?"

For the first time in her life she speaks aloud what has plagued her ever since her mother banged open her bedroom door that terrible scary night. "When she said, 'I hate you,' was she going off on my dad or did she mean me? Am I the reason she left?

"I don't know why you're more attracted to Rita than me," she tells Marcel one morning when he pads into his white cave and leaves her talking to empty space. She laughs. She doesn't really mind when he spends their time together ignoring her or standing at the end of the cage nearest the kitchen because he knows Rita is there. That's good for her too, not being the center of attention. Accepting that. She doesn't feel jealous or neglected when, after Lana's session, Marcel spies Rita, rears up on his hind legs, and presses into the bars for Rita to scratch his chest. Mostly he's attentive and clearly, it seems to Lana, listening. No matter what he does, she feels his acceptance, the privilege of being in his company, his calming force.

Lana hasn't confessed everything to Marcel, not about her dad, but her heart is lighter. One day when their time together is over, she recites the Serenity Prayer: "Marcel, grant me the serenity to accept the things I cannot change; courage to change the things I can; and wisdom to know the difference."

When she is finished, Marcel is more still

than she has ever seen him, and he is brilliant at still.

Tracee means to deal with the diamond necklace. But how? Lana has always solved her problems, but Lana doesn't know about the necklace, and Tracee is scared to tell her in spite of Lana's new, slightly mellower personality, which Tracee doesn't trust. Something as simple as going to the police hasn't occurred to her. She wants a way for it never to have happened in the first place. Disappear, poof, like magic.

If Tim knew, he would leave her.

She is convinced, because one night after making love, Tim tells her about his dad, who died in a freak military accident when he was in training. "His name was Kyle," says Tim. "Kyle Shane Wilson."

"Cool name," says Tracee.

She plays with his hair. She loves the wavy curls and how tangled they are. She loves lying naked skin-to-skin, although Tim is insatiable and usually gets another hard-on minutes into cuddling. "Is that how you know Clayton? From your dad?" she asks.

"He's always been kind of an uncle, keeping an eye out. Before the army my dad worked in a furniture factory and perfected this way of making mattress springs using nylon cord tied in special knots. He was a true craftsman. He made the springs by hand. They last forever. I swear, the beds at my mom's are firm to this day." He rolls over and presses in between her legs.

"I'd love to try them. We should sleep there some night. If it's okay with your mom."

"I know what she's going to say when she meets you," says Tim, beginning to thrust. " 'I love her to pieces.' "

For the first time in their lovemaking Tracee simply goes through the motions. Reality intrudes. How could his mom ever love a kleptomaniac to pieces, especially if she knew the whole of it, if she knew about the necklace? Why would she ever want her son, whom she surely loves to pieces, involved with a criminal? A fugitive from justice. Someone who is going to jail.

No, Tracee cannot tell Tim.

She could tell Rita. That's exactly what she will do. Every day she decides that anew — *I will tell Rita* — but she doesn't because she is so, so happy and doesn't want to spoil it.

Tim often works the bar now with Clayton. This means that when Tracee picks up an order, she can lean across the bar and kiss him. She's having so much fun that she starts saying cheerful waitressy things like "Coming through" when she is carrying a tray loaded with drinks, or "You betcha" when someone asks for a refill. Lana complains to Marcel, "Tracee balanced a tray on her head last night." The gripe sounds so obviously petty when she tells it to the big cat that she immediately forgets about it.

One night after closing they all hang out, sitting around a table while Marcel sleeps. Tracee sips her favorite, ginger ale; Rita, orange pop; Lana, her usual Pepsi. Clayton and Tim share a pitcher of beer. Everyone has worked hard and nobody talks much or needs to.

"I suppose you don't want to go for a ride?" Clayton asks Rita.

She shakes her head.

"How about TV at my place? I bought a flat-screen."

"No, thank you," says Rita. "But it's kind of you to offer."

Clayton takes a final swallow and sets the glass on the table with a little more force than he intends. He has meant to act nonchalant in an effort to regain his edge, as if Rita's hundredth rejection has rolled right off his back. "I'm hungry. You know what — I'm barbecuing. How about that? I'm

260

setting up a barbie in the back. We'll have us a little late-night snack." He takes off.

Tim kisses Tracee as if he is departing on a long voyage before he heads across the room to clean up the bar.

The three women are left alone together.

"I have to thank you," says Rita. "That you picked me up was the most fortunate thing that ever happened to me. I never did believe in miracles, but I'd have to call that a miracle for sure. I'd left Harry before. I left him three times before. But he always found me. 'You're the wife of a minister, Rita. You're the wife of an important man. We have to set an example with our marriage, and you have to come home.'"

Rita closes her eyes. Tracee is sure she's having a memory of Harry berating her, shaking his fist at her to do the right thing. Lana remembers how plain and colorless Rita was when they first met her, and that's how pale Rita turns now. "I hope he never finds me, because I know I'll have to go back. Harry tells you what to do and you do it."

"But you're different now," says Lana. "You're brave. Fiery. You dance with a lion."

"You haven't met Harry."

"Maybe he thinks you were kidnapped," says Tracee.

"He knows I'm fine."

Lana grips her arm. "Imagine not going back. Not ever. Because I bet Harry is the reason you don't think you have an imagination. Remember how you said that? And look at you now with Marcel. Everyone has an imagination unless it's stomped out of you."

"You can't leave," says Tracee. "What would we do without you?"

"But we're leaving," says Lana.

"Oh, right. I forgot. What made you leave?" she asks Rita.

Rita shakes her head, marveling in retrospect. "It was like the cage door was open. He was late getting back from church because of a christening, and I was preparing Sunday lunch."

"Potato salad?"

She smiles. "Just seasoning it. I'd made it the night before. I looked out the window and saw a plumber's truck. Not the local man — I guess they needed someone on Sunday. I thought, 'That's my getaway car.' It was like a fever came over me: 'Now's your chance, get out now.' I put down the paprika, took my purse, left my ring on the mantel. I had to tug to get it off, and for a second I wondered if I would leave at all, because I didn't want that ring going with me. Funny, why would that stop me? Well, I did get it off — caught the plumber as he was driving away, told him my car battery was dead, and asked if he'd mind dropping me at Keene's Grocery. It's right next to the highway. A couple of hours later you found me."

"You found us," says Lana. "Are you sure Harry wants you back? You left. You must have embarrassed him in front of the whole congregation."

"Harry's big on forgiving, unfortunately. I mean, I only left him." She considers that for a moment. "I admit that without so much as a note I walked out the door, but it's not as if I broke a commandment. If I broke one of the ten, then maybe . . ."

"Isn't doing it with someone else one of the ten?" says Tracee.

"You mean adultery?"

"You could sleep with Clayton."

"I know this is hard for you both to understand, being so young and fresh and hopeful, but I don't want another man in my life. Except Marcel."

39

Clayton pushes all the back doors open.

Rita loves it when the wall is gone and the outside and inside get mixed up together. Marcel can smell the trees and grass and whatever other marvelous odors the wind brings, which tonight include steak sizzling on the grill. Sure enough, he wakes and stretches. The moon is one of those middling three-quarter moons, indistinct in shape, and only the brightest stars shine, the rest obscured by a veil of clouds. The air is humid. Gusts of hot wind spring up now and then. They smack down the flames on the barbie. Seconds later the flames leap back to life when the wind dies with the suddenness of a hand making a fist. Behind Clayton and his barbecue there's nothing, the world literally disappears. And yet far off, as if on the other side of a black and bottomless sea, spires of tall, pointy firs wall in the night.

"How do you like your steak?" he calls to the three women as he throws several of Marcel's meals onto the grill.

"Bloody," says Lana.

"Medium for me. Same for Tim, right?" says Tracee as Tim goes to clean the rest-rooms.

"I might be a vegetarian now," calls Rita.

Even from this distance she can see Clay-ton deflate. He gets an allergy attack, pulls out a kerchief, and blows his nose.

Rita relents and goes to join him. "Make mine medium-rare. And please toss a raw one to Marcel."

"Coming up."

"We should keep Clayton company too," says Tracee, but Lana holds her back.

"We are leaving here, you know."

Tracee chews her lip.

"My car's repaired."

"It is?"

"Pretty much."

Tracee pulls away and goes outside.

Lana sits alone and fidgets, her face a snarl.

Marcel pads to the corner of his cage nearest the great outdoors. He inhales the delicious aromas, preoccupied with supper. Not that it matters. Not that he could help Lana. She is off and running.

"Are you okay?" Rita calls to her.

She doesn't answer.

"I thought she was cured," says Clayton as Lana begins pacing and banging into things, probably intentionally.

Rita shakes her head.

More furniture is banged.

"I suppose no one changes all at once," says Rita. "It wouldn't be reasonable to expect that, even with a miracle worker like Marcel."

"I guess not," says Clayton.

Tracee moves into the field behind Clayton. She knows what's coming. She's seen it before. Lana's about to blow the roof off. Still, Tracee recoils involuntarily and drops her plate when Lana kicks over a chair and charges out, screaming, "I'm here because of you. I screwed up my whole summer because of you."

"Sorry," says Tracee.

"I'm not fresh and hopeful," Lana yells at Rita.

"Yes, you are," Rita replies placidly. "And Tracee too. She's so happy with Tim."

"Tim's her toy. She is stuck here. Stuck and bored."

"I love Tim," says Tracee.

"No, you don't."

"Yes, I do."

She heads inside to safety, to find him, but Lana grabs her arm. "I didn't wreck my summer for you to fall in love with Tim."

Tracee bursts out crying. Tears come so easily. She cries before she knows what she feels, a crybaby's preventive strike so Lana will go easy on her. But then she screams, "No one made you get in the car and hand over your keys. No one made you come along."

"I came to take care of you. Because you can't take care of yourself. Because you screw up other people's lives. Because you're a mess. You always have been."

Rita stands between them, unsure of what to do. She puts out her arm to Tracee, who falls into it, sobbing on her shoulder.

Lana rages off into the field.

"Fuck, fuck, fuck, fuck," she screams.

She wants to howl. She hits herself first on the arm, and when that doesn't satisfy, she slaps her chest until it hurts. Tracee is a bitch, a selfish bitch Lana has wasted her life trying to fix. Trying to make up for the fact that her parents were so self-absorbed they forgot to come home. She's hapless, the little thief. Where would she be without Lana? How futile it is trying to make a dumb girl smart. "I'm smart. I'm the smart one," Lana tells herself.

She hates everyone.

Maybe even Rita.

For an hour she stays there, and for an hour they leave her alone. The air is lousy with mosquitoes, which she continually slaps and swears at. She desperately needs some OFF! or one of the antibug lanterns that make it so pleasant around the barbecue. She'd rather be bitten to death than borrow one.

"Someone better get her," Clayton says eventually, and so Rita approaches close enough for her soft voice to carry and says, "Lana, we're leaving."

Rita and Tracee are already in Tim's car when she shows up. She squeezes into the back. Tim holds the door as usual.

On the drive home Lana is hostile, the atmosphere toxic. No one speaks.

When they get out, Lana sprints ahead and enters the room before anyone else has reached the stairs.

Rita finds that her research on lions helps her maintain her composure when she and Lana are alone together. If a wild animal is angry, Rita knows not to engage. A lion can be stubborn or moody, and if he resists it's best to stay away until his mood changes. In her interactions with Marcel she's never needed these bits of wisdom. With Lana it's another matter.

Rita is practicing dance moves, waving paper towels, rehearsing her role in the tricks with Marcel, when Lana comes out of the bathroom, still dripping from the shower and wrapped in a towel.

"Look at this." Lana pulls a charger out of her purse. "I bought it today." She plugs it in, pleased in a furious way, and sets her cell phone in it.

She sits on the bed and shakes her head so her wet hair slaps her face. "I'm getting my car back. Any day now."

Rita tosses the paper towels up in the air to see if that might be an effective dramatic close to the show, although probably nothing is more effective than her bowing to Marcel and Marcel bowing back.

"In a few weeks," says Lana, "we're going to be able to pay back the cost of that wedding dress. Tracee stole it."

"I know," says Rita. "Do you think I can stop wearing a bra? I hate it. It feels like a harness. I get welts. Do you think anyone would notice?"

"Everyone would notice, but so what? You're a star. How did you know the wedding dress was stolen?"

"It's got that plastic button attached, the kind that sets off alarms when you leave the store. What about the necklace?"

"What necklace?"

"Diamonds. I tried it on once. Spied it in Tracee's purse and couldn't help myself. My goodness, they sparkle. A row of little stones in the most unusual shape. I'd never seen anything like it — well, why would I? And gold between. I assumed, because of the dress, that the necklace was also —"

Lana springs off the bed before Rita finishes the sentence. She tears outside in her towel and raps on Tim's door. "Tracee. Tracee, open up."

She tries to see through the window but the blinds are closed. They're probably having sex, she concludes, and is about to pound harder when she hears the sound of a motor, swings around, and looks down over the railing.

Tim's car is pulling out of the lot.

"Tim, Tracee, stop. Tracee!" Lana rushes down the stairs but the car turns onto the street and vanishes.

An hour or so later, on a lovely road shaded with oaks and lined with well-cared-for modest homes with wooden porches and blooming gardens, Tim's car turns into a driveway.

Tim hurries around to help Tracee out. He wraps her arm into his. They approach the front door together with formality. The house is dark. It's nearly three thirty in the morning. Only the porch is lit.

Tracee smiles nervously at Tim as he presses the bell.

A light goes on upstairs, then downstairs. A woman opens the door and peers through the screen. "Good grief, Tim?"

"Hi, Momma," says Tim. "I'd like you to meet Tracee."

40

May Wilson, a tall redhead in a silky pink bathrobe, pushes open the screen door and smiles widely. You'd think Tim had just done something remarkable, like climb Mount Everest, instead of showing up at three in the morning with a strange woman. His mom looks as if Christmas has knocked on her front door.

"Tracee." She claps a hand to her heart. "I am so happy to meet you. Please come in. Oh, Tim." She throws her arms around her son, takes a break to appreciate his face, and hugs him again.

"What's going on?" a man hollers.

Tracee looks up the stairs. On the landing there is, no other word for it, a hottie in nothing but boxer shorts.

"Hi, Gil," says Tim.

"Tim brought Tracee home," says May. "You two don't move. I have to put on my face, be right back." She hurries upstairs.

Gil pats her ass as she scoots by.

"I'm going back to bed," says Gil. "Hope that's okay."

"Sure, Gil," says Tim.

"How's everything? You all right?"

"I'm fine."

"Nothing to worry about?"

"Better than that."

"Good."

"Who's that?" whispers Tracee as soon as he disappears.

"Gil's the only one that can fix Clayton's Chevy. He and my mom have been together ages, ever since she started keeping the books at his repair shop."

"How old is he?"

"Hard to tell with Gil, he's pretty preserved. Works out too. I don't know. Younger than my momma for sure."

May sticks her head over the banister. "I mean it, don't show her around yet."

They hang out just inside the front door, both of them tongue-tied, Tim because this is such a momentous occasion, Tracee for the same reason and because her stomach is in knots. She sneaks a peek into the living room. "So pretty and stylish you wouldn't believe it," she imagines telling Lana. "White walls with a big window in front, and it seems like the flowers on the front porch — these hanging red flowers — are actually inside." She even imagines Lana scoffing and Tracee insisting she knows what stylish is, she's in a position to judge, she's seen lots of different living rooms at Clarkson's. There's a striped rug, the furniture is wicker, which explains why Tim favors it, with big square red cushions, and there are sunflowers. Tracee counts three vases full. The room is neat, but every available surface, several small tables and a three-tiered shelf hanging on the wall, is chock-full of objects and photographs artfully arranged, all of which turn out to have special meaning.

May comes clattering down the stairs in clogs, blue jeans, and an oversize T-shirt advertising Gil's Auto Repair. She's dolled up now, her wavy shoulder-length hair brushed, a slash of bright orange lipstick. "My eyebrows are on but not my lashes. I hope that's okay."

She takes Tracee on a guided tour through a parade of Tims, snapshots from infancy — May groggy in a hospital bed holding her fuzzy-headed newborn — to his graduation from Raleigh Community College, where Tim, grinning in his cap and gown, is flanked by Gil, his ripped body stressing the seams of a slim black suit, and his mother, glamorous in a turquoise minidress and sunglasses, her hair blowing backward in the wind. A photo of Tim, a toddler sitting on his dad's shoulders, makes Tracee want to cry. His dad is in his army uniform and Tim is holding on to his dad's head, squishing his hat. There's a clay ashtray that Tim made in third grade, with a clay blob in the center that May tells her is a tree, a heart-shaped red candy box with a felt top, and a small wooden box with "To my mom" burned into it. "Woodworking class, how old were you?" says May.

"I don't know," says Tim. "Ten, I guess."

Tracee is particularly struck by one photograph of Tim as a teenager. Although she can't articulate why, she understands how alike she and Tim are, which gives her an additional surge of affection and belonging, from seeing him standing under goalposts in his football uniform, the shoulder pads like huge weights on his skinny frame, his face in shadow lost inside the large helmet.

"I kept the bench warm," says Tim.

"He played two games, don't listen to him."

Tracee picks up a color eight-by-ten in a silver frame. She can't believe what she's seeing: May Wilson, younger than Tracee, posing in a white one-piece swimsuit with a tiara on her head and a banner across her front: "North Carolina."

"Wow," says Tracee.

"Long time gone," says May.

"You really were Miss North Carolina?"

May mimes the same radiant smile in the photo.

"You were so gorgeous, well, you still are. Can I have your autograph?"

"You've got my son, isn't that enough?" May breaks up. She has a bright, loud voice, and her laugh is loud too, like she's not afraid to be heard far and wide.

Tracee looks to Tim to see if maybe she was out of line asking for an autograph, but Tim is only beaming, because his mom and Tracee are getting along. "Did you try for Miss Universe?" says Tracee.

"Miss America," says Tim.

"I got eliminated on the first round. I never had to sing. What a relief, I was terrified."

"Was that your talent?"

"I was going to sing 'Moon River,' such a pretty song. I had a warbling way of doing it, lonely and sad. I practiced for hours. Do you know that song?"

Tracee shakes her head.

"Come on, let's have pancakes." May herds them into the kitchen. "Tim, set the

276

table. Tracee, you sit and relax. The sponsors, supervisors, I don't know what to call them — they boss the contestants around much more than you know — thought I should do 'Moon River' because it was unusual and had a story — my daddy taught it to me when I was a little girl. They said that was better than 'Stand by Your Man.' Who knows, because I never sang either."

"Wait till I tell Lana," Tracee says, certain that Lana will not call Tim a rube when she hears about his mother.

"Who's Lana?"

"My best friend."

"Tim, honey, get out the griddle." May scoops flour out of a canister and sets efficiently to whipping up a batter. "I got this new griddle from credit card points. I've been waiting for you to come home to try it." She cracks eggs with a clack of a knife and beats them with a fork. "Isn't there buttermilk? — thank God, yes — and take that melting butter off the flame before it burns."

"Tim told me how popular you are."

"Me?"

"She's everyone's favorite," says Tim.

"Oh, no, Rita is."

"Hey, you're the most popular one at The Lion and everyone knows it," says Tim.

Could that be true? Tracee wonders.

"Well, I'm glad business is booming," says May. "Clayton finally caught a break."

She lets the batter drip off the spoon, seems to decide it's ready based on that, and turns on the heat under the griddle. "Now we wait," she says. "Nothing worse than a pancake cooked on a griddle that isn't hot." She puts a tall pitcher of sun tea on the table and also offers beer. Tim takes one. "Pancakes and beer, why not?" says May. Tracee is relieved that Tim's mom keeps the conversation going, because she is worried about doing or saying the wrong thing, even though she isn't sure what the wrong thing would be in such a friendly place.

"I used to watch *Wheel of Fortune*," says May. "I wanted to be Vanna White in the worst way. She got so far on what? Nothing but looks, and I figured the pageant route was the way to go. I could win money, be famous, and see the world. Wanted to visit Egypt and sail down the Nile. I wanted to go on a safari. Then I won Miss North Carolina. Spent the year being a spokesperson, telling teenagers to follow their dreams, doing the parade thing waving from cars. Met Tim's dad at a harvest festival in Raleigh. The next thing I knew I'd settled down. Tim, you always wanted bear pancakes, didn't you, and now you're bringing Tracee home. How fast is time?"

"What's a bear pancake?" says Tracee.

"One big pancake and two little ones for ears," says May. "I'll make you one."

Later, when they are in Tim's bedroom, lying under a *Star Wars* poster, squished into Tim's single bed, Tracee marvels about it all. "You never told me, why didn't you, you're modest. So is your mom. If I won Miss anything, it would have gone to my head."

They make love silently, not wanting to be heard or to disturb. Their bodies undulate only slightly, a ripple in water, and the struggle to contain their passion to the smallest of movements heightens it. Their climax is a shudder that seems to go on forever.

Afterward they lie together, sticky with sweat and blissful.

Tracee pokes him. "Tim, don't fall asleep. You can't sleep here. Your mom made up the couch."

Tim moans and pulls her closer.

She wants to tell him her deepest fear. She wants to confide about her parents, about how disappearing they were, taking off, never bothering to leave a note, as if she didn't exist. And how, now that they've moved away from Fosberg, she never hears from them. What she doesn't understand the most, what really gnaws at her — if they could forget her so easily, isn't that her fault? She wants to ask Tim, "Am I forgettable?" She wants to ask him because she knows he'll say, "No way," or, "Hell, no," or, "Where'd you get a crazy idea like that? I could never forget you." But all she says to Tim is, "Your mom was so happy to see you."

"She's my mom," says Tim, swinging his long legs over the side of the bed and sitting up. He strokes Tracee's hair. He could look at Tracee's face forever, she's so beautiful, and everything she feels shows right up on it. "Do you know the Theory of One?"

"No."

"Come on, sit up."

They shift back against the headboard, naked, with the blankets pulled up to their chins, facing Tim's bureau with his robot collection on top, including a vacuuming one he showed her earlier that can Dustbust a table. The Theory of One, he explains, means that all you need is one person to make a difference in your life. "You can have the world's most awful life," says Tim, "but if one person believes in you, you'll be okay. With me it was my mom.

She's my champion, always in my corner. It was her idea to start the driving school."

Tracee struggles over the theory. *Did I have a one?* She reasons it out. Lana did. Her dad was her one.

"Are you sure about the theory?" says Tracee. "Because Lana —"

"According to the Discovery Channel it pretty much works. She's sober, isn't she?"

"Yes, but her one doesn't speak to her."

"How come?"

"I'm not sure."

"It usually works," says Tim.

"Is someone being there for you the same as being your champion? I didn't have a champion but I had Lana."

Tracee doesn't want to be someone without a one. She doesn't want to be someone with zero. It seems doomed.

"I would like to be your one," says Tim.

"Isn't it too late?"

"Hell, no. I'm your one."

41

The first call Lana gets on her charged-up cell is from Bill. He wakes her at eleven thirty in the morning. He has to tell her who he is twice because she's still logy from a Tylenol PM. And thank God for it or she would have obsessed about Tracee and the necklace all night.

"Your car is ready and waiting," says Bill.

He picks her up and drives her to the gas station. Even though she's fifty dollars short on the repair costs, he tells her to forget it, and watches with pride as she circles the car, strokes the gleaming new front grille, opens and closes the new driver's-side door, exclaiming at how perfectly it works. "What a beautiful job. It's newer than when I bought it."

"I was able to match the paint too," says Bill. "Got lucky."

He hands her the keys. She slides in behind the wheel and rests contentedly for a moment, the vinyl familiarly hot against her bare legs. She turns the key, gives it gas, and listens to the motor hum. It's like she has a friend back.

"I owe this to Rita," she tells Bill. "If it weren't for Rita . . . I'm in her debt."

"I'm sure you'll find a way to pay her back."

"I don't see how."

She waves and drives off, heading for The Lion. Her mind starts buzzing the way it always does when she drives, flitting from one thought to another, how she lost it last night, how she went utterly south. She needs Marcel. She needs a visit. She needs to hang out with him before confronting Tracee. Before last night's backward slide, Lana had gotten in the habit of talking to Marcel even when he wasn't around — she doesn't call it praying. She tries it now. *Marcel, help me turn my brain off. Slow me down. Marcel, please help me not get in a total fucking rage* — desires that fly right out the window when she reaches The Lion and finds Tim's car in the lot (along with Clayton's), which means Tracee must be there too, since she and Tim are glued together.

Lana pulls in and steams.

Inside, Marcel is chewing on a beef bone

that May brought him, and May, Tim, Tracee, and Clayton are gathered at the bar. Tim is setting up the bar for later, when they open, while May, having a beer and tossing back peanuts, regales Clayton with the events of the night before. "I've got to say, I've never seen anybody as suited as these two. We talked until practically dawn, didn't we?"

Tim and Tracee nod.

"Then we all went to bed."

"The beds were amazing," says Tracee. "Tim's dad made the springs."

"Clayton knows that, honey. He's got one of Kyle's beds too."

"And we picked blackberries this morning." To prove it, Tracee shows off her hands, still stained purple.

For Tracee it was a sweet night and a sweet morning, maybe the sweetest of her life, until Lana charges into The Lion and without so much as a hello announces, "I have to speak to you, Tracee."

"This is Tim's mother," says Tracee. "May Wilson. May, I'd like you to meet my friend Lana Byrne."

"Tracee, right now," says Lana.

"I'm busy."

"Tracee."

"It must be an emergency. Excuse me."

She goes to join Lana, who has moved some distance away. "How rude are you?" whispers Tracee.

Lana only glances at the group and moves farther off.

Tracee follows. "I'm not speaking to you."

Lana walks into the kitchen and disappears from sight. Tracee throws a confused look to Tim and follows her in. "What is it?"

Lana closes the door. "Diamonds."

It takes a second to register. "Oh."

"Oh?"

"I forgot about them."

"You forgot?"

"It slipped my mind."

"How?"

"I don't know. I guess." She rubs her chin, hesitating before apologizing. "I've been happy."

"Do they know you took them?"

"Tim and his mom?"

"The store. Did they see you? Did they catch you on some sort of camera?"

"It was a stand. A booth. You know, that antique mall on Route 9. Fifty dealers."

Lana sighs with relief. "So no camera. Not in town. Nobody we know."

"The Hofstadder booth."

"Karen Hofstadder's parents? Did they

see you, Tracee? Think."

"I don't know."

Lana's heart is racing, a familiar feeling, the excitement that comes from Tracee's messes. Lana has to solve the problem. She is needed. She is alive. "How much is that diamond thing worth?"

"It's very small. Short. A choker, kind of."

"How much?"

"They always jack up the prices at those antique places."

"Tracee?"

"Three thousand dollars."

"Three thousand dollars? That's burglary. That's a felony. They're going to come and get you."

"I know." Tracee swerves one way, then the other, a crazed animal in a small pen. "What about Tim?"

"Yeah, well."

"He's nice, he's so nice, and I'm — I'm going to throw up."

"Please don't," says Lana.

A loud, guttural blast. Marcel. His roar doesn't blow the door open but it seems as if it should have.

"Weird," says Lana.

They listen. They wait. Nothing more.

"He almost never roars," says Tracee.

Lana laughs. "Rita probably just walked in."

"It didn't sound friendly."

"Like you'd know," says Lana, although it didn't sound friendly to her either.

"You know how Marcel wore my veil and now . . ."

"And now what?"

"First Tim put the veil on his head, okay. And now his mom is there and Marcel roars. That's that thing, what do you call it?"

"Nothing. It's called nothing. If Marcel's doing anything it's because of Rita. Or me."

"You?"

"He's my higher power."

"Huh?"

"If you weren't with Tim all the time you'd know."

"How does that work?"

"None of your business."

"Why can't it be about me? Why isn't anything about me?"

"Everything's about you."

"I don't still steal."

"Of course you still steal. It doesn't go away."

"Why not?"

"It's a compulsion."

"Yours went away."

"It didn't go away. It's always there. And drinking's not a compulsion. I don't think. I'm not sure. It's not the same."

"But you don't do it anymore." Tracee struggles, trying not to get defeated the way she always does when Lana argues with her. "Why can you not do yours but I can't stop mine?"

"I'm not discussing this. Look, you're safe for now." Lana opens the refrigerator, finds a peach, and starts devouring it in quick, squirrelly bites. "Let me figure this out."

Tracee cracks open the door, wincing as she turns the knob, hoping it won't make a sound.

"What are you doing?"

Tracee puts her eye to the sliver of a view, needing to see Tim's face, missing him suddenly and awfully, needing something like forgiveness when he doesn't even know the crime. All she sees is Marcel's big head, those piercing eyes staring. At what? She shifts. Is that Tucker? In his uniform? Tucker with another man, older; his back is to her. Who is he? Perhaps the police chief? Perhaps a plainclothes detective from up north, like Maryland?

Tracee backs away.

"What?" says Lana.

She raises a limp finger to point. She has

lost the power of speech but then she finds it. "Police."

Lana shoves her aside and leans in to look. "Not necessarily for us."

"Tracee, get out here," Clayton shouts. "You too, Lana. Tucker wants to talk to you."

42

Lana and Tracee burst out the back door. Tracee, her arms flailing, has no idea where to go and stops for a moment before taking off after Lana, who is running hell-bent across the lot.

She yanks open her new car door, slides in, jams in the key, starts it up, waits for Tracee to hop in.

She speeds down the road, heading for the Tulip Tree Motel, taking curves and corners like a race-car driver — the blazing noon sun boring in the windshield causing her to blink and shift constantly, while Tracee, twisted around, keeps her eye peeled out the back, expecting a black-and-white to turn up at any moment, siren wailing, red light whirling. "Nothing, still nothing, nothing," she squeals, an anxious, breathless commentary.

Finally they are rushing up the stairs.

"Where is it? Our room or Tim's?"

"Ours," says Tracee. She trips on a thick shred of peeling paint, stubs her toe, and is hopping when she catches up with Lana, who cannot find her key. Lana dumps her purse on the concrete, locates the key, hands it to Tracee, and piles everything back inside while Tracee opens the door. Lana pushes her in, closes the door, and keeps watch through the blinds as Tracee rummages in the bureau drawer and comes up with the choker.

"Let me see." Lana holds out a flat hand.

Pinching one end, letting it dangle, Tracee lowers the delicate chain into Lana's palm.

Lana plays with the necklace, moving it in snakelike patterns, watching the stones catch the light and reveal with the palest pink sparkle to be not false but true. Even the links amaze her. Not the bright yellow wiry stamped-out loops of a trinket, but each tiny link irregular, shaped by hand, twisted ropes of burnished gold. This little necklace is so powerful it takes Lana right out of reality. It stops time. She glances up to catch Tracee's eye and they bond, an acknowledgment of illicit pleasure. An object of such simple beauty and value is something so out of their league.

"I have to try it on," she says in a hoarse whisper.

She stands in front of the mirror while Tracee fastens the catch, which itself is a marvel. A tiny gold arrow that fits into a loop when turned sideways, and remains in place when the loop is turned.

The necklace, snug, sits high on Lana's neck. The half-moons stand up in a row. They are so bright that it seems to Lana like an optical illusion, some freak astronomical occurrence when a person sees not one moon but many. She shifts very slightly back and forth, causing them to throw off sparks in all directions. The light transforms. Her cheeks blush pink, her dark eyes flash, her coppery skin glows as if tempered with hot oil.

"Oh," says Lana.

"I know," says Tracee.

"They're like itty-bitty headlights. Only . . . magical."

"I know."

Lana swoops her hair up and, standing taller, lengthens her neck, angling her firm, strong chin slightly to profile. How fresh she looks and yet sophisticated. As if she comes from money. A city woman, not a small-town girl trying to pass.

"Undo it," she says with urgency. "They're too powerful. I could get hooked on diamonds."

Tracee unfastens the chain and tucks the necklace back in the drawer. Lana snatches it out. "Not buried in your underwear. That's the first place they look." She sticks it under the bed pillow, fluffs the pillow, knocks it aside and grabs it back.

She slips it under a chair cushion. Changes her mind. Stashes it under a box of tissues. The box falls over. Drops it inside the box. Digs it out.

"Can they just come in and search?" says Tracee, keeping an eye out the window.

"If they have a warrant. You know, 'search,' as in 'search and seizure.'" Lana prowls, hunting for a hiding place. "You're cooked."

"Don't say that."

"We both are. I'm an accessory after the fact."

"What fact? You know so much about the law."

"It's true, I do. Tucker would love to arrest me."

"How could I do this to Tim?"

"At least you're not pregnant. Oh my God." Lana rushes into the bathroom. "Where is it? I put it here. What did you do with it?"

"What?"

"The condom. I put it here. Next to the Noxzema. Standing up. Looking jaunty. I remember when I put it here, I thought, 'This looks jaunty.' " Lana bends to see behind the toilet bowl. "It's there, yes! Come here. Can you reach it?"

Tracee, with her slender hands, manages to coax the small square packet from where it fell, wedged between the wall and a plumbing pipe. Lana tries to tear it open. "God, what's with this plastic?"

"Guys use their teeth," says Tracee.

"Oh, right." Lana bites the edge and rips it. She slips out the condom, unrolls it, and pulls to stretch it. Very gently. "It's not too elastic. It must be old. Older than us."

"What are you doing, anyway?" says Tracee.

"You'll see."

She manages to enlarge it a little more. "Okay, hand me the necklace."

Lana tries to thread the choker into the condom, but, like a balloon with no air, the rubber sides stick together. Gingerly she attempts to widen the rim while Tracee threads it in. No success.

"Wait, I know." Holding the condom under the faucet, Lana lets water trickle in until the condom becomes a half-filled saggy and soggy balloon. She holds the rim open and the choker slides in.

She swings the condom cheerfully. "Would

you ever know? No, you would never know."

She tears back to the bed. "Rumple, Tracee, rumple."

"It's unmade. It's already a mess."

"Make it more."

Tracee shoves the covers around, jumps on the bed, rolls, kicks a bit, and rolls off.

Lana slips the condom between the sheets. "Not quite in plain sight but practically. Are they here?"

Lifting a broken blind, Tracee peeks out. The lot is quiet, empty. Every so often a car passes by on the street. "Not yet."

"Throw a thong on the floor."

Tracee takes one from the drawer and flings it. It lands in front of the bed.

"Perfect," says Lana.

43

A Toyota creeps slowly along Winstead Road and turns into the parking lot. It passes Tucker's patrol car and Clayton's Chevy Bel Air and swings around to the front door, where it stops abruptly. Rita gets out. "Thanks for the ride, Debi."

"Anytime you want to go to the library, just call. I love to drive. I'll drive anywhere. Tell Marcel hi."

Rita hefts out some books and nudges the door closed with her backside.

"Need help?"

"I'm fine. Thank you again."

She walks into The Lion and stops cold.

She knows who he is before he turns around. Of course she does. Every woman knows her own husband. Besides, thirty years together breeds a lot of familiarity.

Tucker and Clayton see her before Harry does, and when they fall silent, Harry swivels on his bar stool. "I found you," he says.

The books tumble from her arms onto a table. She busies herself a moment stacking them, straightening the edges, and when she looks up, Harry is ambling toward her. In his middle age he's grown slow-moving and bowlegged, she'd forgotten that. Even the discovery of his missing wife doesn't produce a lot of speed. "You look different," says Harry, "with your hair and all, but it's still you."

Rita gets a feeling of helplessness, a sickness in the pit of her stomach that maybe she doesn't know her own mind, or if she does, she doesn't have the nerve to speak it. She focuses on Marcel and that helps, making a beeline for the big cat, who, in expectation of her company, strolls over to the cage door.

"I'm not coming home, Harry. I'm a lion tamer now."

"I heard that. From Tucker here."

"I put some keywords into Google and up popped your disappearance," says Tucker. "In the church monthly."

"I guess there's no hiding these days, is there?" says Rita.

"Amen to that," says Harry.

She bolts for the cage.

It's a standoff — Rita, her key out, ready to unlock the cage door, Harry wondering if one step closer will drive her inside.

"I brought the kids," says Harry. "And your grandkids. They went off to the Truck Museum. Should be back by now." He abruptly changes directions, moving in his molasses-like way to the front door, which he opens. He lifts an arm and waves.

Clayton is watching as if this is a play unfolding. It might not even be happening to someone he knows, much less someone he fantasizes about day and night. He doesn't like Harry. His face is like granite. He's barely cracked a smile, although why would he smile, having arrived to corral his renegade wife? Before sitting, he dusted off the bar stool, and Clayton felt his disgust as he eyed Lana's artful arrangement of liquor bottles. He asked for a lemonade, as if The Lion looks like a place that serves lemonade, not a man's drink, and Clayton doesn't trust anyone who squints indoors, where there is no sun. Harry sat with his back to Marcel, who roared when he entered. Perhaps Harry understood what was apparent to Clayton: Marcel took an instant dislike. That roar had bite. It wasn't like any sound Clayton had heard from the animal before. Marcel's ears pressed back; his lips curled in a snarl. And while Harry didn't acknowledge the lion, Marcel's eyes settled on him and stayed there until Rita came in. While they waited, Harry mostly let Tucker do the talking. He sipped his ice water (his second choice), adding only religious punctuation, a "God willing" or an "Amen." Tucker wondered how Lana, Tracee, and Rita had "joined forces," as he put it, but Harry wasn't curious. "God has his reasons," was all he said, and then asked his only question: "How do you keep the place sanitized?" Clayton explained the hosing system. Then Harry asked a second question. "Has my wife been imbibing spirits?" Clayton only shrugged.

All color drains from Rita's face when Harry swings the door wider to let in her three grown sons, their wives, and three grandchildren under the age of six. They remain bunched together in the doorway, not certain what exactly is expected of them and silenced by the large, peculiar tentlike environment that includes a lion and their grandmother, looking unfamiliar. "Hi, Grandma," shouts the youngest, a pixie in denim overalls.

Rita gets in the cage with Marcel. She does it so swiftly and unself-consciously that it produces barely a ripple of astonishment. "Go away, because I'm not coming back."

"You want to leave us all?" says Harry.

"You can come visit anytime. Although not too often. My life is very busy."

"Your sons have to pay for babysitting now. A stranger takes care of your grandchildren."

"I'm sure not a stranger," says Rita.

"The garden's all weeds."

"All the gardening books are on the second shelf directly below C. S. Lewis. Just look up 'weeds.' Everything here is blooming."

"Stop being foolish. It's time to come home."

Rita knows what's next: a death knell. She says it along with him. "All is forgiven."

Marcel rises up behind her.

Everyone screams.

His enormous head looms over hers and his bushy mane hangs down, grazing her shoulders, a thick, hairy cloak. Except for Clayton, no one doubts he will bite her head off.

Tucker draws his gun. "Come on out, ma'am."

"No," says Rita.

"This is for your own protection. Come out or I'm going to have to shoot the cat."

Marcel starts sniffing her hair — a medley of deep, noisy snorts and dainty sniffs. The grandkids start giggling. The youngest tugs

300

her mom's hand, trying to pull her closer.

"I got this," says Tucker. "I'm taking care of this." He holds the gun now with two hands, as if to take better aim, although what's really going on is that his gun hand is shaking and he needs the other to steady it.

"Don't go shooting Marcel to prove you deserve your badge," says Clayton.

"Stay out of this."

"Just 'cause you passed out drunk and let a girl steal your police car."

"That wasn't my fault."

"Whatever," says Clayton. He drops some quarters in the jukebox and hits "Bamboleo."

"Bamboleo, Bamboleo." *Come dance with me, go wild, fill my heart with fire* — Rita doesn't have any idea if that's what the Spanish words mean, only that the words mean that to her. They are an imperative. She begins to salsa, undulating and swiveling a do-si-do around Marcel. His tail snaps back and forth, whisking now and then across her bouncing, swaying, unmistakably no-bra breasts.

Her family is transfixed. Harry flinches every time Marcel's tail brushes across his wife's bosom.

Tucker lowers his gun.

When the song ends, Rita places her finger on Marcel's nose. A gesture of peace and respect. She turns toward her family, distant, clustered together on the other side of the room, and bows.

"The devil is at work here," says Harry.

Rita sags, the life socked out of her. She might as well say it, he probably won't get it, he might even interpret it as a compliment when for her it's the ultimate tragedy. "Oh, Harry, you're so unpoetic."

She stands motionless and weak as he approaches. He leans in, his face inches from the bars. She sees his eyes clearly. Because they are deeply set, she hadn't noticed the sleepless dark circles under them. His face crumples. His lips are trembling like a child's. He starts to cry.

She was expecting to be lectured or bullied. She wasn't prepared for this. She feels sorrier for Harry than for herself. She always has.

The youngest grandchild yanks free of her mother, streaks through the bar, runs up and sticks her skinny little arms through the bars and around Rita's legs. "Please come home, Grandma."

"Honey, don't," says Rita, disentangling. "Don't put your hands in a lion's cage."

44

The clan piles into the van. The children argue about who gets to sit in what seat and next to which mom, dad, aunt, uncle, or cousin. Inside The Lion, Rita collects her stuff. There isn't much, a sweater on a hook in the kitchen, a mug she picked up for tea between shows.

She wraps the mug in paper towels and then, puzzled, stares at the lumpy object as if she doesn't recognize it. She lays it on the counter; it rolls sideways. She unwraps it and sets it down again.

Behind her Clayton watches, leaning against the door. "Divorce the stinker, marry me."

Rita turns. "I didn't realize you were here. I don't think I need this. I guess I have all the dishes I need."

He straightens up and scratches an eyebrow.

"I have to talk to you about Marcel,"

she says.

"There's an offer on the table."

"I appreciate that, but . . ." She shakes her head.

"It stands."

"Thank you."

Rita pushes open the screen door, steps into the sunlight, and takes in the view. In the beginning, when she first worked at The Lion, she would look out the kitchen window in this direction, appreciating the pale blue late-afternoon light, occasional feathery wisps of pink clouds, while she set out the glasses, getting ready for the bar to open. Later, when she walked Marcel, this was also her vista: the field of wild grass, the rise beyond that she and Marcel climbed each morning, settling at the top, ready to greet the day. She always had a hopeful feeling, a surge of happiness at hearing the birds. Their liveliness was infectious. Marcel's ears would flick forward. The first time she wondered, *Was he hearing something new, or rediscovering sounds he hadn't heard in years?* Sometimes Marcel buried his head in the wet grass, the way a person might thrust his nose into the petals of a fragrant rose, letting the scent overwhelm his senses.

"Not out here," she says, changing her mind. "I can't bear to talk here."

She turns back inside, takes a seat at the kitchen table, waits for Clayton to take the chair across, and addresses him solemnly. "Marcel needs the great outdoors. He needs a garden. Will you fence in the back field outside the accordion doors?"

"Why are you leaving?"

Rita simply stares at her hands, which are clasped together in front of her, resting on the tabletop. "Perhaps you could build a pathway from the cage so he can get from his cage to the outdoors easily. He likes to be outside, especially in the morning."

"Harry is a deep, cold grave."

"I married him," she says flatly.

"Not a federal crime."

"He's lost without me, he often tries to pretend not, you know, inside he's a small and lonely man, I think. This has been . . . it's been a vacation. A dream. Extraordinary. But I'm not young. I made choices. I have responsibilities. I was pretending I didn't. That I had no past, no commitments. But I do. Everyone does. Will you do those things for Marcel? Give him a garden?"

"I'll start tomorrow."

His hands close over hers. " 'Did you ever see a robin weep / When leaves begin to die?' "

"Excuse me?"

"Hell, if I knew it was poetry you wanted."

"Was that poetry?"

"Hank Williams."

"Oh. I like that."

She slips her hands out from under his. "Thank you for everything, Clayton. Do you think you might return my library books? There's one called *Cat Watching*. It's about house cats, but maybe there is something useful in it. You might understand Marcel better. If you want to read it, it's not due for two weeks."

"I'll read it cover to cover."

"And . . ."

"What?"

"Marcel might like a chicken with the feathers on. He could pluck it before he ate it and that would keep him busy."

"A live chicken?" says Clayton.

"No, not live. I'm worried that he's bored. He might enjoy plucking. It makes sense. You know lions rip the fur off their kill."

"I didn't know that. Consider it done."

"And a femur?"

"Whose femur?"

"A cow, I suppose. Once a week he needs to gnaw on a femur bone."

"I'll be sure he gets one."

"Thank you." Rita stands and pushes her chair in neatly, much as she did when she first arrived, erasing her own presence. She goes to the door that joins the kitchen to the bar. Marcel has parked himself at the side of the cage nearest the kitchen, in the corner where he always waits for her. Far away, at the open entrance to The Lion, Harry blocks the light.

"We're waiting for you," he calls. His familiar reedy, needy voice barely conceals a hint of triumph.

"We have to stop at the motel and pick up the rest of my things."

"I know. I'm just saying I'm anxious to get the job done and get home."

"I'll be out in a minute."

As soon as Harry leaves, Rita wraps a hand around one of the thick iron bars of the cage and then, with her eyes, follows the black pole up to its spiked point. Marcel, inside the cage, breathes heavily. "You are patient," she whispers. "Will that to me." She runs her hand along from bar to bar, crossing to the cage door. Marcel follows along.

She unlocks the heavy padlock, lifts it off for the last time, and steps inside.

Recalling what she has read, she knows she can't try this head-on. Marcel might interpret it as aggression. If you want to hug a lion, approach from the side, that's what it said. She stands next to Marcel so that they are both facing the same direction. She is seeing the world as he sees it: someone locked in looking out. She knows this feeling well from her confined life as Harry's wife. There is a comfort in the familiar even when it's deprivation. This old friend, she thinks, is back to stay.

She slips an arm around Marcel's neck and, with her other arm, circles around. She buries her head in his mane. It's thick and bristly and smelly in the mustiest way. She closes her eyes and hopes she will remember the feeling.

She steps back outside and refastens the padlock. Marcel presses forward, his nose against the bars.

"It's been an honor to know you," says Rita. "You are a king — noble and kind the way a king should be. And you're a wonderful partner. You've made me happy."

Marcel roars. The force of his breath knocks her backward into a chair.

Rita remains where he's sent her, astonished. Marcel lowers his head in a deep bow, and now she knows he knows she's leaving.

Rita rushes out.

45

Tracee, the lookout, has stopped looking.
It's been at least an hour; the cops have not
shown up. Her attention tends to wander,
apparently even under circumstances such
as these. She has slid down the wall to a
catcher's crouch and, in this unexpectedly
comfortable position, has been taking a
mental meander through her latest lovemaking with Tim, the stirring and quiet nature
of it. *I could never, ever,* she thinks, *in a million years be worthy of him.*

Lana, slumped now in the chair, one leg
flung over the arm, drifts too, considering
the summer, her father, her life. She has a
cool, damp washcloth that she idly moves
from one spot on her arm to another, pats
her forehead with it, wipes the back of her
neck. She's chewing Dentyne Ice — she
consumes a few packs a day. *Soon I will give
this up,* she thinks. *I will swear it off in a big
way and find something else. Something else*

to fill the void. She cracks the gum loudly.

"Do you want to go to Disney World?" says Tracee.

"Now?"

"No, just sometime."

"I've never thought about it."

"I'd like to go."

"I'm sure Tim would take you."

"I wonder if May and Gil would like to go."

"Who are they?"

"Tim's mom and her boyfriend. I didn't really get to talk to Gil, because he went back to bed. Families are always going to Disney World, it seems like. Lana, Tim's mom is so nice. She's the nicest person. She was a Miss North Carolina. She was in the Miss America pageant."

"You're kidding."

Tracee smiles widely. "I knew you'd be impressed."

"Tim's mom?" Lana says incredulously.

"He's cute," says Tracee, derailing Lana from the direction she's taking — some mention of how you'd never think someone who looks like Tim, whom Lana once referred to as "goofy guy," would have a beautiful mother.

"Sure. Of course he's cute. How far did she get?"

"Not too far. She didn't get to sing."

"Still . . ."

"I know. She's still gorgeous, isn't she?"

Lana tries to remember. "I barely looked at her, I was so angry."

"Do you really think I'm a mess?" says Tracee.

"What?"

"I'm a mess. You're right, I am."

"No, *I'm* a mess," says Lana. "I blame everyone else for what I am. For what's wrong with me. Marcel . . . something about hanging out with him makes things clearer, but then I lose it. Turn me loose and I lose it. I'm sorry I wailed at you."

"It's okay."

"It isn't really. You're just used to it. I cleaned out his checking account."

"You what?"

"My dad's. I stood behind him at the bank while he tapped in his code. Snuck his ATM card one night, you know how he kept his wallet on his bureau, emptied his pockets and put everything there, wallet, change, keys. . . . I used it and returned it. He never knew, well, not until he went to the bank again. Easy as pie."

Lana's a thief. Lana's a thief like me. How astonishing. How awful, and yet Tracee can't help herself. She feels something else too. A flutter of happiness.

"What?" says Lana, noticing some thought passing through Tracee's brain from the subtlest indicator, a brightening of her eyes.

"Nothing. How much did you take?"

"Enough. I drank it away."

"No wonder —"

"What?"

"Just no wonder he doesn't talk to you."

"Yeah. No wonder."

Lana fusses in her purse, produces a pack of Dentyne Ice, pops out several pieces, tosses them in her mouth, and crunches. "This gum thing is an addiction, you know. Addiction morphs."

"I still don't really understand," says Tracee.

"Addiction is something you're stuck with for life." Lana attempts to sound cheerful about this.

"I mean about your dad?" Tracee moves over to perch on the edge of the bed, facing Lana. She wants to take her hand, she wants to hug her, but now Lana has that hard look where her jaw stiffens.

"He figured out I was drinking. He figured out everything, that I'd flunked out, all the lies." Exasperated at having to explain and hearing her own agitation, Lana gives up. She ripped off her dad and stole his pride in her. She can't cry. She won't let herself. She has no right. Still, she's wobbling the way she does when she's loaded, when she can't keep a fix on her feelings. *Just say it,* she tells herself. S*ay it as if it means nothing.* "He told me I had to get straight."

"Straight?"

"Sober. Or he wouldn't help me out, I couldn't come home. So I took his money, got him back. Besides, I had to stay juiced."

"I'm sorry."

"He wasted his life on me. I finally proved I wasn't worth it. Good for me."

"Why didn't you tell me?"

"Why didn't you tell me about the necklace? Just hiding the ugly parts of ourselves, right?" Lana gets up quickly, walks to the window, and lifts a blind.

"Peter will drive the van. You and I will ride with Tucker. He knows the way."

"I know the way," says Rita.

"I'm sure he knows it better," says Harry, getting into the front seat of the patrol car, leaving Rita to get herself into the back, which isn't a problem, since it's a four-door, except it leaves her standing alone in the parking lot looking straight at Marcel's tree, and all she can think is, *I'm never going to see him lounging along a petrified branch, his head hanging over, smiling down at me.*

"That tree is an eyesore," she hears Harry say as she opens Tucker's door and checks out the inside. There's a metal grate separating the front seat from the back. It must be there for safety, she figures, to prevent a crook from beaning or strangling the cop who is driving. She's traveling in a cage. Is she leaving the way Marcel arrived?

They roll out of the lot and turn onto Winstead Road for Rita's last trip from The Lion to the Tulip Tree Motel. Harry sticks a hand out the window, waving for their family to follow, although he has already given instructions to that effect.

"My wife is grateful to you, Tucker, for saving her," says Harry, and, summoning his more resonant preacher voice, adds, " 'The cowardly, the unbelieving, the vile, the murderers, the sexually immoral . . . they will be consigned to the fiery lake of burning sulfur. This is the second death.' "

"Whoa," says Tucker.

"The Bible. Revelations."

"And I thought I was only tracking down a runaway wife."

"Before this strange occurrence I had no complaints," says Harry.

"Not many men can say that about their wives."

"Are you married?"

"Not even close. But one day I hope to be, sir."

"I'll put that in my prayers."

Tucker glances into the rearview mirror at Rita's face, as pale as soap. "What did make you take off, if you don't mind my asking? I should put it in the report."

Rita opens her mouth but Harry answers first. "A madness."

She wraps her arms across her chest, squeezing herself tight. The back of Harry's head appears a mite flat. Definitely, for a head, flat. None of their sons inherited that, thank goodness. "How many criminals have sat where I'm sitting?" she asks.

"Don't hold yourself above them. That's prideful," says Harry. "Don't answer her either, Tucker. It only satisfies a wicked curiosity."

"Speaking of," says Tucker. "Gotta say I'd like to know, how did you join up with the others? The younger ladies."

"We met . . ."

Rita sees his head turn sideways, awaiting the rest of her answer, but her thought vaporizes. On the highway. *We met on the highway* was all she meant to say, but it's gone.

"Doesn't matter, does it?" says Harry.

■ ■ ■ ■

"No police, no warrant, no search. I guess we overreacted." Lana squints out the window into a glaring sun, trying to ascertain what, if anything, is going on in the parking lot, whose dirty gray surface gleams like silver. Everything out there is shimmering in the heat, and there is absolutely no sign of life except for a patrol car on the street coming this way, followed by a white van. They both turn at the sign, TULIP TREE MOTEL.

Lana throws herself back in the chair. "Police."

Tracee screams.

"On the bed, get on the bed. Tracee, now!"

Tracee flops down. There they stay, nearly paralyzed. Imagining the police car parking, the trek up the stairs. Hearing the balcony rail rattle the way it always does when someone approaches. Waiting for the knock. Knowing it's a second away. Expecting it. Still, when it comes they nearly leap out of their skins.

Lana counts to three, walks to the door, and opens it. In spite of coming face-to-face with Tucker and seeing Rita as limp as a dummy, she finds herself distracted. The one who pulls her focus is the grim older man with thinning black hair and a clerical collar.

"This is Harry," says Rita.

He puts out a hand.

Lana, thrown, takes a second to reciprocate. His grip is wet. He's sweating. "I'm Lana. And this is Tracee," she adds, sensing Tracee behind her, closing in for a better view.

"If you're all set, I'll take off," says Tucker.

Take off? Lana and Tracee exchange the briefest of looks.

"Thank you for your help," says Harry. "God bless."

Amazed, Lana and Tracee watch Tucker hustle down the stairs. Is this possible? Should they ask? Why in the world did he want them before? Why had Clayton summoned them? But the answer is in front of their faces. Tucker needed them because he wanted to ask about Rita and her whereabouts.

Something that is now unnecessary.

"I'm going back," says Rita. "I've got to pack up."

Her voice is a deadly monotone. She can barely drag her feet across the room to the closet, where her few thrift shop dresses hang. Sliding the door, which scratches on its runner, giving everyone a shiver, she stops short of exposing the white wonder, Tracee's stolen wedding dress. Still, her few things occupy much more space than they need. Rita fingers the mint green dress, the one she usually wears for her act.

Harry pulls out a drawer in the bedside table. "No Bible," he says.

"This isn't a motel anymore," says Lana. "It's rooms by the month."

Rita lifts out the hanger. Already this gaudy, bright thing seems to belong to somebody else. "Why would I need this?" she says softly.

"You don't," says Harry.

Lana looks back and forth from Rita to Harry. Rita appears to be inches shorter, and she is short to begin with. It seems as if Harry has been pounding her like a nail into the floor.

"Are you leaving the place this way?" says Lana.

"Excuse me?" says Rita.

Lana takes the dress from her and hangs it back up. "This room is a pigsty. Your pigsty. Tracee and I came back this morning after spending the night at —"

Rita looks at her curiously while Lana tries to figure out where she and Tracee might have been. "A religious retreat near . . ."

"Eg-ger-sten-ton," says Tracee.

Lana turns to Harry. "We left your wife here all alone while we went to meditate and pray, and this morning we come back and what do we find? Your thong." She pinches it off the floor and tosses it onto the bed.

"My thong?" says Rita.

"Her thong?" says Harry.

"It's not mine. I don't have bows on mine, do you, Tracee?"

"No."

"But —" says Rita.

Lana cuts her off. "She's embarrassed in front of you," she tells Harry.

"So what if you wear a thong and no bra," says Tracee.

Harry takes a quick look-see outside the door. Can anyone hear them? The balcony is empty. He ambles a short distance in each direction to be sure, and checks the whereabouts of his brood. The grandkids are below, playing tag in the lot.

Meanwhile Rita whispers to Lana, "What's going on?"

"You're not leaving," says Lana.

"I have responsibilities."

"What about Marcel?" Lana grabs her by the shoulders and shakes her. "You cannot go back to being that pasty half a person we

picked up on the highway. Not on my life."
Abruptly she releases her as Harry takes a
step in and shuts the door.

"Look at the bed," says Lana.

"The bed?" says Rita.

"Are you leaving it this way?"

"I won't," says Rita, utterly confused but
always helpful.

"Don't you dare make us make your bed,"
says Lana.

"Of course," says Rita, "whatever you
want."

"Stop arguing," says Lana. "You slept in
it, make it." She yanks the covers down.
There is the condom.

They all stare. Lana, as if startled, throws
the covers back on.

The silence that follows seems long
enough for the sun to have risen and set.

Harry lifts the blanket and top sheet, leans
down to peek under them again, and lays
them back down.

"We'll wait outside," says Lana.

"I can't forgive this, Rita," says Harry as
soon as they are alone. He purses his lips.
They start to move silently.

Rita grabs a pillow and whacks him.
"Don't you dare pray for my soul."

"Someone has to."

"Not you."

"Better you're not around the children."

"My children are grown. They can bring my grandchildren to visit anytime. If you have a spark of decency, you won't interfere." She goes to the door to let him out but he blocks her way. His eyes narrow and darken. For an instant she thinks he's going to seize her and kiss her, a dreadful notion. And ridiculous. There's never been an ember of passion in Harry. He gets only sterner when crossed. "You're going to hell," he says.

"Don't push me, Harry, or I'll tell you what hell is." Rita presses past him and turns the knob, showing him the way out.

The moment he's gone, her legs buckle. She reaches for the bureau to stabilize herself and works her way over to the chair. She buries her head in her hands, not surprised to find she has not a tear to shed. "I'm free," she says under her breath, and looks up to see Harry standing there.

"Oh," says Rita. "What?"

"Who is the other man?" he says. "Is it that man in the bar?"

"I have many admirers," says Rita.

"So, anyone then? Anyone and no one special?"

"Marcel."

"Marcel?"

"Marcel."

"Does he have a last name?"

"I really don't know."

Harry shakes his head, marveling at the depth to which his wife has sunk. "Is he foreign?"

Rita smiles. "Yes. African."

Lana and Tracee do not trust that Harry is gone until he actually is. They hang over the rail until the van has disappeared down the road and around a curve. Only then do they return to the room. Rita is not there. The covers on the bed are folded down. There is no condom.

"Rita," calls Lana.

She comes out of the bathroom.

"I flushed it," she says.

46

There is a sign on the door. Written in pen, a hasty scribble on a piece of white paper taped on with masking tape, impossible to make out until you get close. *No More Shows.*

Rita rips it off and enters The Lion.

Marcel shoots out of his white cave. Rita has never seen him move so quickly. He paces frenetically, and as soon as she gets close, he rears up at the bars.

"I'm back," she says again and again as she scratches his chest. He twists his head this way and that so she can get at his ears, trying to rub against her, and all the time she hears, like a fine-tuned engine idling, the soft rumble of Marcel's purring.

"Well, now," says Clayton, coming in from the kitchen, hearing the rumpus. "I knew you couldn't leave an old cat."

"You know how you're an object to some
people," says Lana. "No offense, but you're
a curiosity. They don't see you the way Rita
does or the way I do now. I think that's what
I did to my dad. I didn't consider what it all
must have meant to him. Mom bolting.
Raising me. He never really dated, at least, I
didn't know about it if he did. I was so full
of my own stuff. Barreling along. What
about him? What was it all like for him?

"If he ever wants to be my father again,
I'll ask him.

"The other day I put on a necklace, and
when I looked in the mirror I was a different person. Not someone scraping by, but
someone with a life. Ever since then I've
been thinking. I'm smart. I had a scholarship to the University of Maryland. I don't
have to have a job that I need to wash off at
night. Suppose I went to work in an office?
Got a job with benefits, where I could get

promoted. Earned enough to buy myself a diamond necklace. Why not? Why couldn't that be me? Before I screwed up I was prelaw. I know a lawyer isn't worthy like a doctor or brave like a lion tamer, but I'd be good at it. I love to argue. I always have. Lots of presidents have been lawyers. Not that I want to be president. I'd probably start a war with every country, I'm so obstreperous, but I bet I'd be great in court. I know that's a pipe dream, but if I take extension courses at night and get back into college, it won't only be good for me but maybe my dad will understand. I'm not who I was. He didn't waste his life on me —"

Lana breaks down.

She crashes onto the tabletop, burying her head in her arms. *You have no right,* she tries to stop herself. *You have no right.* But she's gone, giving in to years of pent-up guilt, despair, and regret. Rita, wondering at the noise, at the thundering misery, walks in and tiptoes back out, knowing Lana would never want to be seen this way. In pieces.

Marcel listens the way he does, accepting without judgment.

When her torment finally ebbs, Lana, tearstained and wrung dry, drives back to the Tulip Tree and sleeps for twelve hours straight. She sleeps dreamlessly right through her shift at The Lion, and when she wakes up she feels good.

48

The giant metal spool tips sideways, falling into a rut. Rita, red-faced, blowing upward at her bangs, pulls it upright while Lana and Tracee push from the other side. "Clayton said I should wait for his help before I hassled with this thing, but I'm anxious to get going." She takes a second to retie the laces on her new boots, double-knotting them, and then reties the red kerchief around her head that keeps her hair off her face. Seizing the metal handle with both hands, she tugs. The wheels pop out of the rut and spin. The spool bounces over rocks, leaving a trail of red string as Rita clomps through the grass, marking the perimeter of Marcel's garden.

"Clayton said I can make it as big as I want, well, as much as he owns. I figure an acre at least."

"We're leaving Saturday," says Lana.

Rita halts. "Oh, my goodness. I wasn't

thinking it was coming so soon, but of course it is."

"Classes start next week."

"What am *I* going to do?" says Tracee. "What's *my* plan?"

"You'll find something, Tee. We both need jobs."

Across the field, the backside of a truck edges onto the grass. Clayton unhooks the doors, throws them open, and he and the driver climb in, getting ready to unload rolls of wire that will be Marcel's fence. He waves at Rita. She waves back.

"Did you call your sons?" asks Lana.

"I called Lucas. He's always been the most sensible. He's my middle one. He's coming for a weekend in October, for Melanie's birthday. She's turning four. I apologized. I didn't say a proper good-bye to them, to any of them. I wasn't thinking clearly." She yanks the spool and continues her trek. "Next week I'll call Andrew and Peter. Give them time to cool down, that's what Luke suggested."

"Tracee hasn't broken up with Tim yet." Even though Tracee is there, Lana says this as if she isn't.

"I don't want to," says Tracee.

"It's my fault," says Rita, keeping an eye on the spool to make sure it's unraveling properly. "If only you still had the necklace, you could return it."

"Returning stolen goods doesn't make you not guilty. It's evidence. It proves you did it," says Lana.

"I suppose I knew that," says Rita. "Wishful thinking."

"Maybe it's even better that you flushed it. Not having it makes it harder to prove Tracee's guilt."

"I am guilty," says Tracee.

"The law's not that simple."

"If I'm guilty, how could I be not guilty?"

"It happens every day."

Tracee suddenly sinks to the ground.

"Whoa," says Lana.

"What's the matter?" says Rita.

"Are you having a sugar attack?" says Lana.

"No." Tracee pries a mini-box of raisins out of her pants pocket, opens it, plucks out a few raisins, and eats them. "But if I was, I'd have these. The P 'n S got a truckful delivered and no one's buying them. Buzzard told Tim, 'Take a hundred.' Tim stored them under the bed. We've got enough for the winter."

Lana doesn't say they won't be here. Tracee is now splayed backward on the wet grass. She hasn't been eating much. Her face is thinner; her large round eyes seem larger, pitifully so. She's been a terrible waitress for the past week too. Forgetting everyone's order. Needing to kiss Tim every five seconds. One night Lana found her in the kitchen, staring vacantly, like she'd been towed in and abandoned or her battery had died.

"That's a very wet place to lie," says Rita. "And it's in the sun. Let's sit over here." She points to a small fir that provides a circle of shade. "It's time to take a break anyway. It's always a good time for a break."

Lana offers Tracee a hand, pulls her up, and steers her over. "Sit here, lean back against the tree. That's good. Good for you. Wait, let me brush the grass off the back of your shirt."

Tracee settles down again, stretching her long skinny legs in front of her. Her knees are rosy. "Why are my knees red?"

"Knees sometimes get that way," says Rita. "I don't know why, but they do. Then it goes away."

"The garden's going to be great," says Lana.

"Do you think so?" Rita unfolds a square of paper, presses it flat on her lap, and reads, " 'Jackalberry tree, gum tree eucalyptus, elephant grass, candelabra tree.' Don't they have romantic names? They're all plants from the African savanna. 'Jarrah tree, kangaroo paw.' Clayton says we'll find someone at a botanical garden to advise us, there's a couple in the state, and we'll find out what plants available here come the closest. I'll move Marcel's tree in too. He won't be happy without it. Whenever he rubs it he purrs. Well, of course he doesn't really. Lions can't purr, according to the experts. But he makes a wonderful rumbling noise, and if you ask me, he's purring."

"Marcel's lucky," says Tracee. "What more could he want?"

"The wild," says Lana.

"What's so great about that? Why is everyone always acting like the wild is so great?" says Tracee.

"Who?" says Lana.

"I don't know. Just maybe it's not so great. Eat or get eaten."

"Lions don't get eaten."

"Unfortunately, they do," says Rita. "By crocodiles. If they have to cross a river."

"See," says Tracee, whose misery is making her less compliant. "Marcel has love. A safe place."

"You have that," says Rita.

"Not if I leave Tim. I have to leave Tim." She recites this like a mantra, hoping it will take. "Last night we were . . ." Tracee loses her train of thought. It feels as if her brain is unraveling. "Last night Tim and me were with his mom and Gil and we went to the amusement park, the weekend one they set up in the parking lot at the intersection of 3 and something. Gil was knocking down everything and so was Tim. At the booth where you throw a baseball and the pins fall down. I didn't know Tim could throw like that. He won me a teddy bear. A big one. It takes up the whole chair, you know, in our room. His mom wants to teach me to cook. She said, 'I'm going to teach this girl to cook.' When we walked, she linked her arm in mine like we were related."

"Are you in love with Tim or his mom?" says Lana.

"Both."

"You barely know him."

"That's not true."

"Seven weeks, that's all you've been together."

"I've known him forever, that's how it feels."

"Maybe it will all work out," says Rita.

"How could it all work out?" says Tracee.

"I don't know," says Rita. "I just wish your problem would vanish."

"How?"

"Perhaps Marcel could help," says Rita.

"You are certifiable," says Lana.

"Sometimes he gets the ball rolling. Remember how he ate Tracee's veil?"

"What ball did that get rolling?"

"I can't say for sure. I just have a feeling about it."

"What am I going to say to Tim?" says Tracee. "I don't want him to know anything about the necklace. It's not fair. He could end up like you two — an accessory."

"An accessory?" says Rita.

"After the fact," says Lana.

"It's my mess, not his." Tracee pulls in her legs and wraps her arms around them. This is such a pretty view. She's never been such a far distance behind The Lion looking back at it. All those planks and metal bits going every which way. There are so many angles that no matter how many times she sees the building, she never gets bored. Sometimes it seems like it belongs in a circus; other times she thinks a witch might live there. Other times it's startling, even beautiful. Other times it seems like what it is: one big junk heap with doors.

"We're going back to Maryland," says Lana gently. "And you have to break up with Tim because it's the only decent and fair thing to do."

"You know what Tim said. He said the thing to do about my stealing was just to tell everyone in Fairville that I'm a kleptomaniac. It's not a big town. Everyone knows everyone, and they're friendly. Then if I take something people will just say, 'No big deal, Tracee the kleptomaniac took it.' And I can give it back."

"That's actually smart," says Lana.

"He tried it on Clayton. Clayton was cool about it."

"Clayton knows you're a kleptomaniac?"

"Yes. And you know what he said? He said, 'Well, she's a damn good waitress.' You underestimate Tim," says Tracee.

"You're right, I do, and I apologize for that. And probably that solution might work for the wedding dress. Confess and pay. We've got the money now. But that won't work for the diamond necklace. You're over your eyeballs in that one. Break up in a public place, Tracee, and then it won't get out of hand. Tell him it's a summer romance. He caught you on the rebound."

"But Tim knows my feelings. He knows they're deep." Tracee blinks. She blinks and blinks, squeezing her whole face each time she does it.

"Stop it, Tee. You haven't done that since we were kids."

"I still sometimes do it."

"Don't, please." Lana scoots closer and puts her arm around her best friend.

Tracee burrows into Lana's shoulder. "He's my one."

49

Tim lopes along Fairville's main drag. He's a little late and hoping Tracee will be in front. Waiting. She always throws herself at him as if they haven't seen each other in months. He likes to pick her up and swing her around, she's so light. But he doesn't see her.

He bursts into the Drop In — that's the way he arrives everywhere now that he's with Tracee. Full of enthusiasm. Flying high. He spots her mop of curly black hair. She's in the far-back booth, facing away, unusual, since there's a slew of booths in the front where it's sunny and you can look out the window, which Tracee loves to do. She likes to sit at the counter too sometimes because of the pictures hanging behind it. Cindy tacks up snapshots of her customers' tobacco plants and there's always a new one. It makes Tracee giggle to see tobacco plants in people's front yards mixed in with all the black-eyed Susans, coneflowers, and whatnot. ("Everyone grows their own," Tim explained.) Dimly all this registers, weird her sitting back there in the gloom, but he doesn't assign it any significance until later, when he obsessively relives his trauma again and again. He greets Cindy as well as Rich McPherson, whose son, Dwight, Tim taught to drive. Tim never, ever thought Dwight would get the knack of it — he had an unusual depth-perception problem, sometimes nearly bumping other cars when he braked, other times leaving space for an entire county between him and the vehicle in front.

Tim slides in next to Tracee and puts his arms around her. Tracee wiggles back against the wall. "Sit over there." She points across the table.

"How come?" He still steals a kiss.

"Tim, please."

He takes the seat opposite and then notices a pile of shredded napkins and Tracee's serious face. He's never seen her like this. Stern, tight-lipped. "What?" says Tim. "You're not breaking up with me?"

Tracee flinches.

"Holy cow, you can't be. Tell me you're not."

She says it straight out and fairly loudly.

"I can't be with you because —"

"Stop. Don't finish that sentence."

"I can't finish. I don't know how . . ." She falters and then summons her determination again. "Lana's going back to Baltimore tomorrow."

"Don't say you're going. You're not going."

"I'm going."

"You mean it?"

She nods.

"You can't mean it."

Tracee looks down. She can't bear Tim's pleading eyes.

"If I had every girl in the world to pick from, you're who I'd pick. You over everyone."

"You'd want me more than anyone, anyone in the world?" says Tracee, her heart bouncing.

"Hell, yes. Is it the other guy?"

"Huh?"

"That guy before."

Who is he talking about? Then she remembers J.C., and it's like recalling a stranger she once passed on the street. She shakes her head.

"We're making plans. What about Disney World? I thought we could get a place together — do you want to get married first, is that it? I'll do whatever you want. The Lion's packing them in. I signed up three more driving students. Doesn't matter, does it?" He slams back against the booth and digs his hands into his hair like he wants to pull his head off. "Why?"

Tracee feels as if she's underwater. Tim's a blur, a puddle of a person, and she can't breathe.

"Why?" He smacks the table. The shakers topple. He swipes them off, shocking them both.

"I have to go with Lana. She needs me." This is her only line of defense, but at least it's true. Lana does need her. Lana has always needed her as much as she needs Lana.

"She doesn't need you."

"Yes, she does."

"No."

Tracee finds herself shouting, "Is it impossible that someone should need me? Like I'm no help to anyone?"

"I need you," says Tim quietly.

"Leave," she wails, covering her face with her hands, and when she looks again, to her horror, he has.

When Tim shows up for work at the Pick 'n Save, he's so discombobulated he can't figure out how to get in the door and keeps pushing it instead of pulling it. Tami, despite her preoccupation with the tabloids, notices that, for the first time ever, Tim doesn't inquire after everyone, asking her and the other employees how they are and how their day went. He breaks the price stamper. He walks into a display of supersize V8 juice cans, crashing it. For an hour he sits dumbly in front of a computer screen, barely aware of why he's there — he's supposed to assign and post the next month's shift schedule. On his break he tries to eat a snack of Ritz Bits, but chewing and swallowing is more than he can manage. After that he spends a while in the stockroom punching and kicking a cardboard box, bruising his knuckles. He's got a headache. It seems like the fluorescent lights are drilling holes in his eyes. Every so often he moans, seemingly for no reason. Still, when Ronald phones with a bogus tale about how he can't make his shift because his refrigerator broke, Tim, who could find a sub, decides to stay.

He finally leaves the P 'n S at three a.m., every miserable second of his breakup with Tracee still running on a continuous loop in his brain. It's a fantastically beautiful night, stars by the bushel, a full moon taunting him. Tim can't bear it. He stands at his car, lacking the will to get in and drive back to the motel where Tracee used to be waiting, snuggled in bed, her legs kicked out over the sheets, her arms wrapped around both pillows. Hearing the door close, she'd open her eyes and smile, and Tim would jump on the bed, tearing off his clothes, and they'd make love. He can't imagine a tomorrow without Tracee.

He intends to drive to the Tulip Tree but finds himself heading instead to The Lion, his old late-night refuge. He parks, drags himself to the door, and unlocks it. The metal doors clanking open don't disturb Marcel, who is sleeping.

Tim goes to the bar and draws himself a beer from the tap.

He sits down at a table, the rickety chair squeaking as the seat shifts on its uneven legs. Still the lion sleeps. He's got a life now. Whoever thought Mr. M would have a better life than him? Not that Tim begrudges it. He just never expected the lion to find happiness while he found the opposite. *You never know what's in the cards,* thinks Tim.

He sticks his long legs out straight and drinks his beer slowly while he waits for wipeout, a feeling of exhaustion so deep that he can return to the Tulip Tree and pass out before his head hits the pillow.

Marcel's nose wiggles. He yawns. He rolls onto his stomach, lifts a paw to bat an ear, pulls his legs under him, and lumbers up to stand.

"Hello," says Tim.

Again Marcel yawns; this time his jaw drops open wide enough to fit in a small car. His long, bright pink tongue hangs out between his fearsome incisors.

Tim yawns and sticks his tongue out at Marcel.

Marcel cocks his head and emits something that sounds like a bark.

Tim cocks his head and barks.

Marcel tilts his head up and lets loose a thundering call of the wild. Tim does the same. The loud, shapeless noise commences from his diaphragm, gains strength in his lungs, and blasts forth, fueling Tim with energy.

Marcel's legs bend under him, he sinks down on his haunches, rolls back onto his side, snorts a few times, and falls back to sleep, but Tim misses this because he is running out the door.

Tim speeds back to the Tulip Tree, drives to a spot directly across from number nineteen, parks, and gets out. The entire building is dark, every single window. It's nearly four a.m. The only sound is the relentless tinny rattle of cicadas.

He takes a few steps backward until he has Tracee's second-floor window fully in his sights, throws back his head, and roars.

Lana fumbles for a light switch. Tracee pops up. Rita wonders for a second if she's awake or dreaming of Marcel.

Another roar and then another.

The women stumble to the window. Lana yanks the cord, jamming the blinds to the top in a bunch, and they all crowd in to see what's happening.

A few cars looking like large boulders sit here and there in an otherwise deserted landscape, and in the near distance a tall, lanky, awkward young man is silhouetted black against a streak of pale and misty moonlight. With his arms wide, willing Tracee to him, he sends out his mating roar, unearthly bellows of lovesick yearning.

Tracee swoons.

"It's a lion's serenade," says Rita.

Lana pulls Tracee away. "Don't watch. Don't fan his flames. It's not fair."

Tim sees the light in the window extinguish, his hopes snuffed out. His arms drop to his sides; his chest aches, whether from exertion or heartache, who can tell. He trudges up the stairs, lets himself into his room, and kicks the door closed behind him. The teddy bear is waiting, its white button eyes shining in the dark. Tim forgot about winning that stuffed bear for Tracee. She'd carried it clutched to her breast, rubbing her cheek against the fur while she told Tim how amazing he was, how she never thought he could throw a baseball like that. He knocks the bear out of the chair, sinks down on the bed, flops down flat, and stares into the bleak. He has no idea how long he's there. His mind is blank.

He hears a light knock.

The knock comes again.

Tim takes his grabber pole and uses it to turn the knob and open the door.

There is Tracee in her wedding dress.

For a second he thinks he is having a hallucination.

"Will you take my dress off me?" says Tracee.

Tim clamps her skirt and tugs her over.

When Tracee is right next to him, he props the pole upright and simply lies there looking at her. "Undress me," she pleads, extending a hand to help him up.

Tim runs his hands over the satin, beading, and lace, and over her body. He kisses the nape of her neck and nibbles along her collarbone. He cradles her face in his hands and kisses her eyes. He turns her around. It takes him a while to locate the zipper, artfully concealed under a lace pleat, but then he undoes it and the dress collapses in billows around her. She's naked beneath.

Tim lays the dress carefully on the chair and then picks Tracee up and lays her carefully on the bed. She takes his hand, kisses the tips of his fingers, and then places his hand between her legs. She instantly shudders.

Tim joins her on the bed and they begin again.

50

The next morning Tim wakes up alone and sits up with a start.

Tracee, wrapped in a blanket, is sitting on the chair. "The reason I can't be with you is because I stole a diamond necklace and they might come for me and by accident it got flushed down the toilet so I can't even give it back."

"Holy cow," says Tim.

"I have to turn myself in."

51

There's no answer at the office door. Lana raps again. "Marlene?" she calls. She tries the rusty knob. It turns. She sticks her head in. The TV, on but mute, immediately sucks her in as a man demonstrates the many attributes of a salad spinner while an 800 number flashes beneath.

Marlene is not on the Barcalounger or anywhere else.

Lana looks around.

An unwashed coffee mug on the counter contains some milky dregs. Recent, Lana figures. She fiddles with a pen, which is attached to a string that is nailed to the counter, punching the point in and out. Does it work? She scribbles in a margin of the *Fairville Times*. It does.

She needs some blank paper, something, some way to leave a note. Pressing her palms onto the countertop, she hefts herself up and leans over to see if there might be a drawer or shelves on the other side. Crouched behind is Marlene.

"Oh, hi," says Lana.

Marlene's frightened beady eyes stare up at her.

"Are you hiding from me? Oh, shit, shoot — I'm trying not to swear — are you? I came to apologize. For the way I treated you. God, you're so scared you're hiding from me. I come in peace. I owe you big-time. Thank you for not throwing me out, even though I deserved it. Even though you need the money and probably couldn't, it was still nice. I was cruel. Being frightened to go outside is no joke."

Marlene blows some air into her cheeks, inflating them. She straightens only enough to thump backward onto her bottom.

"I'm not going to do anything crazy," says Lana. "I'm leaving today. Tracee and I. Rita's staying. I know Rita told you. I'm sorry. I'm truly sorry for the pain I caused you." Lana pushes back and off the counter, leaving Marlene her privacy. "I'm going to close the door and leave the place the way I found it." She backs out of the office. "I'm not taking anything. I'm out now," she says as she pulls the door shut.

Because the entire town square is blocked

off in preparation for a parade of soapbox derby cars later in the day, Tim is forced to park behind O. Henry's, the used-book store. It hasn't been open for months but still he leaves a note of apology on the windshield before leading Tracee on a shortcut through the alley. They hurry to the police station and collide with Tucker rushing out.

"We're here to see you," says Tim, holding Tracee's hand tight.

Tucker walks backward away from them. "Can it wait?"

"Huh?" says Tracee.

"Is it an emergency?"

He takes their silent astonishment as a no. "I'm due somewhere, and if I don't show up the chief will fire my ass. You know my dad. I'll be back." He spins around and sprints, leaving Tim and Tracee alone in the doorway under the American flag, which droops low enough to graze Tim's head.

"His dad?" says Tracee.

"The chief."

"The chief's his dad?"

"Nearly everyone on the force is kin. Come on, maybe someone else is here." He pulls Tracee inside.

"Morning, Ginny," he says to the dispatcher, noting that, in the corral behind her, the six police desks, which face one another two by two, are empty.

"Everyone's out," she tells him, "as if you can't see for yourself." She douses a tissue with nail polish remover and rubs the pink off her nails. "Don't report me for this." She laughs. "Smell that, sugar." She offers the open bottle to Tracee for a sniff. "That's a real sinus clearer, isn't it?"

After chitchat about her kids, Ginny opens the swinging gate and invites them to pull chairs from other desks over to Tucker's desk and wait.

They sit there, Tracee shifting back and forth from her toes to her heels, rolling the chair forward and back. The office is quiet except for some static coming over Ginny's two-way radio. Tracee leans in close to Tim. "Do you think I'll have to go to jail?" she whispers.

"If you do, I promise I'll visit every week-end."

She plays with Tucker's stapler, pounding it. "Orange jumpsuits, that's what prisoners wear. And cuff links."

"You mean handcuffs?"

"Sorry, I'm sorry. I'm . . ." She can't think of the word, any word. She lets the thought go. She imagines Tim and her on visitors' day, a glass wall between them, talking on the phone. "How long would I have to go to prison for?"

"It's a first offense," says Tim. "Don't go there yet."

Her leg jiggles. She yanks and twists her hair. Tim raps his knuckles impatiently on Tucker's desk. He smiles encouragingly at Tracee, whose face is spotted red with anxiety. The minutes drag on.

"I'm feeling like we should just take matters into our own hands," says Tim.

"I blame everyone. Everyone else. For things I do. Trouble I cause." Lana's voice quavers. She didn't expect when she asked the leader if she could address the AA meeting that doing so would unmoor her. "Thank you for letting me speak, by the way, I mean speak but not be 'the speaker.' " She uses her fingers to put quotes around the word. "To let me say something to everyone. I know it's not normal."

She's prepared. She's been over this territory already with Marcel. She's nicely dressed. She bought new jeans and a pink blouse that she found at Goodwill. Not normally her thing to wear pink, but it's flattering. Her hair is clean, and because she borrowed some of Rita's cream rinse, it's shiny too. Tracee has trimmed it, eliminating its most egregiously chopped parts. Although it's still several different lengths, it no longer appears to have been mutilated. Even so, even well dressed and mentally prepared, confronting a whole roomful of people she mistreated is proving difficult. The police chief is sitting on her far left. She forces herself to look at him, to apologize straight to his face for barging into AA to scream that Tucker's getting suspended was all his fault. And to suggest that AA should kick him out. However, the chief appears not remotely interested. He's preoccupied, watching the door, which opens.

Tucker takes a step in. And stops.

Lana feels dizzy. He has come to arrest her. He has probably already nabbed Tracee. Lana feels so guilty for all her bad behavior that she almost extends her wrists to be cuffed.

"Is there a problem, Officer?" says the leader.

Tucker's voice is a mumble but everyone gets the drift. He's here for the meeting.

Lana's legs go weak with relief. She wants to fly across the room and hug him. She wants to shout, "I love you," even though she doesn't and the thought has never before crossed her mind.

"Welcome," says the leader. "Why don't

you introduce yourself?"

"Why?" says Tucker. "I know everyone."

"That's just how it's done," says Lana. "Like, 'I'm Lana and I'm an alcoholic.' "

Tucker screws his face into a knot. He buys time scratching his forehead. He knows he has to come out with it. His dad gave him no choice: AA or quit the force. Besides, his dad is fixing him with a stone-cold stare that would make a killer confess. "I'm Tucker," he says. "I have a problem with beer."

The leader indicates a stack of literature on a manicure table. "Help yourself after the meeting. Take a seat anywhere you like."

Lana waits until he is settled. "I . . . Let's see . . ." She tries to remember what she's already said. The pierced guy gives her an encouraging thumbs-up and Lana pushes on. "I owe everyone here an apology. I stole from the donation hat, and when you called me on it, I hated you. I hated every single one of you. Well, not you, I didn't hate you," she says to the pierced guy. "What's your name? I know I've heard it."

"Ben."

"Right, Ben. I didn't hate you but I hated everyone else. And Tucker, I almost wrecked your life. I'm sincerely sorry for that. I was . . . No excuses. No more excuses. I'm trying to be less impulsive, less destructive, more respectful."

Several members nod. All of them have their most supportive and positive faces on. The feeling in the room is inspiring, uplifting. Lana has never experienced anything like it before. *They're rooting for me,* she realizes. *Even Tucker.*

"I'm leaving today. Tracee and I are driving back to Baltimore this afternoon. I'll go to meetings and hopefully . . ." She stops herself. She knows not to make predictions. "Rita tamed a lion. All I have to do is keep a little monkey off my back. How hard can that be?"

"Thank you. This is mighty kind," says Tim.

"Just press this button and when you hear a dial tone, dial out. The chief will be gone another half hour at least." Ginny closes the door to the chief's office, giving them privacy.

Tim phones Information. "They're listed," he tells Tracee. He presses in the numbers and hands her the receiver.

"It's ringing," she says. She waits, chewing her lip. "Hello," she says loudly, then lowers her voice, embarrassed. "Mrs. Hofstadder, it's Tracee. Tracee Lynn Hobbs. Karen's friend."

"Hi, Tracee, how are you?"

Tracee makes a face at Tim, like *How do I do this?* but keeps going. "Fine. Mrs. Hofstadder —"

"Karen's not here. She got married. She and Greg are living in Dover."

"I stole from you."

"I'm sorry, what did you say?"

"I stole from you. That's why I'm calling." Now that she's out with it, she races. "I stole a diamond necklace last May. I'm at the police station in North Carolina. I'm going to turn myself in but I thought you should hear from me directly because I know you and I was chatting right at you when I slipped the necklace into my pocket —"

"Just a second."

"She said, 'Just a second.'"

"You're doing great," says Tim.

"Should I say anything about flushing it?"

"Keep it simple. Just say you don't have it."

"Tracee, this is Randall, Karen's father."

"Mr. Hofstadder, I am so, so sorry."

"Lenore says you're at the police station?"

"Lenore?"

"My wife."

"Oh, yes."

"Did you talk to them?"

"Who?

"The police."

"Not yet. We're going to."

"Don't."

"What?"

"Are you sure you haven't told them anything?"

"I'm getting confused. I think you better speak to my boyfriend."

Buoyed by all the hugs and good wishes from her new friends at AA, Lana arrives at The Lion honking her horn. She bursts through the doors. "It went great," she shouts to Rita, who is in the cage tapping a tambourine, dancing with Marcel.

"Wonderful," Rita calls back. "I knew it would. I'll be right out. I'm still favoring Julio and so is Marcel," she tells Clayton, who punches another tune on the jukebox.

"I figured," says Clayton. "But give me a chance."

Lana plunks down on a bar stool and spins.

"How do you like your cake?" says Rita as she locks the cage. "Yours and Tracee's. It's in that bakery box."

Lana lifts the top and peeks in at a layer cake with pink frosting, red roses, and green leaves. *Come back soon,* it says.

"I love it. It's pink, I'm in pink." She looks

down at her blouse. "What was I thinking? Pink?"

"But the meeting went well, that's the important thing." Rita settles on the stool next to her and clips up her hair. "Oh, I'm a mess. I get all sweaty working with that animal."

"Everyone was forgiving. I had an amazing experience. 'Come back soon.' We will. I hope we will."

Rita lifts the cake out of the box and sets it on the bar. "Clayton ordered it."

"No big deal," says Clayton.

Lana can't help but notice how easy Rita and Clayton are together. But she doesn't say that. She wouldn't dare. She might jinx it.

Clayton folds open the back doors, letting in fresh air and a sunny view across the field. A warm wind whips the grass, bending it toward Marcel, who, in his deliberate way, ambles in that direction, to the far side of the cage. The wind ruffles his mane. His tasseled tail scoops up.

"That whole field is going to be his," says Rita. "How about that?"

Lana spins again on the stool, feeling young and light and free.

"May I cut you a slice?" says Rita.

"Let's wait for Tee."

"I'm here," Tracee calls, waving both hands, bouncing and bobbing around Tim, who is solemn but busting with something, something big. They're back together, that much is clear. More even, thinks Lana. "Did you get married?"

A grin breaks across Tracee's face. "I turned myself in." Her hands fly up and drop down helplessly. "Well, I tried to. I tried."

"She did," says Tim.

"We went to the police station."

"To get booked," says Tim.

They are brimming with excitement to recount this tale, and even though they already know it, they are as excited to recount it to each other as to everyone else.

"Tim said I had to face it. Face the music. But the place was empty. We bumped into Tucker, but he was in a rush to get somewhere. He asked if it was an emergency. It really wasn't. So we sat and waited and then Tim —"

"You did it," says Tim.

"It was your idea." Tracee can't help herself, she crows, "I called the Hofstadders. I thought about you." She beams at Rita. "You walking into the lion's den. You with Marcel. That's how I did it. You were my inspiration."

"Well, now," says Rita, too surprised to say anything else.

Tracee spies the cake. "I'm starving. Could I have a slice?"

Rita cuts one. Tracee takes it in both hands and makes sounds of intense pleasure while she greedily gobbles it. "Sorry, I'm hungry. It's delicious. I didn't eat before, I was so nervous."

"Tracee, come on, then what?" says Lana.

"Lenore answered, Karen's mom. I told her who I was and she said" — Tracee licks her fingers — " 'Hi, Tracee, how are you?' She was happy to hear from me, so I knew right off she had no idea I'd done it. I said, 'I'm calling to tell you that I stole a diamond necklace,' and she said, 'Wait one second,' and left me there."

"Left you?" says Lana.

"She just, like, left me on the phone."

"Dangling," says Tim.

"I practically had a heart attack, I was so frightened, well, more stunned and nervous about what might be coming."

"Coming?" says Lana. "Like a SWAT team?"

"What's that?"

"It's not important."

"Then Randall gets on, that's Karen's dad. He says, 'Leave the police station right now,' or words like that. I gave the phone to Tim and Tim said, 'We're not leaving until you explain.' The way he said it, it was like 'Tell us or else.' No one would mess with Tim the way he said it." She loses herself for a second looking at Tim, who can't take his eyes off Tracee, never can. "Anyway, so he told us."

"The insurance," says Tim. "They'd already collected."

"But why would that matter? So what, they collected. I still stole it. It doesn't make sense."

"None," says Tim.

Everyone wonders about that except Lana, who bites her thumb. She's wondering about something else.

"I was hoping secretly," says Tracee, "you know, hope against hope, that they hadn't reported it and they'd let me pay it back, although it would take ages, but they didn't even want that."

"They must have gotten more than it's worth," says Clayton.

"Huh?"

"Let's say they said it's worth six thousand. And they collected. It's better all around if Tracee doesn't show up."

"That's so dishonest," says Tracee. "I can't believe the Hofstadders would do something like that."

"They probably think they're just working the system."

"I have no respect for them," says Tracee. "None whatsoever."

"You're not coming with me," says Lana.

Tracee gets a jab from Tim but says nothing.

"You don't have to now, right?"

Tracee opens her mouth, but the speech she prepared in the car is gone. She can't recall a word of it.

"Who would like a slice of cake?" says Rita.

No one answers.

Clayton takes a seat and folds his arms across his chest. He watches Tracee's eyes flick nervously from Tim to Lana.

"I am," says Tracee faintly. "Going to stay." Her voice gains confidence.

"But that's great," says Lana. "How cool, fantastic it all worked out. It worked out just the way you hoped. You have to stay, no question. You're in love. Tim's great. You are, Tim. It's wonderful." She knows she's babbling but can't stop. "Wow, what a relief. I bought Marcel something. Beef patties." She looks around, confused — where is her purse? She yanks it up from the floor. "They're somewhere in here." She reaches in and comes up with an eight-pack. "A going-away present. Well, I'm the one going. I mean a thank-you present." She fumbles with the wrapping.

"Here," says Tim. "Let me help."

He rips off the plastic. "Eight patties. How about that, Mr. M?"

"Would you give them to him?" Lana asks Rita. "I'm nervous to."

Rita flips them through the bars. Marcel pounces.

"Could I have a minute alone with him?" says Lana.

"Of course. Absolutely," says Rita. "What a good idea."

She herds everyone into the kitchen. Clayton stops at the bar and draws a Pepsi for Lana, one with lots of ice, the way she likes it. He sets it on a table.

"Give a shout when you're done," says Rita.

The room is suddenly silent save for Marcel, sprawled on his stomach, making quick work of the patties, barely chewing, gulping, licking his chops, licking the floor where they landed, and then licking his paws. He lies there, sated.

Lana drags a chair close to the cage and straddles it. Finding herself unexpectedly parched, she drinks her soda. She loves it when there is no one hanging out here but her and Marcel. Today especially she loves it. Today especially she appreciates this safe place where her thoughts don't distress her and her memories are easier to handle. When, how soon, if ever, will she be back?

She thinks about the summer — her bolt out of Maryland with Tracee, the serendipity of meeting Rita, the car crash. One, two, three, they fell through the window of The Lion. Her friends found happiness. She is going back alone. Better than she was but still with mountains to climb.

Marcel draws himself up to his full height and resettles, lounging the way he often does, on his side with his head held high. He rests his gaze on the young woman sitting in a chair turned backward, trying to appear tough and resilient and feeling anything but.

"I'm taking you with me," she tells him. "All your peace and patience and listening ears. You'll be here" — she holds a fist to her heart — "keeping me sober. Sober and sane."

52

Lana tosses her purse into the front seat of the Mustang.

"Got water?" says Clayton.

"I do." Over her pink blouse she buttons his parting gift — a red cotton shirt with *The Lion* in script on the pocket. "Thank you again for this. I love it."

"Do you have a full tank?"

"Yes." She sticks out her hand to shake, but Clayton wraps her in a bear hug.

She goes to Tim next, to kiss his cheek. It's awkward. They bang heads. "Drive carefully," says Tim. "Don't forget to signal."

"I won't."

"And don't just use the side mirror if you're changing lanes. Look over your shoulder."

"I will. I promise."

Rita opens her arms. Lana falls into them. Rita's soft. Everything about her is soft and warm and comforting.

"Whenever you're feeling low, remember this," whispers Rita. "You saved my life." She brushes Lana's hair off her face, tucking it behind her ears. "You look so pretty."

"I do?"

"Simply beautiful."

"Thank you."

"Don't forget to write," says Rita.

"Of course I won't write. I'll e-mail and text and phone."

"But it won't be the same," says Tracee, pulling her best friend away to have a moment to themselves.

They huddle by Marcel's petrified tree, not knowing what to do or say. How do you separate when, for as long as you can remember, you've never been apart? Lana rubs her hand over the bark. "It feels like plastic. Have you ever touched it?"

Tracee feels it. "Ooh, that's strange."

"Look, he's managed to rub some bark off and it's not really even bark anymore. What an amazing beast."

"Are you going to see your dad?"

"I'm not even going to call. Not until I have something to show for myself. Not until I can begin to pay him back."

"It isn't really that far."

"What?"

"Maryland."

"Only two states."

"Don't ever forget I love you."

"I love you too," says Lana. "I love you forever."

They cling to each other and then at the same instant break apart, each stepping back decisively so that they can do what they have to: Lana can leave; Tracee can stay.

Lana hurries to the Mustang, gets in, and starts it up. She backs out of the space, drives to the exit, and brakes. She checks the rearview mirror and then, as Tim counseled, looks over her shoulder to make sure no surprises are coming up on her left. There's only Tracee, Rita, Tim, and Clayton waving wildly. Rita blows a kiss.

As Lana turns right, heading toward the highway, she hears Marcel roar.

53

The next morning at dawn Rita walks the lion to the top of the rise. The ground, wet from a light rain, is spongy under her feet and she lays a blanket down before sitting. Marcel stretches out beside her.

Together they wait for the sun to spill its gold over the tips of the firs. The birds are raucous. The tall grass yellowing here and there is the only sign on a warm morning that the weather is about to change.

As a light breeze scatters petals from the wildflowers like confetti, Marcel, big kitty that he is, rolls over and bats his paws at the sky.

ACKNOWLEDGMENTS

I owe an enormous debt of gratitude to Katherine Buess of the San Diego Wild Animal Park for advising me and generously sharing her knowledge of all things lion. My appreciation and thanks as well to all the people who read for me and in other ways helped me create this world: Heather Chaplin, Nora Ephron, Laura Geringer, Allan Gurganus, Anna Harari, Lauren Hobbs, Joy Horowitz, Adam Kass, Deneen Zezell Graham Kerns, Natasha Lyonne, Debra Monk, and Nick Pileggi. Also great appreciation to Deena Goldstone and Robert Wallace for their talent, skill, patience, and support; to Jodi Schoenbrun Carter, who knows what I don't and is so very kind to share it; and to my husband, Jerome Kass, whose compass always points to true. I am indebted to everyone at Blue Rider for embracing Rita, Lana, Tracee, and Marcel, and most especially to David Rosenthal, my editor and

publisher. He is all I could wish for —
smart, wise, sensitive, enthusiastic, and ap-
preciative in the most encouraging way.
Special thanks to Dorothy Vincent at Jank-
low & Nesbit, and to Lynn Nesbit, who
wisely guides me and supports me whole-
heartedly. And to my dog Daisy (may she
rest in peace), who started it all, and to
Honey Pansy Cornflower for continuing the
amazement. Also I'd like to thank Maurice
Sendak for writing *Higglety Pigglety Pop!*,
which never fails to inspire.

ABOUT THE AUTHOR

Delia Ephron is a bestselling author, screenwriter, and playwright. Her movies include *The Sisterhood of the Traveling Pants, You've Got Mail, Hanging Up* (based on her novel), and *Michael.* She has written novels for adults and teenagers, books of humor, including *How to Eat Like a Child,* and essays. Her journalism has appeared in *The New York Times, O: The Oprah Magazine, Vogue, More,* and *The Huffington Post.* Recently she collaborated with her sister Nora Ephron on a play, *Love, Loss, and What I Wore,* which has run for more than two years off Broadway, and has been performed in cities across the United States and around the world, including Paris, Rio de Janeiro, and Sydney.

The employees of Thorndike Press hope you have enjoyed this Large Print book. All our Thorndike, Wheeler, and Kennebec Large Print titles are designed for easy reading, and all our books are made to last. Other Thorndike Press Large Print books are available at your library, through selected bookstores, or directly from us.

For information about titles, please call:
(800) 223-1244

or visit our Web site at:
http://gale.cengage.com/thorndike

To share your comments, please write:
Publisher
Thorndike Press
10 Water St., Suite 310
Waterville, ME 04901

32.99